D1472223

FENCE™

DISARMED

FENCE ™
DISARMED

An original novel by
Sarah Rees Brennan
Based on the Fence comics created by
C.S. Pacat and Johanna The Mad

Little, Brown and Company
New York Boston

Little, Brown and Company
Hachette Book Group
1290 Avenue of the Americas, New York, NY 10104
Visit us at LBYR.com

First Edition: May 2021

Little, Brown and Company is a division of Hachette Book Group, Inc. The Little, Brown name and logo are trademarks of Hachette Book Group, Inc.

The publisher is not responsible for websites (or their content) that are not owned by the publisher.

Library of Congress Cataloging-in-Publication Data
Names: Brennan, Sarah Rees, author. | Pacat, C. S. Fence. | Johanna the Mad, illustrator.
Title: Disarmed: an original novel / by Sarah Rees Brennan; based on the Fence comics created by C.S. Pacat and Johanna the Mad.
Description: First edition. | New York: Little, Brown and Company, 2021. | Series: Fence; [2] | Audience: Ages 14 & up. | Summary: "The boys of Kings Row are off to a training camp in France! The team will have to face superior fencers, ex-boyfriends, expulsion, and even Nicholas's golden boy and secret half-brother, the infamous Jesse Coste"—Provided by publisher.
Identifiers: LCCN 2020048438 | ISBN 9780316429870 (paperback) | ISBN 9780316429894 (ebook) | ISBN 9780316429863 (ebook other)
Subjects: CYAC: Interpersonal relations—Fiction. | Fencing—Fiction. | Brothers—Fiction. | Boarding schools—Fiction. | Schools—Fiction. | Gays—Fiction.
Classification: LCC PZ7.B751645 Dis 2021 | DDC [Fic]—dc23
LC record available at https://lccn.loc.gov/2020048438

ISBNs: 978-0-316-42987-0 (pbk.), 978-0-316-42989-4 (ebook)

Printed in the United States of America

LSC-C

Printing 1, 2021

This book is dedicated with deep gratitude to a trinity: Olga Velma, coach of the Pembroke Fencing Club; Paul Quigley of captainly wisdom; and James Stratford, Trinity fencer. Their kind, wise answers to my increasingly bizarre questions brought Camp Menton to life.

1 NICHOLAS

The *salle* at Kings Row was the most luxurious and gorgeous place Nicholas Cox had ever fenced in. He'd first learned to fence back in the city, in Coach Joe's scruffy gym. He'd trained there so much and so hard that whenever he picked up a mask and an épée, some part of Nicholas always expected to walk out onto a wooden floor so old it was gray and worn white in patches, with a shredded rubber mat to mark their field of play, the *piste*. Coach Joe said fencing clubs with grounded *pistes* were only for millionaires.

Here in the *salle* at Nicholas's new school, they had grounded *pistes*. The floorboards were glossy—but never slippery—and even and gleamed like gold. The sections of the two-meter-wide strip that was their *piste* were marked clearly with light gauge metal. The differences didn't end there. At Coach Joe's, there had been no historical swords fixed to the wall, no twirly wedding-cake twists at the corners of the ceiling, no triangular window with gold leaves swaying on the other side of the glass.

But, worst of all, Nicholas had not had a partner at Coach Joe's.

Nicholas and Seiji stood facing each other, in *en garde* position.

"*Allez,*" commanded Seiji, who insisted on acting as referee during their practice bouts. His eyes were steady through the mesh of his mask. The long, light lines of their foils were poised.

Nicholas attacked. Seiji parried. Nicholas barely managed to parry Seiji's riposte in turn and swung into another attack as quickly as he could. Nicholas's speed was his advantage; he didn't have Seiji's skill, polished into glass over years of expert training. Every time one of his rough lunges made Seiji retreat, or even hesitate, Nicholas's blood thrilled.

Seiji's next riposte landed.

Just then, the double doors of their *salle* were flung open, and Eugene rushed in. Eugene Labao was a big guy, but he walked softly.

Right now, he wasn't *talking* softly.

"Bros!" he yelled. "Big news."

Nicholas turned his head. Seiji made a small impatient sound from within his mask.

"More proof of your total inability to focus, Nicholas?" he asked.

2

"I'm focused," Nicholas promised, and lunged.

Parry, riposte, engagement, change of engagement, steps, and swords. Like a dance Nicholas could win, and he wanted to.

"Seriously, guys, I know you're doing your thing, but this is important," Eugene said.

"Halt!" said Seiji in a ringing tone.

He took off his mask and fixed Nicholas with the steel-cold stare that had made another student cry in class last week. Nicholas grinned over at him. Seiji used that stare on him at least once during every practice bout.

Seiji gestured with impatience. Even when he wasn't holding a foil, Seiji seemed ready to parry the world's attacks until it admitted defeat and surrendered.

"What is your news, Eugene?" he asked.

Eugene raised a well-shaped eyebrow, a slightly sardonic expression on his face. "It's not my news, bro. It's Coach's news. She says it's big, and we need to report to her office immediately."

Coach's office was one of Nicholas's favorite rooms in Kings Row. It was small and cozy, and she had cool posters of sabers on the walls. When Nicholas once asked where she'd gotten the posters and if he could get some with épées, Coach Williams made a sour face and told him not to talk to her about épées.

She wasn't making a face now, though. Her dark eyes were

sparkling. She was a vision of joyful impatience, tap-dancing her fingers on her desk as they took their seats.

As soon as they were settled, Coach Williams burst out with "Have you heard about Camp Menton?"

Nicholas looked around the room for a clue. Their team captain, Harvard Lee, was already sitting in front of Coach's desk, and Assistant Coach Lewis was in the corner with her notebook. Assistant Coach Lewis always took very meticulous notes.

The last member of their team, Aiden Kane, wasn't here. Now that Nicholas thought about it, Aiden hadn't been around much lately.

Harvard gave Nicholas a reassuring smile. Their captain was like that, always ready to carry the whole team on his capable shoulders. He never made Nicholas feel stupid for the gaps in his fencing knowledge. He'd drill with any of them whenever they asked.

Harvard seemed as though he was about to fill Nicholas in when Eugene spoke up: "I've read about Camp Menton! It's a totally famous European fencing camp, on these amazing training grounds in France. A bunch of their fencers went on to represent France and Germany and England in the Olympics."

Eugene and Nicholas had both started reading up about fencing so they would be more informed. Nicholas wished he'd gotten to the book Eugene had.

"Yes, everyone knows that." Seiji spoke flatly.

Eugene looked slightly offended, so Nicholas defended their teammate. "Like you know so much about French fencing."

"I know a great deal about French fencing," Seiji claimed.

"Really, how?" Nicholas demanded.

Seiji raised his eyebrows in the way that made him look extra imperious. "I lived in France for a year?"

"Oh yeah," said Nicholas. "Forgot that."

It was weird, sometimes, remembering how different from Nicholas's life Seiji's had been. Spending a year in France sounded as fabulous and distant to Nicholas as spending a year on the moon. France and everything about it had always seemed like a symbol of ultimate luxury. Nicholas only had a passport because one of his mom's boyfriends made a promise that he'd take them to Paris. His mom had believed him, because Nicholas's mom always believed the boyfriends, but she was also always fooled. That boyfriend never even took them to the arcade.

Since Nicholas had fallen in love with fencing, France seemed even more special. The *salle* was called that because of the French term for weapons room—*salle d'armes*. And *épée*, the foil they fenced with every day, was the French word for sword. But Seiji Katayama, US Olympic prospect and fencing prodigy, knew all that. Seiji knew everything. For him, seeing Nicholas and Eugene memorizing this stuff must have been faintly puzzling. Fish didn't try to learn about water.

No wonder Seiji and Nicholas hadn't gotten along the first

time they'd met. Or the second. Seiji had kicked Nicholas's ass on the *piste*, then been standoffish, which Nicholas now knew was simply Seiji's way. At the time, Nicholas had been infuriated. But he hadn't been able to stop thinking about the way Seiji fenced.

Seiji, and wanting to prove he could be as good as Seiji someday, was part of what inspired Nicholas to try for a place on the Kings Row team.

Seiji and Nicholas, in a world that made sense, would have stayed as distant from each other as the sun and the moon. In *this* world, though, they had both come to Kings Row, and they'd been assigned to each other as roommates. It hadn't been easy at first, but who wanted easy? Fencing wasn't easy. Winning gold was never easy.

Not that Nicholas had ever won gold. But he would. And being friends with Seiji was *like* winning gold.

Harvard nodded approval at Eugene, who glowed. Coach Williams swept on excitedly.

"Exactly, Eugene. Camp Menton is a highly prestigious training camp. It's different from any other. It's the breeding ground for champions. The camp used to be restricted to EU fencers only. A few years ago, they allowed some other international teams to participate, but Camp Menton has never been open to US fencers." She paused for thrilling effect. "Until now.

"This is the first year a few select American high school teams have been invited," she continued. "Kings Row, along with several of our rivals for state. Please tell me you can all come. This could be what gives us the edge we need to win."

Harvard was the one who spoke up. Their captain was the best fencer aside from Seiji, and he was great at dealing with people, which was...not one of Seiji's strengths. Nicholas knew everyone at Camp Menton would like Harvard. Their captain was the coolest.

"Coach," Harvard said in a low, thoughtful tone, "there's the issue of cost."

Their coach's face fell, as though she'd been so excited that she hadn't even considered this.

Oh. Yeah, that made sense.

"Other state teams are attending?" Seiji asked in a sharp voice. "Which ones? Exton?"

"MLC and Exton," Coach admitted. "Of course, it's not mandatory to attend Camp Menton! None of you should feel you have to go. It's an honor to be invited. I only wanted to tell you guys about...the honor."

She didn't sound convinced, though, and Nicholas didn't find her convincing. Kings Row had never won state. Nicholas had really been hoping this would be the year—showing everyone that he really did deserve that scholarship.

And if Nicholas's father found out, he might be proud.

"I don't need to train at Camp Menton," Seiji said sharply. "I can train here."

Eugene sighed. "Yeah, I guess we can train here. Still, it would be amazing to go."

7

"If you want to go, then go," snapped Seiji, as if the solution was obvious.

There was a silence. Eugene stared at the floor with sudden fixed concentration.

"Be serious, Seiji," said Nicholas, because he deeply enjoyed offending always-serious Seiji when he said that. "It costs millions of dollars to go to France."

Seiji's eyebrows judged Nicholas. "Thousands at the most."

Nicholas shrugged. "Same thing."

"Mathematically speaking," said Seiji, "no."

"Practically speaking, Seiji," Nicholas riposted, "yeah. Doesn't really matter how much it is if you don't have anything."

Seiji paused, brows now drawn together in a vehement black V, as though he were solving a complex calculus problem.

Eugene's head hung low with embarrassment. Harvard laid a hand on his shoulder. Eugene didn't have as much money as the other kids at Kings Row, but he still seemed pretty rich to Nicholas; Eugene said it was all relative. As the resident scholarship kid, it was obvious to Nicholas that fancy European trips were out of the question. Nicholas didn't understand what was so embarrassing about that.

It felt like they were disappointing Coach, though.

"Sorry, Coach," Nicholas added.

"No, Nicholas," said Coach. "There's nothing to be sorry for."

"Seiji and I were having a practice bout," Nicholas offered. "We'll get back to it."

"You do that," said Coach, and when everyone got up, she held up a hand. "Hang back, Captain, would you? I want a word."

Harvard sat back down, but the rest filed out of the coach's office, in lower spirits than before. There'd been other guys who'd tried out for the fencing team, good guys and good fencers like Kally and Tanner, who could've afforded a trip to France easily, but they hadn't made the cut.

"Do you want to go to Camp Menton?" Seiji demanded abruptly.

"Sure." Nicholas tried to smile. "Same way I'd like to fly around in a private jet or have superpowers. Have I told you what my superhero name would be? I've figured out a cool one."

"No, Nicholas," said Seiji. "For the last time, I don't want to hear your superhero name. Do some drills. I have to go make a call. I mean, *take* a call."

"From who?" Nicholas yelled after him.

The call had to be from Seiji's dad. Nobody else ever called Seiji. Even though Nicholas thought Seiji was very cool, he was pretty sure he was Seiji's only friend. Seiji seemed to generally dislike people and didn't even talk to his former fencing partner.

Seiji's dad had started calling more over the last few weeks. Nicholas didn't listen in, but he could hear from the other side of the shower curtain Seiji'd hung up in their room that the calls seemed oddly brief and businesslike. But it must be nice to have your dad call you. Nicholas's dad didn't even know who he was.

Nicholas glanced over at Eugene, but he was already slinking

9

toward the gym, obviously crushed that he couldn't go to Camp Menton. When upset, Eugene liked to lift his feelings away. Nicholas headed out. It was almost sunset, and when he could, he liked to be outside for the magic hour.

Nicholas had been at Kings Row for weeks now, longer than he and his mom had lived in some of their apartments before getting evicted. He'd never, for any length of time, lived anywhere like this. He'd never even dreamed of a place like this.

When the sun set on the sprawling buildings, the mullioned windows shone as brilliantly as gold, and the redbrick glowed crimson. Nicholas could go outside and sit in the open on the lawn, like he was doing today, or wait under the shadow of the trees, and just marvel that this school was his.

He didn't need Camp Menton. He had this.

He loved Kings Row. He loved fencing. He loved—

Just then, his reverie was interrupted by Seiji marching toward him.

"I thought you would return to the *salle* and practice your footwork!" said Seiji sternly. "Come back with me at once."

Nicholas stretched as he scrambled up from the grass. "Don't know why we're suddenly in a hurry, but okay."

"There's no time to be lost!"

Sometimes, Nicholas saw what people meant when they said Seiji was "very, very, very intense." Mostly, though, he thought people were being ridiculous.

Seiji accelerated, dodging and weaving around the throng of

Kings Row students who just hung out in their free hours. Nicholas tried to catch up and almost slammed right into Aiden, the last member of the Kings Row team, who was leaving a dorm room that wasn't his.

"Watch where you're going, freshman," Aiden snarled.

Usually when Aiden appeared anywhere, his fan club fluttered around him like adoring bluebirds, and the sun danced in his hair. His voice was typically warm and amused, like he was mentally on a tropical beach.

This evening, it seemed as if a tropical storm had arrived, sending the tourists running and turning the white sand gray. Aiden's hair, normally imperfectly perfect, was wild. It looked as if someone had pressed ash-covered thumbs under both his eyes, leaving dark marks beneath them. He was buttoning up his wrinkled uniform shirt, concealing a string of small bruises running up from his chest to his chin, as though he'd been hit multiple times with the hilt of a sword.

Nicholas truly had no idea why anyone would be getting dressed in somebody else's room, let alone how someone would get those bruises. But somehow even those things weren't as weird as the blankness in Aiden's eyes.

Nicholas shook his head.

Aiden. What was up with that guy lately?

2 HARVARD

"Hang back, Captain, would you?" Coach Williams said. "I want a word."

That was Harvard's first sign something was very wrong.

When Coach was in a good mood, she'd yell, "Yo, Harvard!" and maybe toss something at his head. Harvard would always catch it and grin. Sure, she was stern when it came to discipline, but otherwise she was pretty chill.

Seeing Coach Williams this serious made Harvard want to run away.

Harvard was captain, though, so he couldn't do that. Instead he braced himself and waited for whatever came next. He usually liked it in the coach's office, where they would sit at her big, battered desk and sketch plans for the team's future.

Today Assistant Coach Lewis was sticking around, too, wisps of ruddy brown hair escaping from her ponytail. She shot Harvard a covertly sympathetic glance over her glasses, then straightened up. She never stayed behind for captain-to-coach meetings. If Coach Williams needed backup, that was even more proof this was bad.

Coach Williams gestured to the chair across from her. Harvard sat and Coach Williams sighed.

"This isn't about fencing," said Coach. "Well, only tangentially. It's about a member of the team, and I think you know who."

Coach paused, leaving a space for Harvard to fill. Harvard wished he didn't know who Coach meant. He had a sudden desperate urge to hear Eugene was setting fires in the gym.

Instead he turned away, to the window, and said to the glass rather than his coach: "Aiden."

Even saying his best friend's name sent a strange, shuddering pang through Harvard. It was like a story Harvard had read as a child about a broken magic mirror. The shards had flown in all directions and hit people—some in the eye, some in the heart—and the small, cold, jagged pieces had stayed in them and twisted. Those who'd been hit had to learn to live with those sharp, cold reminders that something magic had been broken and couldn't be fixed.

"The man himself," said Coach. "Have you seen him lately? Because I haven't since he no longer comes to matches, to practice, or, so I'm told, to class. He didn't even come to this meeting. Eugene couldn't find him."

Harvard crossed his arms and tilted back in his chair. If he'd been Aiden, that would've been a cool move of lazy insouciance.

Since he was Harvard, he felt vaguely unbalanced and almost immediately restored the chair to its rightfully steady position on all four legs.

"Aiden says he's living his best life."

"He's sneaking out to meet guys. And I say 'sneaking out,' but it seems like he wants to get caught, or at least doesn't *care* if he's caught. He's had detention every day for a week," said Coach. "At least he gets some sleep in there. He certainly doesn't *look* like he's living his best life. Do you have any idea what's going on with him?"

"I . . . ," said Harvard. "Not exactly."

He swallowed, fidgeted, and bit his lip. He didn't do well with guilt. When he was younger, and he was home alone and broke something, he waited on the porch so he could run to his mom and confess as soon as possible.

He'd never kept a guilty secret. Not until now.

"Do you want me to read out all the Kings Row rules Aiden has broken this week?" Coach Williams gestured. "Lewis has a list."

"I do have a list," the assistant coach agreed sadly. "It's extensive."

Harvard shook his head. He didn't want to hear it.

"Is it my fault?" wondered Coach Williams aloud. "Am I a bad role model?"

"You're doing great, Sally," the assistant coach contributed supportively. "You're the best role model!"

Coach drummed her fingers meditatively on the surface of the desk. "I certainly haven't dated the entire state of Connecticut, as seems to be Aiden's dream."

"You totally could, Sally." The assistant coach continued to validate Coach Williams. "Um. Anyone could tell you that! Anyone would say the same thing."

Coach Williams was frowning, dark eyes narrowed as she focused on the problem of Aiden. The assistant coach sighed and pushed her glasses up her nose. Harvard's stomach roiled, sick with guilt.

What he couldn't tell Coach was that Aiden's behavior was all Harvard's fault. Harvard was a fool about love who'd messed up the very few dates he'd ever gone on. It had been *Harvard's* idea to practice dating with his best friend, and it was Harvard who continued being a spectacular idiot and fell in love with his best friend over the course of three days. Brilliant, beautiful Aiden Kane, who wanted to date the entire state of Connecticut.

Harvard had tried to make things right. He'd reassured Aiden that he only wanted to be friends, that their friendship was the most important thing. He'd made sure Aiden knew he was free to do whatever he wanted.

Only it seemed now that what Aiden wanted was to go absolutely wild. Harvard couldn't figure out if the recent bad behavior was Aiden making clear that he couldn't be tied down, or—and this suspicion made Harvard feel worse than anything else as he lay alone in their room through the long, cold nights—if Aiden had simply been bored out of his mind for the handful of days they'd pretended to date, and was seizing his chance to have fun again.

"We had an emergency meeting about Aiden," said Coach Williams. "The principal called Aiden's father. You know Aiden's father."

Sadly, Harvard did. He thought it was a pity that *Aiden* knew Aiden's father.

"His father is opposed to any discipline that would stay on Aiden's record, like suspensions," Coach Williams went on. "He said he would rather withdraw Aiden from school. Of course, it won't come to that, but I don't even want to think about it. Do you understand, Harvard? You have to get Aiden to calm down."

Harvard could barely speak, but he managed in a low voice: "Yeah."

He understood.

Coach Williams ran a hand through her springy Afro, dark-and-silver curls catching on her fingers like rings. "I hate to put this on you, kid. But I've tried sitting him down myself, and I just got a cat-eyed stare and too-cool-for-school jokes. You're the only one who can talk sense into him."

Harvard had always been Aiden's best friend. Since they were little.

"I'll do my best," promised Harvard.

He always really tried. He couldn't let these wild new feelings for Aiden—feelings that were his problem alone—get in the way of being a good captain or a good friend.

He excused himself from the coach's office and made his way back to the dormitory. His own room was empty, with no sign of his roommate. Harvard wasn't surprised. Aiden hadn't slept there in days. He and Aiden, at the start of the year, had pushed their beds together so they could talk and watch movies more comfortably. The only occupant of Aiden's side of the bed was Aiden's teddy bear, Harvard Paw. Harvard had given him that bear in preschool, and Aiden had always fussed over it and treasured it. Until now. The teddy bear was flung carelessly to one side, abandoned. Much like the room. Much like Harvard himself.

It had reached the point where Harvard missed Aiden so much that he'd gone home and brought back his album full of postcards from all the outrageous vacations Aiden had ever been on. Aiden always wrote postcards to Harvard every day when he went abroad and texted Harvard every day when they were both at home. They had never really been separated before now.

Okay, that was enough of that. Harvard turned right back around to head for the *salle*, where he could run drills alone, but he found his freshman teammates there already. Seiji was barking orders at Nicholas at the top of his lungs. Cute kids. Nicholas was getting a lot better. Apparently, Seiji's unusual teaching methods really worked on Nicholas. Other students who only *witnessed* Seiji's lessons had been reduced to tears. Harvard withdrew silently, leaving them to it.

Instead of a running a drill, Harvard walked around the school, hoping to spot Aiden somewhere. There were a few students here or there, coming back inside as dusk fell, their dark-blue uniform jackets blending with the deepening blue of the evening sky. None walked the way Aiden did, or had long honey-colored hair that could be tied up in an elegant knot or could fall down all around you like a curtain at the theater.

Being at Kings Row usually made Harvard happy. He'd chosen this beautiful, small school where he could get to know everybody's names, where they could run through the long paneled halls and across the velvet-smooth lawn underneath the leaves. He'd talked Aiden into coming here so they could be roommates at last and best friends always.

Falling in love with Aiden shouldn't have changed everything.

Harvard thought about it all the time, and he couldn't talk about it to anyone. Who could he tell? He always told his best friend about his problems, but now Aiden *was* his problem. His parents loved Aiden: He didn't want that to stop just because Aiden had accidentally broken Harvard's heart. His friends were Aiden's friends, and they knew how Aiden was. They'd think Harvard should have known better—after knowing Aiden for so long—than to add his name to the endless list of Aiden's lovestruck victims. Even Coach Williams would laugh at him.

Coach Williams literally made people do suicide runs if they said "Aiden dumped me" in front of her. And Aiden hadn't even dumped Harvard, because they hadn't been truly going out in the first place. This was pathetic. Harvard felt like a big joke.

When it came to fencing, Harvard didn't have Seiji's consummate skill or Nicholas's raw potential. What he had was determination and patience. He kept a level head, and he worked on mastering a move, and he made sure he succeeded.

He could master this feeling, too. He should concentrate on what mattered: teamwork, being captain, being a good friend. Aiden couldn't give him the slip forever. Even if he had to corner his roommate, Harvard would make Aiden see reason.

Maybe this break would be good for them both. Eventually things would be just the way they'd been before. If Harvard kept calm and stayed sensible, it would all work out. Nothing had to change.

3 AIDEN

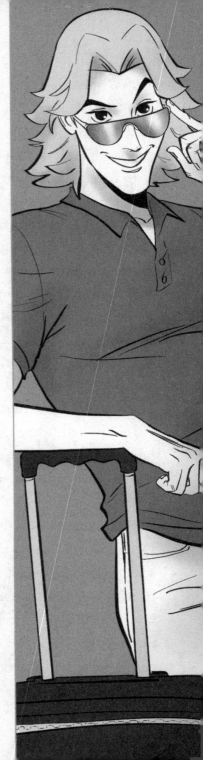

"O n second thought," announced Aiden, slamming the door on the awful world in general and Nicholas Cox's awful haircut in particular, "come over here and kiss me, What's-your-name."

Aiden's head hurt. His whole body hurt. He'd been sleeping badly in unfamiliar beds for days. He hadn't slept last night, though he'd skipped class and fallen into a fitful doze at some point today. Unfortunately, the owner of last night's unfamiliar bed had returned and disturbed him.

The owner of last night's unfamiliar bed blinked over at Aiden now. He had eyes like a wounded sheep's. Seeing someone else's suffering infuriated Aiden. He wasn't here for more pain.

"You don't remember my name?" the other boy asked.

"Were you laboring under the mistaken impression you were memorable?" bit out Aiden.

The resemblance to a wounded sheep increased. Whatever— this guy had kicked out his roommate for a chance to spend time with Aiden. That made him a lousy roommate, and he deserved everything he got.

There was a sour taste in Aiden's mouth, but he almost savored it. Aiden kept doing this lately. He'd always had a sharp tongue, but there was a difference between a needle and a sword. In the past, Aiden had known when to stop. He'd tried not to say anything that would ever disappoint Harvard if it got back to him.

To be fair, Aiden still *knew* when to stop. He just...didn't stop when he should. Who cared?

He prowled toward the boy now.

"If you let me kiss you," Aiden murmured as he dipped his head down toward the other boy's, "you're pathetic."

The boy trembled and turned his face up for the kiss. It wasn't a kind kiss. His hands shook as he clung to Aiden.

Had Aiden seemed the same way when he was with Harvard? *Did I like him too much? Was I too obvious?* Aiden wondered sometime later, once it was night. He sat on the ousted room-mate's bed, pushed up under the window, and stared out at the black-veiled trees. The lake beyond gleamed by the light of the moon, as the moon had shone for an owl and a cat in a tale from one of Harvard's storybooks. The owl and the cat had sailed

22

away for a year and a day in a pea-green boat. Aiden only got fairy tales at Harvard's house. His dad and his many stepmothers were too busy. Harvard's mom used to read books to them both when Aiden stayed over, and that was Aiden's favorite story.

Aiden had hurt his flings in the past, but he'd always done it by being thoughtless. He hadn't cared much about his wannabe suitors, but he had never *wanted* to hurt them.

Now he *did* want to, with a viciousness that surprised him. Aiden wanted to hurt anyone within reach, including himself. He was especially furious with himself.

Ever since his growth spurt, Aiden was used to his mind and body being on great terms. He treated his body right and kept his hair fabulous. In return, his body remained cool and composed in even the most stressful of situations.

He didn't understand why, now, in his time of need, his body had betrayed him so completely.

Harvard had said he only wanted to be friends. Aiden had given him what he wanted. Everything back to normal, pretending like they'd never kissed, never touched. He'd thought he could do it, for one evening, for the duration of one night. They'd gone to sleep like they always did, in beds pushed up together.

Aiden had woken in the early hours of the morning, with his arm twined around Harvard's neck as though it belonged there, his face nuzzling into the crook of Harvard's shoulder. Thank God Aiden had woken up before Harvard. He'd thrown himself out of bed and onto the floor, then snatched up his uniform and gone looking for the first boy he could find. Anyone would do.

Finding a new fling had always worked to make Aiden feel better in the past. But now it wasn't working in the slightest.

Every time he went to kiss a guy, Aiden had to fight the urge to turn his face away. Kisses had once felt like playing, but now they felt like defeat. There was nowhere he felt comfortable enough to sleep. He didn't dare go back to his room, and it was horrifying to sleep near anyone else. Even if he tried, he would inevitably jolt out of his doze, heart hammering in a panic because something was wrong, and would have to spend too many sick moments figuring out what it was. He was always in the wrong place with the wrong person. It was as if Aiden's every instinct had been rewired over the duration of a handful of days.

A few times, he'd been unguarded enough to flinch from a kiss, or his fling had caught him being too obviously miserable. What was Aiden supposed to say? *I hate being touched by someone who's not Harvard? I hate you for not being Harvard?*

He'd thrown himself into misery instead and hadn't come up for air. Why would he do that when he just wanted to drown?

Aiden was so tired his eyes burned, but he didn't close them. Whenever he shut them, he saw that evening again and remembered what an idiot he'd been to hope. He'd run to Kings Row, intent on confessing his love to Harvard. But before he could even get the words out, Harvard had said he couldn't imagine anything worse than being in love with Aiden.

What a moment that had been. Aiden was well aware of what most people thought of him, but he hadn't thought his best friend agreed.

Luckily, Aiden hadn't had the chance to confess his love. What an exercise in humiliation that would've been. He didn't even know why he'd thought it might work: He'd spent years following Harvard around. He'd followed him to Kings Row.

Aiden smiled mirthlessly to himself.

He didn't care if everyone thought he was awful. That was better than the truth.

Being unrequitedly in love with your best friend since you were *a little kid*? That was pathetic. Aiden Kane was determined to be anything but that.

He was the one who'd made the rule that he wouldn't date people on the fencing team. He was the one who'd broken the rule. He deserved whatever he got.

If you're going through hell, keep going. That was a quote from a British politician with a face like a cranky bulldog.

Aiden had to keep living like this, had to keep going through the deep charring feeling underneath his breastbone. It felt as if his heart were being burned away.

That was the whole point. Once his heart was gone? Problem solved.

4 SEIJI

Seiji couldn't believe he was doing this.

The worst thing was that he couldn't even blame anyone else. He was the one who'd had the bright idea to run off and call his father.

Koichiro Katayama was a very busy man, so Seiji tried not to bother him, but ever since Seiji had asked him for help over a certain matter involving Nicholas, his father had been calling more frequently. It was peculiar. His father didn't seem to have anything much to say.

"How are they treating you at Kings Row?" his father inquired once.

"They *aren't* treating me," Seiji answered. "I haven't sustained any injuries, and I haven't been ill."

"Ah," said his father. "Making friends?"

"More friends?" Seiji returned in horror.

"Never mind," his dad replied. "How's Nicholas?"

His father always asked. Seiji would tell him about Nicholas's fencing progress, which was dismal, every time his father called. At least that was a pleasant part of the conversation. He'd known his father would become more interested in fencing one day.

He understood his father would rather have a social butterfly for a son, but Seiji had enough trouble with the one friend he'd accidentally acquired without heaping more disasters on himself. Still, those weekly awkward talks with his dad meant Seiji felt he could call him, when the next trouble regarding Nicholas arose.

So he walked out onto the grounds at Kings Row as the sun set, dialed his father's number, and caught him playing golf.

"I'm sorry, I'll call you back later," Seiji said at once. "Focus on winning."

Seiji hadn't wanted to come to Kings Row. He'd always expected to accompany Jesse Coste and attend Exton: a far larger school than this one, with an elite fencing team and high gray walls surmounted by tall gray towers. But Seiji was getting used to it here in this small school, where everything was old-fashioned in a way that was classic and cozy at once and where he hardly ever sat by himself in the dining hall. His father's voice was steady and reassuring in his ear.

"Don't worry about that. It's just a game, Seiji. Winning's not the most important thing in the world."

"I don't understand," said Seiji.

"I know you don't," his father returned. "Someday you might. For now, let's talk. Did you just want to, uh, chat?"

His father was attempting a more casual way of talking to him lately. He was trying to be "down with the kids," Seiji thought, and it was horrible. Seiji himself had never been "down with the kids."

"Why would I bother you if all I wanted was to exchange pleasantries?" asked Seiji. "We can do that during winter break. No, I'm calling about something important. This is about Nicholas."

"Okay, wow, it's happening," said his father. "Right, Seiji, let me just move away from the others, give us some privacy. Listen, guys, save me something from the drinks cart—"

"You don't need to leave your friends."

Seiji was starting to feel unnerved.

"They're not my friends, they're business associates. I barely like them," his father said, then speaking away from the phone, "Sorry, Jock, didn't mean for you to hear that." He transferred his attention back to Seiji. "Doesn't matter! What matters is *you*, Seiji. I think I know what you're going to tell me. I'm so glad you feel able to share this with me! Thank you. I, ah—love you."

Seiji cast a hunted look around the courtyard. He had the irrational wish to climb up a chestnut tree and escape this emotional conversation.

"And I'm sure I will love Nicholas," his father continued.

"Why would you do that?!" asked Seiji. "He's annoying, and he's bad at fencing!"

There was a long pause on his father's end of the line.

"I'm sure he has . . . qualities," his father said at last. "The point is, I hope you know that you can always tell me . . . whatever it is you have to tell me. I'm accepting. I accept you. I just found it difficult to swallow the idea of Jesse."

"Why are you bringing up Jesse?"

Seiji's throat narrowed a small but crucial amount when he was forced to discuss Jesse Coste, his former fencing partner and the reason he was attending Kings Row. The mysterious obstruction in his throat made it difficult to speak clearly and show that Seiji was perfectly all right.

"No reason," said his dad. "I'm sorry. Let's never talk about Jesse again. That would make me very happy. Tell me about Nicholas!"

"Do you remember me saying that he was socioeconomically disadvantaged?"

"That doesn't matter," his father assured him.

Seiji lifted his eyes to the sky. He knew his father was intelligent. He wasn't sure why sometimes he said foolish things.

"Obviously, it does matter. That's why I'm calling you. To tell you about Nicholas." Seiji paused. "And Eugene."

"Eugene!" his father exclaimed. *Who is Eugene?*

"He's also on the fencing team," said Seiji. "He lifts weights. He has . . ." Seiji considered. Nicholas said Eugene had "an army of brothers and sisters" but Eugene had rolled his eyes when Nicholas said that. Seiji didn't know the truth. "Potentially twelve siblings. He says *bro* frequently and makes excellent protein shakes. I don't know anything else about him."

A silence followed, the wind dropping leaves one by one onto the grass. Perhaps he'd praised Eugene in overly glowing terms, but Eugene was a teammate and always friendly.

"He sounds nice." His father's tone was doubtful. "Well, I'm an open-minded and modern man. Tell me whatever you have to tell me about Nicholas . . . and Eugene. . . ."

"It's really the whole team," said Seiji.

On the other end of the line, his father made a strangled noise. Seiji heard him cover the phone and yell out muffled apologies to other golfers.

"Go on," his father encouraged him after this eventful break in the conversation.

"I want you to sponsor the Kings Row team to go to a prestigious training camp in France," Seiji said. "Nicholas wishes to go, but he can't afford it."

He didn't like it when Nicholas wasn't able to have things Nicholas should have. It was as though someone had cheated in a match to gain an unfair advantage, except it seemed as though someone had rigged *life* to make it easier for them and harder for other people. Seiji disapproved of unfair matches.

"Right," his father responded cautiously after another and less eventful pause. "Uh, Seiji, why not have me pay for just you and Nicholas to go?"

"Eugene's poor as well," Seiji answered. "Not as poor as Nicholas, but his family can't send him to France."

"I suppose he has all those brothers and sisters . . . ," his father murmured.

Seiji had no more to say about Eugene's family. "More importantly, if you sponsor the whole team, it's a gesture of support to the school and doesn't single out Nicholas. He might feel awkward or as though he owed me something if he perceived himself as an object of charity. He has to think this is something that would happen whether he was at Kings Row or not."

"You're learning a lot at this school," said his father.

"I don't know about that," said Seiji. "It's vital for me to have fencers of my own caliber to have practice bouts with, and there isn't anyone like that at Kings Row. That's why we must go to Camp Menton."

And there was the silver lining, gleaming like an épée in the light of their *salle*. In France, there would be plenty of elite fencers to face. He'd had many excellent matches in France in the past. The only time he'd been so evenly matched in the US had been with . . .

But Seiji didn't want to think about Jesse.

His father offered, in a careful manner, "If this fencing camp is so prestigious, will the Exton team be attending as well?"

The fact his father was worrying about that was awful. It made Seiji feel as though he'd left a gap in his defense, so obvious it could be spotted by anyone, and now he was sure to lose.

"Yes," Seiji said in a clipped voice.

"*Jesse's* going to be there."

That stupid obstruction was back in his throat. Seiji refused to let it interfere with his speech. He kept his voice stern and convincing as he said, "I can handle Jesse."

That had to be true.

"But you don't have to 'handle him.' You shouldn't do anything that will hurt you. Winning's not that important. It's just—"

"Just a game?" Thinking of Jesse made Seiji's voice sharper than he'd intended. "You already said that. Why do you enjoy sealing a deal or opening a new factory? It's not about money. We have enough of that. It's about winning. You keep score, the same way I do."

He expected his father to be insulted by the comparison. Instead, he sounded oddly pleased.

"Never thought about it that way," his father admitted. "Ah well, the child of a hawk is a hawk. I take your point, Seiji. I don't like losing, either. I only wish...I never want you to feel trapped. You should decide when the victory is important. Don't let anyone choose your fight for you."

When his father talked about feeling trapped, Seiji remembered the humiliation of losing against Jesse in that one match where he'd let his feelings get the best of him. Never again.

"I think the Olympic selection committee might choose my match for me," said Seiji.

Seiji didn't know why everyone else was always missing the

obvious. There were times in life when you had no choice but to fight.

"I'll let you win this conversation," his father told him, laughing. "I imagine you win most of them."

"No, I don't," Seiji said gloomily. "Nicholas never listens. He just keeps talking, and he does whatever he wants!"

"I must meet Nicholas someday soon," Seiji's dad added.

"Why would you want to do that?" Seiji was baffled. "I really don't think you'd have much in common."

"We have you in common," said his father.

Seiji stared fixedly up at the fall-gold leaves. "About what you were saying earlier."

His father coughed. "Ah. Yes, some crossed wires there. I can see how a lot of the things I was saying probably didn't make sense to you."

At least he knew!

"I just wanted to say I . . . hold you in high regard as well," said Seiji. "But I'd rather not talk about it."

His father's voice went soft. "All right. Then we won't. Consider your request granted. I'll sponsor the team. Enjoy France. I must get back to winning my golf game."

"I thought it was just a game and it didn't matter?"

"It *is* just a game," said his father. "That I am going to *win*."

Seiji found himself giving the phone a small smile after he'd hung up. It was bizarre but oddly nice to think he and his father were alike in some ways. And it was good Nicholas would be pleased about going to France.

Then he did some mental arithmetic about how the travel time to France was going to cut in on his fencing schedule, and it became clear that going to France was a terrible idea. Seiji rushed Nicholas back to the *salle* and tried to do as many drills as possible.

That night, Seiji lay in his bed on the properly ordered side of the room and frowned over at the yellow ducks on the curtain he'd hung up to keep Nicholas's chaos away from him. The ducks fluttered in the night, taunting him.

Chaos awaited in France. He would be forced to think about how it had been when he lost his match to Jesse and fled to France because he felt as though he were in exile. He would have to see Jesse at camp as the new captain of the Exton team. Seiji and Jesse had once planned to lead the Exton team to victory together.

Why had he done this? Just because Nicholas wanted to go to Camp Menton. Just because Nicholas hadn't been trained the way he deserved. Why was it up to Seiji to make that right?

What had Seiji been thinking? He must have lost his mind.

5 NICHOLAS

Coach Williams summoned them to her office again the next morning. This time it was before breakfast, when the rolling green lawn outside the windows was still silver-sheeted with dew. Seiji had only just dragged Nicholas out of bed, and Nicholas was still yawning and tugging his tie into a non-crumpled-leaf shape. He didn't feel mentally prepared to be in trouble.

When they arrived at Coach's office, Harvard was already there. His shoulders were slumped, and Nicholas thought he seemed tired, but then Harvard looked up and gave Nicholas a smile. Nicholas beamed back. The captain mustn't like mornings, either. Nobody with sense liked mornings.

Eugene came into the office next. He fist-bumped Nicholas, but Nicholas was so tired he missed the fist bump and ended up punching Seiji in the arm instead. Seiji glared.

Then Coach dragged in Aiden and closed the door behind them. Harvard's back went sword straight. Aiden's hair and clothes looked even more wrecked than they had yesterday. Nicholas wasn't the fussy kind like Seiji, but he had to wonder if Aiden had forgotten what hairbrushes were.

Was the *whole team* in trouble? Nicholas guessed they were. They didn't have a match on the schedule yet, so he didn't know what else it could be. He supposed Aiden *had* been in detention a lot lately. Nicholas had seen him there, sleeping on a desk with his head cradled in his arms.

Granted, Nicholas saw him there because he, too, had been in detention, but he only had it the regular amount. In fact, he was in detention less lately than ever before! Seiji's rigorous training program meant Nicholas didn't have much time to break the rules.

But this time he must have broken some rule by accident. That was easy to imagine. What was difficult to imagine was the captain breaking rules. Maybe Seiji and Harvard had been summoned so they could be disappointed in Nicholas together? Nicholas waited in dread.

But when Coach finally sat down at her desk, she was smiling. Her goodwill seemed to suffuse the whole room, like light glancing off a blade.

"Good news, team! Thanks to a very generous donation from

Mr. Katayama, the whole fencing team will be attending Camp Menton. Pack your bags, kids. We're on our way to France."

Eugene leaped to his feet and gave a cheer. "Bro! I mean, Coach... Coach bro. Wow!"

On his feet, he scanned the room for an outlet for his enthusiasm and settled for giving Nicholas a double high five. This time, Nicholas didn't miss.

"Right, that camp in France," Aiden said carelessly. "Is that this weekend?"

He was leaning back in his chair. It was weird how Aiden, even with his clothes and hair a mess, made something like leaning back in a chair look cool. Maybe that was why he had a circle of fans who followed him wherever he went.

"Lost track of time?" Harvard asked, his voice strained.

"I was playing around," drawled Aiden, stretching. "All work and no play makes... someone a dull boy."

Nicholas shot Aiden a shocked look. Aiden made mean jokes frequently, but never to the captain! Harvard shrugged and glanced away, though, so maybe it wasn't a big deal. Harvard must be used to Aiden's jokes.

Nicholas's train of thought was derailed by the sheer pressure of Seiji's gaze. Seiji's stares were often unnerving, but this particular one felt as if there were holes being bored through Nicholas's face.

"Nicholas!" Seiji snapped, as though he were a highwayman demanding Nicholas's money or his life. "Are you pleased?"

"Oh my God," said Nicholas, totally forgetting Aiden's weirdness as the revelation sank in. "Yeah! I can't believe it! Are we actually going to France? Not to brag, but I have a passport."

"They don't give poor people *passports*?" demanded Seiji, who'd led a sheltered life.

"Only forty-two percent of Americans have a passport," Coach informed him.

Most of the team seemed startled to hear this. Nicholas rolled his eyes. Rich kids. Who cared, though, he was going to France!

"Coach," Nicholas blurted out, "may I be excused?"

"I suppose you can, Cox." Coach was glowing. "Pack light; get ready to train hard."

"Totally, Coach," Nicholas assured her. Then he jumped up, grabbed Seiji's sleeve, and dragged his roommate out of the office.

Nicholas and Seiji careened down hallways, which were all walnut paneling and white plaster, adorned with portraits of gray-haired dudes, as Nicholas searched for the shortest person in Kings Row. Other students scattered out of their way, terrified by Seiji's baleful stare. Seiji had strong opinions about his personal space. Another student had once patted Seiji's arm in class. Five minutes later the poor guy'd asked to go to the infirmary because he'd developed a headache in the ensuing icy, outraged silence.

"Nicholas, it's ridiculous to drag me around the place," Seiji complained. "Nicholas, I've pointed out frequently that—"

That was when Nicholas spotted his quarry. He let go of Sei-ji's sleeve and pounced on Bobby Rodriguez.

"Bobby!" he yelled. "Guess who's going to France!"

He grabbed Bobby in a hug. Bobby hugged him back enthu-siastically. Then the pair jumped up and down together. Bobby was wearing a turquoise ribbon in his hair today, and several sparkly turquoise earrings. He looked cool; that was nothing new for Bobby.

Bobby beat Nicholas's chest enthusiastically with his small fists. "You're going to Camp Menton? Nicholas, that's amazing! You're going to have so much fun. A foreign country, all those fencers..." Bobby paused to consider. "You know what? I'll go, too!"

Nicholas blinked. "What? How? I mean, you're not on the team and it's—it's expensive...."

"Please. I'll just ask for this to be an early...Arbor Day pres-ent. My parents will totally say yes," said Bobby with a grin. "Plus, I know everything about Camp Menton! They let friends and family attend as part of the audience during training so stu-dents don't have to travel by themselves. I'm a friend! We'll have so much fun!"

"Yeah!"

Nicholas beamed. Bobby was as frenzied about fencing as Nicholas was. It was the first thing they'd bonded about.

"Besides, you'll need support," said Bobby. "Camp Menton is supposed to be totally intense and hard-core."

"Yeah, I can handle that," Nicholas assured him. "And then I'll use my new skills to win at state!"

"I know you will! We'll learn so much! I heard a German fencer came back with his footwork totally transformed—"

"Why are they like this?" Seiji murmured.

"Not sure," grunted Bobby's best friend, Dante, leaning against the opposite wall.

Bobby noticed Seiji was there and stopped doing his happy dance. Nicholas was left doing a happy dance by himself, which must have looked kinda dumb. Bobby was never subdued except when he was around Seiji, because Bobby was so wowed by Seiji's fencing prowess. He went quiet and blushed whenever Seiji spoke to him. Nicholas understood the feeling but thought Bobby should get it together. The weird silences were making Seiji believe that Bobby disliked him, and Nicholas wanted them all to be awesome friends.

"Hi, Seiji." Bobby pulled on his ribbon and went red. "I didn't see you there. I mean, not that you're easy to overlook! You're very . . . striking. . . ."

Seiji obviously didn't know what to do about being called "very striking." He stood with his back held stiffly to the paneled wall. Nicholas was pretty sure this particular aloof stare from Seiji meant he was feeling awkward.

"Sorry we were so loud!" Bobby added. "I know you hate that."

Nicholas made a rude noise. "Whatever! I'm gonna be loud

about the coolest thing that's ever happened to me, next to coming to Kings Row and winning our match against MLC."

If he learned amazing tricks at Camp Menton, there would be even more victorious matches in his future. Coach Williams thought this camp might be their key to winning at state.

Nicholas could tell Seiji was happy about France, too. He was looking at Nicholas, and there was a faint curl of satisfaction to Seiji's mouth that might have been a smile on someone else.

"It's good that you're pleased," Seiji said decisively.

Bobby was smiling, too. Unlike Seiji, Bobby's smiles were unmistakable, bright as his ribbons and earrings. "Dante, you'll come, too, right?"

In some surprise, Nicholas turned to the taller boy. Dante Rossi nodded in Bobby's direction, then returned Nicholas's look impassively. Dante's face was neutral. It usually was.

"I thought you didn't like fencing?" Nicholas asked.

He wasn't sure why anyone would feel that way, but he'd absorbed that Dante did.

Dante nodded again.

"Then, uh . . . ," said Nicholas. "Not that we're not glad to have you, but why would you come?"

Dante's gaze drifted over to the turquoise beacon of Bobby's ribbon. Nicholas wondered why Dante was looking at Bobby, then realized he must want Bobby to answer for him. Dante and Bobby were roommates and the type of best friends who did everything together.

"Dante has family in Italy, so he can have fun with them," Bobby explained.

"Uh, but we're going to France," Nicholas pointed out.

"The town the camp's based near, Menton, is on the border between France and Italy. It's a half hour drive to get to Italy and this city called Ventimiglia, where Dante's cousins live." Bobby gave Dante an affectionate look. "So he can visit them *and* be at the camp to hang out. And he can even watch the fencing! He's actually getting way more into fencing."

Bobby's back was turned to Dante. Bobby didn't see Dante slowly but vehemently shaking his head, his wavy dark hair tumbling every which way. He didn't argue with Bobby's statement, though. Dante was a guy of few words.

"Dante and I always have fun when we travel together. When we pack," said Bobby, "we always keep space in both suitcases to bring back many cheeses! Dante loves cheese."

This time Dante nodded. A terrible realization descended upon Nicholas.

"Oh my God," said Nicholas. "Can't stay here chatting, guys. Gotta go! Seiji, I have to pack for France. Seiji, what should I bring to France?"

"Clothes," Seiji said flatly.

Nicholas was already dragging Seiji back to their dormitory. Nicholas had read somewhere that French people were into fashion. Bobby would fit right in, but Nicholas didn't own any fancy clothes. He did have a lot of black T-shirts. Maybe those would work? Black was cool, right?

Nicholas tossed the question over his shoulder as he barreled through the door to their room, number 108. "Do people wear a lot of black in France?"

Seiji pulled his wrist out of Nicholas's grasp. "I never noticed."

The morning sunlight was pouring with equal brightness into both halves of their dorm room, Seiji's half with a neatly made bed and alphabetized books, while Nicholas's half contained a colony of socks under his bed. Nicholas knew Harvard and Aiden pushed their beds together so that they could watch movies and chat. He didn't think Seiji would ever go for that, since Seiji insisted that the duck-patterned shower curtain they'd hung up in the middle of their room must stay there for the preservation of his sanity.

Nicholas paused halfway toward the duck curtain, arrested by a sudden thought.

"This is so nice of your dad," he told Seiji. "What made him think of doing this?"

"I don't know, Nicholas," Seiji snapped. "How should I know? I wouldn't, because I haven't spoken to him recently. He gets wild ideas all the time. It was a strange whim of his, I expect. Maybe he's regretting it now."

Nicholas shrugged. "Well, I think it was great of him. Your dad seems really cool."

"He's a well-respected businessman," said Seiji, but he had that faintly pleased look on his face again.

Sometimes Seiji got testy about his parents. Nicholas wasn't sure why. With the way Seiji spoke about them, it was as if he worried he was disappointing them, but obviously nobody could be disappointed in Seiji.

Maybe it was just that the Katayamas were occupied with running their car-making empire, and they didn't get the chance to spend a lot of time with Seiji. That must be sad for their whole family.

"Say thanks to him from me," Nicholas said. "I mean, not that he'll know who I am. But, like, from a teammate of yours? Since that's what I am? Let him know I wanna say thanks."

If it wasn't for Seiji's dad, there was no way Nicholas could've ever dreamed of going to Camp Menton. Mr. Katayama didn't realize what he'd done, didn't know how much it meant, but he'd given Nicholas a better chance of winning at state.

Seiji said distantly, "He knows who you are."

Truly this was a great day. Nicholas brightened further. "Yeah?"

He *was* Seiji's roommate, and they fenced and spent a lot of time together. It made sense that Seiji might have mentioned his name, even if he was just listing off his team members.

"I constantly tell him how terrible you are at fencing."

"Wow, Seiji!" Nicholas grumbled. "Thanks for nothing. Next time you mention me, could you tell him that I'm really improving?"

"I might if you actually were," said Seiji, so Nicholas was forced to go over and shove him.

It was cool to think that Seiji's dad was somewhat aware of Nicholas having a place in Seiji's life, that Seiji's dad might even remember Nicholas's name from phone calls with his son. Nicholas didn't really understand how it was with dads. Nicholas would have given a lot for his dad to call him, but his dad never would. He didn't know Nicholas existed.

Nicholas had asked often about who and where his dad was when he was small, but his mom hadn't told him for years. So Nicholas had made up a bunch of cool little-kid stories, like that his dad was totally awesome but super busy with important stuff, which was why he couldn't see Nicholas.

He'd always thought, really, that those were just dreams. It had been a shock to find out they were true. To find out his dad was Robert Coste, the finest fencer of his generation, who had long ago attended Kings Row just as Nicholas was now. Robert Coste, who had once won Olympic gold. Nicholas had hunted down a newspaper with an article about Robert Coste's victory at the Olympics and cut it out to keep. The picture was grainy and blurred, with Robert's golden hair blending with the gold of his trophy, but it was the only physical picture of his dad Nicholas owned. That was okay. It was the most important picture possible, because it showed the amazing thing his dad had accomplished.

Robert Coste didn't know about him, and Nicholas didn't

want him to. Not yet. Nicholas wasn't as skilled a fencer as his dad had been. He had to train more and learn better. People had called Nicholas "Zero" after a fencing match gone wrong, and he couldn't have Robert Coste thinking of him as a zero. Nicholas didn't want his dad to be disappointed in him when they finally met.

After all, Nicholas had competition: Robert Coste's other son. Jesse Coste, who had inherited his father's golden hair and shining fencing talent. Jesse, who had been Seiji's fencing partner for years, and whom Seiji hardly ever talked about. Yet whenever anyone mentioned Jesse, or on the thankfully few occasions when they'd encountered Jesse, all the muscles in Seiji's face had gone rigid as though he was in pain.

Nicholas was dreading the day Seiji found out about Nicholas's connection to Jesse Coste. He knew Seiji hated being reminded of him. And it was tough whenever Nicholas considered the fact that he was competing with Jesse not only for Robert's attention, but for Seiji's as well. Seiji wanted a rival with real skill, the type Jesse possessed. Sometimes when Seiji fenced Nicholas, it felt as if Seiji were looking through Nicholas to another fencer who had Nicholas's speed and Nicholas's left-handedness, but who was polished like a trophy. A better version of Nicholas. He didn't want his dad to see him that way.

Jesse had Nicholas's dad. But Nicholas had Jesse's fencing partner. Seiji went to Kings Row with Nicholas, not Jesse's stupid Exton, and he trained with Nicholas every day.

So Nicholas thought he could wait to meet his dad until he was officially Seiji's rival. Once Nicholas was a great fencer, Seiji wouldn't mind Nicholas being related to Jesse, because Jesse wouldn't matter to him anymore. Nicholas would be enough. His dad would be proud of him then.

Maybe if Nicholas excelled at Camp Menton, and Kings Row won the state championship. Maybe if he accomplished that, he could tell his dad who he was.

Nicholas planned to sneak his newspaper clipping of Robert Coste into his suitcase when Seiji wasn't looking. He couldn't go to France without his lucky charm.

6 AIDEN

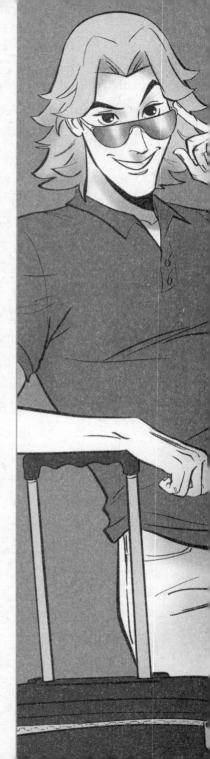

Wow, that had been a lot of horrible joy from freshmen too early in the morning. Being excited about going to France was so gauche. Did people not understand Aiden was *tired*?

"Leave me out of the team meetings next time," said Aiden, sighing as he rose to his feet. "Not sure I have the constitution to bear Nicholas Cox's haircut before breakfast."

"Aiden, do you remember what I talked to you about?" asked Coach Williams in her most ultra-solemn voice.

He had a dim recollection. She'd been using the ultra-solemn voice then, too.

"Not really," Aiden drawled. "Wasn't listening then, won't listen now."

He shut the door of the coach's office. As he made his way down the hall, his phone buzzed in his pocket, but when he slid it out of his uniform pants, it wasn't a guy trying to make a date. It was Rosina, the woman who'd almost been one of his many stepmothers, the one he'd loved. She wanted to reconnect, and Aiden had thought for a passing moment that he'd like to.

Not anymore. Even Harvard, the person who knew Aiden best, found the idea of getting closer to him to be the worst thing he could imagine. So Aiden already knew how reconnecting would end. Better for Rosina to be a little disappointed now than a lot disappointed later. This way, Aiden wouldn't have to *watch* her be disappointed.

He silenced his phone and put it back in his pocket without reading the message. The world was worryingly fuzzy around the edges, and his jaw was aching from clenching it too hard, but Aiden congratulated himself on a personal victory. He'd been in the same room as Harvard and hadn't looked at him more than three times, and now he'd escaped.

"Aiden!" called Harvard's voice behind him.

Aiden never got lucky. Aside from in the obvious sense.

"Hey." Aiden refused to pick up the pace on his sauntering stride. That would look like running away. "You go ahead to breakfast. I'm not hungry."

"Great," said Harvard. "Me neither. I want to talk."

"But I'm starving to death," protested Aiden as Harvard took hold of his elbow and piloted him down the brick walkway running along the quad, back to the dormitory.

Once again, Aiden's stupid body betrayed him, every cell too aware of Harvard's hand—on his *arm*, for God's sake. The cells were all in a rush of warm approval. *Yes, go with Harvard; yes, do whatever Harvard wants, yes.*

He hadn't been back to their room in . . . It had been a while. Harvard had made both beds. Aiden strolled over to the bedside and lay down across them, hoping this looked more like lounging than a collapse. His teddy bear, Harvard Paw, was tilting dangerously off the side of the bed. Aiden viciously crushed the urge to rescue the bear. He wasn't that little kid anymore, clutching his toy, trailing after Harvard in helpless adoration. He refused to be.

He closed his eyes. Oh, he was so tired. Maybe, if Harvard was here but didn't talk to him and wasn't in the bed, *maybe* Aiden could sleep.

"Could you open your eyes and look at me?" Harvard asked.

Aiden's eyes opened without his consciously willing it. Damn his idiot, treacherous body. Harvard was standing a careful distance from the bed. He didn't look wrecked, the way Aiden was. He looked like he always did, tall and strong, broader across the shoulders than the average fencer but able to walk softer than anyone, his black hair cropped close and his brown eyes the kindest in the world. He looked like everything Aiden had ever wanted in his whole life.

"Hey, Aiden," Harvard said in the gentle voice Aiden loved best. "Listen to me for a minute."

"Nah," Aiden responded. "I think I can guess what's going on. Coach told you to make sure your teammate fell in line, and you said, *Yes, Coach*, like a good little captain. But I'm gonna pass. Getting lectured seems like a buzzkill. Life's too short to do things I don't want to do."

"Is there anything you *do* want to do?" Harvard snapped.

"*Hmm*. I don't know," Aiden drawled. "Want to make out?"

Something flickered in Harvard's eyes, turning the gold in them dark. For a shocked, dizzy, delirious moment, Aiden thought Harvard might say yes. Then Harvard's mouth twisted, and Aiden realized the emotion darkening his eyes was disgust.

"I—what?" said Harvard, clearly at a loss faced with Aiden's revolting offer. "No."

Aiden smirked to show he didn't care at all. "Didn't think so."

Harvard sighed as if he found Aiden exasperating. Aiden had always believed it was fond exasperation, but maybe he was wrong.

"Yeah, Coach asked me to talk to you. She was concerned about your behavior. I am, too."

"Why?" asked Aiden.

Harvard frowned. "You just don't seem yourself."

Aiden laughed and made it convincing. "I've been messing around with a lot of guys, neglecting my fencing, and generally having a good time. How is that *not* like me?"

Harvard had no answer for that, Aiden saw to his bitter satisfaction. Aiden was simply living down to everyone's expectations.

The only thing that was different was that now Aiden had crushed out the last remnant of the little kid that trailed Harvard everywhere; that idiot who still hoped.

"I've always been a jackass," purred Aiden. "Nothing's changed. Isn't that what *you* wanted? For nothing to change?"

He had to get up off this bed and out of this room. He couldn't stand to be around Harvard, yet he felt like he couldn't bear to leave. That was why he had to go now.

Aiden decided he couldn't wait to go to France. Surely there would be many opportunities for oblivion there. He just wished he could also take a vacation from himself.

"Hey, bud. What's going on with you?" Harvard asked at last, his voice strained with the effort of being casual. "Let me help."

Okay, bro, be a pal and fall in love with me, Aiden snarled in his head. Only, Harvard had already made it perfectly clear he didn't want to do that.

"For the last time, there's nothing going on with me. I just like to have fun, Harvard." Aiden could almost see his own voice on the air, gleaming and cutting like razor wire. "I know the concept must be terribly confusing for you. Since you're no fun at all."

7 HARVARD

Harvard forced himself not to flinch. It was nothing he didn't already know, and it made sense that Aiden felt that way. Aiden had flings with heirs to Swiss banking fortunes and nights on the town with minor royalty. Harvard's parents were well-off, but Aiden's dad had stratospheric money, and that meant Aiden had access to all the most glittering and expensive entertainments in the world. Aiden clearly regarded their weekend trip to France as forgettable and pedestrian. Harvard himself was as exciting as Aiden's old teddy bear.

Aiden had wasted enough time with Harvard already.

"Sure, I get it," said Harvard. "Have as much fun as you want."

"Thanks for your permission, bud," Aiden returned. He spoke in the light way he always spoke, like the sound of silver bells, but there was a note underneath that sounded like steel.

It made Harvard uneasy, but what else could he do? He wasn't ever going to cramp Aiden's style. That was the whole point. No matter what Harvard wanted for himself, he couldn't be selfish.

Not even if Aiden was going to roll around on their bed, his honey-colored hair spilling across newly rumpled sheets, and murmur in his honey-smooth voice, *Want to make out?* Harvard had to dismiss the warm, lurching impulse to surrender and go over there. He had to sternly banish the memory of when Harvard had made his fatal error. How he'd kissed Aiden, at their door, on their bed, and hadn't wanted to stop. Things like that didn't mean to Aiden what they meant to Harvard. Things like that didn't mean anything to Aiden at all.

You've always been the only one who could talk sense into him, Coach had said. Surely, they still had that between them: that Aiden would trust what Harvard told him, and know Harvard was saying it for Aiden's own good. If they didn't have that, maybe they didn't have anything at all.

"I'm just giving you a word of warning," Harvard urged. "Do whatever you want but try to be more careful. Coach says you're getting into trouble practically every day. She said the principal talked to your dad, and your dad won't put up with you being suspended."

"Great news," said Aiden. "Once again being rich and pretty means facing absolutely no consequences."

"What if there are consequences?" Harvard hesitated. "You could get in real trouble. Seriously, he's talking about taking you out of school if you keep getting in trouble. What if they asked you to leave school?"

"Oh, please," said Aiden. "Who'd do that? I'm so ornamental."

He sounded as though the idea of leaving Kings Row didn't bother him at all. Harvard was hurt enough to fall silent. They'd planned their future together for so long, how they'd go to boarding school and fence together, plotting under their blankets through a hundred sleepovers over the years. Then they'd seen Kings Row, with its quaint old-fashioned classrooms that still had hinged wooden desks and blackboards, with its deep lake and deeper woods. They had walked through the quad for the first time, and Aiden had spun around one of the pillars lining the walkways as he agreed that this was the place.

"You know me, Harvard," said his best friend.

Harvard had always believed he did.

Aiden's cat-green eyes surveyed their room—the beds pushed together, the teddy bear fallen on its side—with indifference that seemed close to contempt. Then his gaze rested on Harvard. His eyes were as flat as they were brilliant, his smile sparkling and cold as a diamond. It was clear to Harvard that nothing he'd said had made the slightest impression.

"I can get out of anything," Aiden claimed.

He'd always been able to reach Aiden. But now Aiden seemed impossibly distant.

"Right," Harvard said quietly. There didn't seem much else to say.

"Right." Aiden's smile showed another blinding facet. For the first time in Harvard's life, he found himself wanting to look away from his best friend. Yet somehow, terribly, he still couldn't tear his eyes off him. "Catch you later, Harvard."

"When?" Harvard had to ask.

"Haven't you heard?" Aiden asked lightly as he strolled out of the door. "We're going to France."

Harvard almost called out for him to return, but he'd realized years ago when guys started paying attention to Aiden that he shouldn't hold Aiden back. He didn't have the right. He'd be a bad friend if he tried. So Harvard watched Aiden go, and he didn't say a word.

When the door closed behind Aiden, Harvard's phone buzzed. *See?* Harvard thought. *I'm fun. I'm popular. Cool people text me constantly.*

The text was from his mom, but Harvard thought his mom was very cool so that was all right. *Have fun in France! Be safe. Maybe you'll meet a nice boy!*

Harvard texted back, *I don't know if nice boys are my type.*

Current evidence seemed to suggest not.

His mom texted instantly: *Maybe you'll meet a boy with a certain je ne sais quoi.*

I don't know, Harvard texted.

Exactly! she texted in return, along with many laughing-face emojis and various other emojis as she always did. Old people, even cool old people like his mom, didn't get emojis. Harvard's mom claimed he was the one who didn't understand them.

His mom was right as usual, Harvard decided, going over to his wardrobe and starting to pack. He included a first aid kit since Nicholas was coming along on this trip. It was best to be prepared. The whole team would enjoy France. He and Aiden would get back to normal soon. Harvard ignored the sick feeling in the pit of his stomach and decided he was looking forward to Camp Menton.

He could have fun, too, *Aiden*.

Fun in a responsible way. He was the captain. He'd made too many mistakes already. Now he had to make the right choices.

8 SEIJI

Seiji couldn't believe he was being forced to waste even more time on this ill-advised French escapade. Yet *someone* had to supervise Nicholas's packing. Nicholas kept getting it wrong.

First of all, Nicholas had tried to pack his clothes in a backpack, which was upsetting. Apparently, Nicholas didn't own a suitcase, so Seiji got out his spare one and insisted he disliked it and was throwing it out if Nicholas didn't take it off his hands. Suitcase arranged, Nicholas then attempted to go to France with no pajamas, so Seiji forced him to pack the pajamas he'd given Nicholas on a previous occasion. He couldn't help noticing that Nicholas didn't wear them.

"Does everyone wear pajamas in France?" asked Nicholas sadly.

"Yes," said Seiji.

Everyone rational wore pajamas,

in every country. Nicholas was basically feral. Nicholas also seemed to have very odd ideas about France.

"What are the people in France like?" he asked Seiji on the morning they were supposed to leave. Nicholas had a hard time getting up early to practice, like he should, but he *would* spring out of bed to pack for the twelfth time.

"They're like people who speak French."

Seiji didn't know what else to say. People were confusing and terrible everywhere.

"I need a baguette." Nicholas fretted.

"They have baguettes in France."

"Then I need a beret!"

Nicholas cast a searching look around the dormitory. He had started stealing Seiji's stuff, which Seiji had decided Nicholas was allowed to do, but Seiji didn't have any berets stashed in his room. Seiji *had* no berets. Seiji needed no berets.

"We will be spending our time in France fencing," Seiji reminded Nicholas. "Do you intend to put a beret on top of your mask? Do you think that would be a good look for you?"

A smile dawned on Nicholas's face. It wasn't a making-a-joke-about-Seiji-in-his-head smile. Seiji was very familiar with those. It was more a sharing-the-joke-with-Seiji smile. Seiji liked those well enough, though he'd never made an intentional joke in his life.

"Might look dashing," said Nicholas easily.

Seiji thought it was possible he would enjoy the upcoming

trip, if it weren't for the constant insidious thoughts of Jesse. Last time, going to France had put an ocean between him and Jesse. This time, Seiji was flying toward him. Memories of Seiji's former life kept intruding.

Seiji had attended many fencing camps, and many international fencing matches, in Jesse's company. Jesse was used to such trips, as was Seiji. Jesse's father usually arranged for someone to pack for them, so they could maintain total fencing focus. International travel had never been complete chaos before. Nicholas's particular and perpetual chaos was new to Seiji, but he was becoming accustomed. He scrutinized the room carefully to see if Nicholas had hidden his pajamas or forgotten his passport. Finding all as it should be at last, he turned to see Nicholas surveying the room with an extremely startled air.

Oh no, Seiji thought. *What now?* But then Nicholas began to grin.

"Seiji!" said Nicholas, beaming. "*Seiji*. You took down the shower curtain."

"Of course I did."

Seiji wasn't certain why Nicholas looked so pleased. Then he worked it out.

"Ah, I see you've misunderstood completely. I *packed* the curtain," Seiji informed him. "We will need it for our room in France."

Nicholas was undaunted. Nicholas was rarely daunted by anything, which was one of his best qualities. Seiji had been informed *he* was daunting, but Nicholas never seemed to feel that way.

"You wanna be roommates in France, too?" Nicholas asked brightly. "Can't bear to be parted from me?"

"I dream of being parted from you!" Seiji shoved Nicholas the way Nicholas had shoved him a couple of days ago, which Nicholas seemed to mean as a friendly gesture. "I simply accept you as an unfortunate fact of life at this point."

Had Nicholas wanted to share a room with his friend Bobby? Seiji understood if Nicholas would prefer that, but Bobby was almost certainly sharing a room with Dante, the tall one who didn't like fencing. Unless Bobby had become tired of Dante's anti-fencing attitude.

"You didn't have to pack the shower curtain," said Nicholas, sudden packing expert. "I think they have shower curtains in France." Nicholas paused. "*Do* they have shower curtains in France? Seiji! Tell me."

Seiji checked his favorite watch, which was faintly pink for Nicholas-related reasons but worked fine. "I suppose you'll have to wait and see."

Nicholas had absurdly poor timekeeping skills, so Seiji had to shepherd him out of the dormitory and toward the bus that would take them to the airport. At the bottom of the stairs, Nicholas panicked about not having enough socks. He made a break for socks and freedom and had to be marched down the halls, which made them late. Everyone else had arrived before them. Seiji had never been late for anything before and was deeply shamed. The bus was already waiting, idling under the autumn trees. As Seiji climbed aboard, he glanced over his shoulder at the old redbrick buildings against the green lawn and gold leaves. The school that was nothing like the school he'd planned on. The school where, as his father wanted, he could choose his own battles.

It was a slightly silly feeling, since they would be back in four days, but Seiji realized he was sorry to be leaving Kings Row.

This school was a refuge for him against Jesse. Here, he wasn't just Jesse's fencing partner, the less shining half of a whole and only there to make Jesse look good.

Seiji wasn't sure who he would be at Camp Menton.

There was a torrent of greetings on their arrival. Coach Williams commanded them to sit down. Harvard called out, "Hey," then told them off in a captainly fashion for being late. Eugene fist-bumped Nicholas, and Bobby waved his arms enthusiastically to attract Nicholas's attention.

"Hi, Seiji," Bobby added in a very tiny voice, when Nicholas and Seiji grabbed the seats in front of Bobby and Dante.

"Hi," said Seiji in a voice that was at his normal level.

He'd noticed Bobby was extremely talkative with anyone who wasn't Seiji. Many people disliked Seiji, but he wished Bobby would hide his dislike better. It made social interactions even more uncomfortable than they had to be.

To cover for the awkwardness, Seiji gazed around the bus, and he spotted Aiden lying stretched out on the back seat, clearly pretending to sleep and thus unavailable for comment. Seiji could tell he was pretending by the tension in Aiden's frame. It was obvious, like a fencer on the edge of losing his match, feigning that he wasn't scared.

There was a line of brightness on the horizon, like a slice of lemon dropped into the sky.

As the bus took a turn down a winding lane, the brightness was lost, and so was Seiji's last sight of Kings Row. They drove toward darkness...and Jesse.

9 NICHOLAS

It was the first time Nicholas Cox
had ever been on a plane, and Seiji
was trying to strangle him. Or, at
least, Seiji had grabbed Nicholas by
the back of his collar while Nicholas
was still walking. The flight attendants stared at Nicholas asphyxiat-
ing, wearing expressions of polite
distress, but nobody stepped forward
to save him.

"You're going the wrong way," Seiji's voice said from behind his back.

"You could've just said that, Seiji,"
protested Nicholas, once he could
breathe again.

"I could have," Seiji agreed with
unruffled calm.

Nicholas had simply been turning
right, following the flood of people
in front of him. The line had broken
down halfway through the long glass
tunnel, and now it was all a rush.

They were like swallows flying south. Except Seiji refused to be a swallow.

"I was going the way everyone else was going," Nicholas pointed out.

"Yeah, but we're in first class," said Eugene. "Which is pretty cool. I've never been in first class before."

Why did planes have classes? Seiji's grip on Nicholas's collar was tugging him to the left, but Nicholas took a swift, curious glance to the right before he followed along.

To the right was most of the plane, row upon row of people.

"Oh, those guys don't have enough room," Nicholas murmured in concern.

"That's business class, bro," said Eugene. "Look deeper."

Farther back it was worse than the city buses at rush hour. People were packed in on top of one another like cans in the grocery store.

"People pay for this?"

"Yeah, the current system leaves a lot to be desired, but you're holding up the line, and that's not likely to help," Harvard said in a kind but firm tone. "Move, Cox."

Nicholas let Seiji pull him into first class. In first class, the seats were so big they looked like beds set in fancy plastic thrones. In first class, there were curtains with tiny fringes.

"Wow, this is nice," Nicholas said, slightly distressed. "I could've gone to sit in the, um, third class."

"They don't call it third class," Bobby told him. "It's first, business, and coach, so the people in coach don't feel any worse about being in coach."

Nicholas raised his eyebrows. "Well, that's not how numbers work. That's like saying *one, cauliflower, bicycle*."

"My father calls coach *cattle class*," Aiden drawled.

He was standing beside Harvard and was apparently angry at the world, as usual these days. Nicholas noticed that Aiden looked exhausted. He could sympathize: He'd been so excited about traveling that he didn't get any sleep last night. Maybe Aiden had been up all night packing!

"You can't sit in coach," Seiji told Nicholas. "You can't compromise your mobility and embarrass me during your matches at Camp Menton. People know we train together."

Nicholas hadn't considered that before, that what he did reflected on Seiji as well as on Coach Williams and Kings Row. He wanted to do well even more now. He wanted to make them all proud.

They filtered to their plastic throne seats. In a stroke of luck, Nicholas was assigned to sit beside Seiji. Dante and Bobby were behind them. Eugene had to sit with Coach. The assistant coach was farther back and seemed disappointed to be separated from them.

Eugene seemed stoked. That made sense, since Coach was pretty awesome. Coach had already sat down and taken out a stack of magazines: *Home and Saber*, *National Saber*, the *Saber Evening Post*, and *Saber Living*.

They weren't supposed to disturb Coach during the flight. Coach had been very firm on this subject. Nicholas wondered if it would disturb her a lot if he asked quietly to borrow one of her magazines.

He leaned across the aisle. "Coach, can I—"

Coach held up her magazine so that Nicholas could see the back. At home in Kings Row, Coach had many sayings that were forbidden, all posted on the wall of the gym. Boys were forbidden to say that épées were better than sabers, or despairingly claim "We lost because of me." If anyone said forbidden phrases, they were punished by having to do suicide runs. On the back of her magazine, Coach had taped a note that read, *COACH, CAN I TALK TO YOU DURING THE FLIGHT?*

Realistically, Coach couldn't make him do suicide runs on a plane. Could she?

Coach's dark eyes met Nicholas's over her magazine. Nicholas subsided back into his plane throne.

"Great choice, Cox," said Coach Williams, and returned to the *Saber Evening Post*.

Aiden had also been lucky with his seat assignment and was supposed to sit with the captain. But since Aiden was a disaster, ungrateful for the good things the world provided him with, he was standing in the aisle, making complaints in a lazy voice that Nicholas had heard one of Aiden's fans call *languid*. To Nicholas, *languid* just seemed like a fancy word for *lazy*.

"Sir, I have to ask you to sit down," said a flight attendant, who looked a bit dazed by Aiden in the way most people did, as if Aiden's face were the equivalent of a two-by-four that struck heads with great force. "It's in the regulations."

Aiden winked. "I have to ask. . . . Do rules really apply to the handsome?"

"Yeah, I'm pretty sure they do," said Harvard, when the flight attendant failed to reply.

"If you recline both chairs and bring down the armrests, you can lower a small pod over yourself and sleep in a luxurious pod bed," the flight attendant offered helpfully. She demonstrated, bringing down Harvard's armrest to create a larger space.

Aiden flushed as though suddenly startled, but with no other spots available, he had no choice but to sit next to Harvard. He gingerly lowered himself into his seat, keeping his eyes focused straight ahead.

Nicholas looked around to share this Aiden-related weirdness with Seiji, but Seiji had produced a book from his bag. On the cover was a woman in hijab, holding a fencing foil balanced lightly against her shoulder. Seiji was already some way into the book and had an air that suggested there would be dire consequences if he was disturbed.

Deciding to disturb Seiji later, Nicholas craned his neck to see Bobby and Dante immersed in a conversation that was mostly Bobby talking and Dante giving nonverbal cues.

Harvard and Aiden seemed to have settled down.

Nicholas turned back to Seiji and tried to get a look at his book. Seiji shot him an annoyed glance, so Nicholas elbowed him. Then the plane, which had been zooming down the runway, jolted into the air and seemed to leave Nicholas's stomach on the runway behind him. Nicholas flailed, yelped, and hid his face in Seiji's shoulder. It was a sudden and shocking feeling, after sixteen years spent on the ground.

Seiji made a sharp irritated noise, then a relenting but still irritated sound, and patted Nicholas awkwardly on the shoulder once.

"Let go of my shirt, Nicholas," he said. Nicholas found Seiji's icy annoyance comforting in its familiarity.

Nicholas kept hold of Seiji's shirt. The plane could lurch again at any moment. He only detached when the flight attendants came by with what was apparently just the first round of free food. They were offered tiny sandwiches and fancy flavored sparkling water in glasses with stems. Nicholas and Eugene had a conversation with the nice flight attendant about what was in the sandwiches and why they were so tiny.

"You eating your tiny sandwiches?" Nicholas asked Eugene.

"Yeah. Don't mess with my protein intake," said Eugene, as stern as Eugene ever got.

Nicholas sighed, accepting his fate, and tried again to peek at the book Seiji was reading. Seiji held it farther away from Nicholas without taking his eyes off the page.

"What's the book about?"

"The life and fencing experiences of Ibtihaj Muhammad. She

was a bronze medalist in the 2016 summer Olympics," Seiji told him. "She's one of my personal heroes and role models. You can read the book after I'm done."

But what was Nicholas supposed to do now? He read the in-flight magazine, which told him more about the plane. Also about many whiskeys and colognes, but Nicholas didn't really care about those. He looked up *fencing documentaries* on the search function on the screen in front of him and got a documentary about building a fence between America and Mexico. No thanks! The only actual fencing documentary was one Coach had already made them all watch six times. Nicholas felt the in-flight entertainment didn't understand how to entertain him.

"The flight attendant said if we recline both our chairs and bring down the armrests, we can lower a small pod over ourselves and sleep in our small pod bed," Nicholas told Seiji. "Want to be in a small pod?"

Seiji turned a page of his fencing book without even glancing up. "I don't."

Nicholas felt a lurch of unease, though that might have been the plane swooping some more. This was all so strange to him, and so obviously nothing new to Seiji.

"Are you still startled by the plane?" Seiji asked.

Nicholas shrugged.

"You can read the book with me," offered Seiji. "But don't ask me to turn a page before I'm ready. You know I like to take my time and make mental notes."

"Totally." Nicholas leaned in against Seiji's shoulder. After a few minutes of interesting reading, he asked, "When do you think you might be done with this page?"

Seiji rolled his eyes, then said, "I'm not eating all my sandwiches."

Nicholas cheered up. He could get used to new situations, like he'd grown to love his school. He was starting to like the plane already. The Kings Row team was going on an amazing adventure. France would be great.

10 HARVARD

Harvard was frustrated. Just days ago, he would've been thrilled to have been seated next to his best friend for the whole trip from New York, to Paris, then to Nice. Before everything happened between them, they had shared seats on other flights, bus rides, and various trips. It was always comfortable, and it was always fun, but now everything was different.

Now Harvard could only think of one of the last times he'd sat this closely with Aiden, when they'd shared a seat on a Ferris wheel on a date. Harvard tried not to reminisce about that day and what came after, but it was hard when Aiden was this close to him for the first time in days.

They were stuck together on this flight to Paris. For seven hours.

The seats in first class were huge,

77

but the flight attendant had lowered the barrier between them so that they could sleep together in a pod. Which, obviously, they weren't going to do.

Who had invented the double meaning of *sleeping together*? It was a confusing and distressing phrase. Harvard had slept in the same bed as Aiden on countless sleepovers, had slept with their beds pushed together since they came to Kings Row. In the olden days, when people had to sleep in the same bed and nothing could happen, a sword might be laid down between them.

Harvard's obliviousness to his own feelings had been the sword laid between them, and now it was gone. Every molecule of Harvard's body was terribly aware of the warmth of Aiden beside him, a fraction of an inch away and impossibly distant.

Be a good team captain, be sensible, don't let anybody down, Harvard told himself, and redirected his attention firmly toward the others. Bobby was singing a song. *"I love fencing in the springtime, I love fencing in the fall—"*

Dante was sitting beside Bobby, a faint smile discernible on his face as Bobby sang.

Seiji cleared his throat. "The high school fencing season typically lasts from early September until late January. Of course, for any serious fencer, it's a year-round commitment. If preparing for the summer Olympics, I agree the springtime would be crucial."

"Um," Bobby said in crushed, flat tones. "That's a great point. Thanks, Seiji."

"It's fine. Did you make up that song yourself?" Seiji asked, relenting and speaking in his *I am taking an interest in Nicholas's friends* voice.

The voice alarmed the other students even more than Seiji's regular voice. Harvard sympathized. Seiji was a great kid, and an even better fencer, but seeing Seiji try to have normal social interactions was like watching the Terminator at a children's tea party.

"Ah...yes," said Bobby.

"Very droll," said Seiji.

"Sorry for bothering you," whispered Bobby, staring at the back of Seiji's head with love that—naturally—flew right over Seiji's head.

Dante's smile had snapped off. Neither Bobby nor Seiji noticed.

"You're not bothering me," Seiji told Bobby. "*Nicholas* is bothering me."

Nicholas, who was taking up half of Seiji's seat because his arms and legs went everywhere, and was eating Seiji's sandwiches, gave Seiji a thumbs-up. "You know it."

Harvard started when a weight hit him unexpectedly, then glanced to the side and realized Aiden had fallen asleep on Harvard's shoulder.

When Harvard moved, Aiden made a low complaining sound that, because something fundamental had gone wrong in Harvard's brain, Harvard found sweet. Harvard shifted so that Aiden would be more comfortable, and sighed inwardly. Aiden really should take better care of himself. It couldn't be all running around having good times with hot boys, Harvard thought, his chest twisting with misery, which he quelled immediately. This wasn't about Harvard. This was about his best friend, and how Aiden should sleep occasionally.

A lock of Aiden's hair, silk soft as a whisper, brushed against Harvard's ear. Harvard endured the torture and turned his attention desperately back on the rest of the team.

Bobby appeared to have cheered up. He and Eugene were telling each other facts about France that they seemed to both know but seemed equally happy to hear. Bobby caught Harvard looking their way as they chattered.

"You know everything, Harvard!" he said enthusiastically.

"Not really," said Harvard.

Bobby sighed admiringly. "And you're so modest. Will you tell us all about Camp Menton?"

Harvard gave Bobby a kind smile, to make up for Seiji accidentally crushing Bobby's tender heart on the reg.

"Sure, I can tell you everything I know about Camp Menton. One thing to remember is that we'll all have to be on our best behavior and train our hardest. They are famous for their discipline and how rigorous their training program is. Some teams have even failed out of training because they weren't able to hack it. Can you imagine the shame?"

Everyone looked alarmed, even sweet Bobby, who wasn't on the team and wouldn't be training at all.

Harvard was sorry to frighten them, but trouble *did* seem to follow the Kings Row team around. This might be a good opportunity to scare the team into watching their behavior. "Maybe it's an urban legend, but I heard one fencer was permanently banned from the camp. Of course," Harvard added, to be fair, "maybe he deserved it. The guy was infamous for his bad temper."

He raised an eyebrow at Nicholas and Seiji, who'd been caught fistfighting in an equipment closet a few weeks ago. Seiji looked icily unimpressed. Nicholas gave Harvard a mischievous grin.

"Sounds like a cool guy."

"Another time, a whole team was thrown out of camp, and then suspended from their school," Harvard went on. "They say it was because they were having parties in their rooms at night, but who knows?"

Bobby's eyes went wide as saucers. "Do you think they were engaging in . . . debaucheries?"

Dante's faint smile was back, except now it was a faint smirk. "What kind of debaucheries?"

Bobby hit Dante in the arm with a small fist. "Wild debaucheries! Don't interrupt me. You talk too much!"

Dante subsided with a grin.

When Harvard's voice sank, solemn and hushed, Aiden made a fretful noise in his sleep. Harvard passed a hand over Aiden's water-smooth hair before continuing, and Aiden settled with a content sigh.

It almost felt nice, until Harvard imagined one of the anonymous boys Aiden was clearly used to snuggling with. Then Harvard felt sick instead.

"So we're all going to train hard and behave perfectly, right, team?" Harvard asked.

"Totally, Captain," said Nicholas with automatic enthusiasm, then bit his lip. "Behave perfectly? Me?"

"Yeah, we might be tilting at windmills here," Harvard admitted with a grin. "But I trust my team can do anything."

Several members of his trusty team looked confused.

"What does this camp expect us to do with windmills?" demanded Nicholas.

"*Tilting at windmills* means trying to fight them," Harvard explained.

Seiji's perpetual frown became more pronounced. "I do not see how you could win a fight against a windmill?"

"That's the point, bro," contributed Eugene. "It's become a saying for people who take on hopeless causes or fight battles they can't win, because they've got big dreams."

"Hey, check you out, Labao," said Harvard. "Unexpected breadth of literary knowledge."

"You can listen to audiobooks at the gym, you know. I've got depths," claimed Eugene. "Many depths. I'm a brocean."

Harvard grinned at Eugene. "I believe in you."

"I'll do my best to behave," promised Nicholas, and sneaked a glance at Seiji. "I don't wanna let anybody down."

Harvard knew he'd keep his word. Nicholas was a good kid, as well as a good fencer. He turned to the window and saw the sea glittering miles and miles below the plane, seeming distant as starshine.

For a moment, when he turned, Aiden stirred. Harvard felt a flash of icy dread that Aiden might wake and be cruel again, and everything would be as cold and strange as it had been for the past few lonely days.

Aiden just whispered, "Hey, Harvard," in his ear. He sounded like he was smiling.

Harvard couldn't help smiling, too. "Hey," he murmured back, soft as a song to send Aiden back to sleep.

Once Aiden's breathing had gone regular as Harvard's heartbeat, he forced his attention off his best friend and back to his team. He was still smiling.

"Enough doom. What are you guys looking forward to the most about France?" Harvard asked the group.

"Did they invent French kissing in France?" Eugene asked. "Kind of interested in finding out more about that at Camp Menton."

Harvard was the captain and the oldest . . . and he'd had his first kiss last week. Now his horrible team had turned the conversation to kissing when Aiden was so close. He could feel his ears burning so hot they might turn to cinders and fall off.

"Wow, Aiden and Harvard just broke up! Don't be insensitive. Don't worry about it, Captain," declared Nicholas, a sweet kid who Harvard might be forced to drown. "I haven't kissed anyone ever. Like, who cares? Busy being awesome at fencing, right?"

"... PleasebequietNicholas...," said Harvard.

To Harvard's intense sorrow, Nicholas kept talking.

"So, Captain—"

"Who's being awesome at fencing?" Seiji asked Nicholas. "Surely you can't be referring to yourself."

Undaunted, Nicholas said, "Have you had your first kiss, Eugene?"

"Waiting for someone special, bro," said Eugene. "Kinda hoping it will be magical. And I hear France is a romantic land."

"We are there to fence!" snapped Seiji.

Thank God for Seiji.

"Seiji, have you—" Nicholas began.

"If I kill you in France," mused Seiji, "will that be an international incident?"

"I can't believe we're not even in France yet," said Coach, "and already I have to make several new rules. No kissing. No killing." Nicholas opened his mouth. Without glancing at Nicholas or even taking her eyes off her magazine, Coach added, "No arguing."

Forbidden to argue out loud, Nicholas and Seiji began to silently fight over the pages of Seiji's book.

Lulled by the sound of Aiden's breathing in the sudden quiet, Harvard fell asleep. He surfaced briefly when they changed planes in Paris, stumbling to their connecting flight, but fell back asleep as soon as they sat down. He stirred when the pilot announced they had lost their slot on the runway and would have to circle Nice airport, and he let himself fall back asleep as they flew in slow sweet circles around in the sun. He woke at the jolt when the wheels of the plane hit the runway and found his cheek resting against Aiden's hair. He was warm and content for a moment, then memories rushed back to scald him, and Harvard jerked away.

Aiden stirred and pulled himself from his spot on Harvard's shoulder. If he noticed Harvard's slipup, he certainly didn't show it as he gave Harvard a tight smile. None of Aiden's smiles seemed sincere these days.

Aiden was the first to rise when the plane came to a halt. He grabbed his suitcase, then stretched as he tied up his hair. Harvard gave him a single glance—the hair scooped up in Aiden's hands was the color of sand in shadow, Aiden's body a carelessly graceful arch against the pale sunlight—then looked away. The first thing Harvard had said during their first kiss, Harvard's first kiss ever, was *I love your hair*. In retrospect, that was so humiliating. Could Harvard have been more of a clumsy fool, making it so obvious that the kiss meant far more to him than it should have? No wonder everybody knew. No wonder Aiden was trying so hard to make it clear he could do better.

Harvard straightened up, shouldered the weight of his bag, and made his way out, too. Nicholas and the others followed him out into warm, dusty-gold air.

They went through customs and, now officially in France, boarded a second bus.

The sun shed brilliance across the deep blue sea, and the bus rattled down the road along the Côte d'Azur toward Camp Menton. Harvard didn't let himself rest. Everything was bright, but the warmth seemed lost.

11 AIDEN

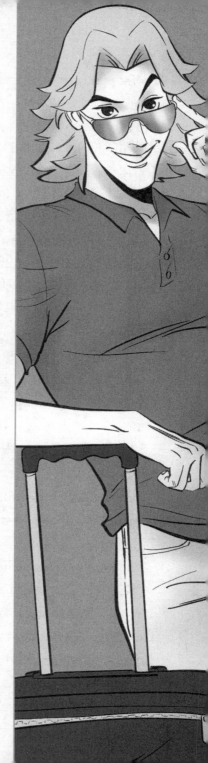

In the dream, he was warm and happy. At first, Harvard's voice seemed a natural part of the dream: Of course he was there. Hearing him tell a story was how Aiden slept best.

Then Aiden felt Harvard's breath halt and his shoulder stiffen under his cheek. Ah, of course. Harvard must feel terribly uncomfortable snuggling with his *buddy*. Since that was all they were to each other. Obviously, Aiden had totally embarrassed them both, and shamed himself, by cuddling up to Harvard in his sleep.

He was tempted to feign slumber for an instant longer, hold on to that feeling of peace and not let go, but since that was pathetic Aiden pretended to stir awake. He pulled away from his best friend's body, barely taking a moment to shoot Harvard a tight-lipped smile. Harvard immediately glanced away, avoiding his gaze.

Aiden's chest tightened. So be it. It was better to just pretend nothing had happened, as if the position they were in was perfectly normal. As soon as the plane shuddered to a halt, Aiden jumped out of his seat so that he could get out of this metal tube and away from Harvard as quickly as he could.

It wasn't Aiden's most graceful exit.

Aiden wasn't great at dealing with rejection. He'd had very little practice, because of being so good-looking. But the plain truth of the matter was that no one but Harvard had been able to hurt him in the past. He'd never loved anyone else.

"It's good that you got some rest," Seiji said in his cool, neutral voice as they waited to gather their luggage in the main terminal. "You can't fence at your usual skill level when not rested. And your usual skill level isn't that high."

Aiden raised an eyebrow. "High enough to beat you that one time, as I recall."

He'd done so by taunting Seiji about Seiji's spectacular loss against Jesse Coste. It wasn't nice of him to remind Seiji of that, but nobody ever said Aiden was nice.

"It won't happen again," said Seiji calmly.

Seiji had a chiaroscuro sort of face, to go with his personality. He was a handsome enough kid, Aiden supposed. He was so far from Aiden's type he resided in a different type galaxy, but little Bobby Rodriguez clearly thought Seiji was the dreamiest. Aiden didn't see the attraction in severe lines, with no warmth or pity to be found anywhere.

"I'm glad you're feeling better," Seiji proceeded. "What Harvard said on the plane was correct. The training at Camp Menton will be rigorous. European fencers tend to be of higher caliber than Americans. I don't want to be embarrassed for anyone from Kings Row, and your behavior has been embarrassing ever since you and Harvard stopped dating."

Aiden's voice almost failed him. "Excuse me?"

It hadn't occurred to him that conclusions might be drawn about him and Harvard. When Aiden had agreed (far too eagerly) to teach Harvard the ropes of dating, he hadn't imagined it would cause much comment. After all, Aiden had dated practically every hot guy in school. What was one more date?

Nobody knew that it had never been real. That Harvard would never date Aiden for real.

Clearly, Aiden was so transparent that *Seiji Katayama*, a guy who probably counted épées to send himself to sleep, knew what was going on.

Seiji's merciless black eyes searched Aiden's face, seeing too much again. "I think perhaps I should not have said that. I was thinking about fencing. I didn't intend to hurt your feeli—"

"My feelings?" Aiden bit out. "Listen up, freshman. I don't have those. Do you have any idea how many people I've dated? And I've never cared about any of them."

Seiji, plainly unable to deal with this situation, looked around for his security idiot, Nicholas Cox. Nicholas and Eugene had gotten their bags first and wandered off while the others waited, only to return a few minutes later holding cardboard cartons of yellow ice cream. Nicholas offered Seiji his wooden spoon, and Seiji made a face.

"That's disgusting. You're disgusting."

Nicholas seemed pleased to have Seiji's attention.

"Bro, we were looking for you to translate our French, but not to brag, we handled ourselves pretty well French-wise." Eugene beamed proudly. "I take Spanish for the easy A," he added.

"The ice cream was free," said Nicholas, offering it again, as though the information the ice cream hadn't been paid for would make Seiji think it was more appetizing.

Seiji waved the ice cream away irritably.

"We were slightly worried, since it's yellow," said Eugene. "Which, nice color! Cheerful. Good vibes. But I'm allergic to pineapples. So we had to check if it was pineapple flavor. We were like, *comment* flavor, my French bro?"

"Eugene said that, but I provided moral French support," supplied Nicholas. "And he said something about perfume? And we were like, we don't want any perfume. We eventually managed to convince him."

"*Parfum* means *flavor*," said Seiji.

"Oh," said Nicholas. "Everything makes sense now. Well, we got the important part. The ice cream is *ananas* flavor, and *ananas* was obvious even to me. Banana ice cream! It doesn't really taste like bananas, but honestly? Neither does banana-flavored gum."

"Wait. Nicholas." Seiji frowned.

Nicholas grinned. "Do you want some after all?"

Seiji recoiled from the persistent ice cream offering.

There was an important detail in Nicholas's chattering, but Aiden couldn't really hear over the humiliated pounding in his own head. If Seiji knew, then everyone knew. Everyone at Kings Row knew Aiden had feelings for Harvard, and they *pitied* him.

Thank God they were in France.

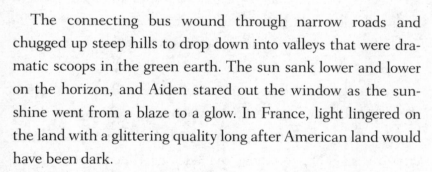

The connecting bus wound through narrow roads and chugged up steep hills to drop down into valleys that were dramatic scoops in the green earth. The sun sank lower and lower on the horizon, and Aiden stared out the window as the sunshine went from a blaze to a glow. In France, light lingered on the land with a glittering quality long after American land would have been dark.

Aiden heard Bobby murmuring something about wild debaucheries. He wouldn't have expected that of Bobby, but wild debaucheries sounded good to Aiden right about now.

The bus was going through the town of Menton, almost at camp. The houses in Menton were as brightly colored as a box of candy, yellow and green and pink. They cast a multihued shimmer on the rippling turquoise waters, colors shifting on the waves like flags in a breeze. Nicholas Cox, who'd clearly been raised by rats in a gutter, had the tip of his nose pressed against the bus window. He seemed totally enraptured, dancing lights reflected in his eyes.

"Seiji, do you see? Seiji, this is so cool!"

Seiji, face impassive, looked at Nicholas.

"Yes," said Seiji. "I like it, too."

Nicholas and Seiji made Aiden feel sick. He wasn't sure if it was because they were so stupid and young, or because they were happy.

Five minutes away from Menton proper lay Camp Menton, a collection of rambling gray stone buildings and more modern houses, built low with their vast windows facing the ocean. The motley assortment of buildings was held together by a ring of lemon trees and a short stone wall.

Ornate gates stood open to welcome them. Beside the gates, there were three people waiting. Aiden recognized one of them, because even though the setting sun reduced everyone to silhouettes, the sight of one silhouette made Seiji flinch.

Jesse Coste.

Seiji and Nicholas no longer seemed happy. Well, being hopeful and young had to end sometime.

"I don't feel great," mumbled Eugene as the bus rolled to a halt.

"Join the club," Aiden snapped.

Harvard helped Aiden get his suitcase out of the baggage

hold. The perfect captain and the perfect best friend. "You ready for Camp Menton, buddy?"

Harvard was calling Aiden that a lot lately. He was making himself clear, Aiden supposed. Maybe soon Harvard would take a leaf out of Eugene's book and start calling Aiden *bro*.

Aiden gave Harvard a glittering smile. "Sure am. But ask yourself this, *pal*: Is Camp Menton ready for me?"

12 NICHOLAS

It had been a long journey, and Nicholas was pleased to spot a woman waiting for them. She had an air of authority and was wearing the black-and-silver uniform of the Camp Menton coaches. He was looking forward to being shown around the camp and then shown to his and Seiji's room. Nicholas was anticipating rest at the end of such a long day.

But, of course, the day couldn't end without taking a wrong turn.

"Seiji! What a totally unexpected surprise," declared a familiar voice. There against the lemon trees and the strange sky stood Jesse Coste.

His father's other son. Seiji's other fencing partner.

"You again," mumbled Nicholas.

Jesse didn't seem to hear him. Jesse didn't seem to even *notice* him. He only had eyes for Seiji.

The Kings Row team stood in the dust kicked up by the bus wheels turning on the narrow road, silently staring at the apparition that was Jesse. Seiji seemed to have turned to wood, his whole attention on the boy in front of him.

Jesse Coste wandered closer, blond as Nicholas's worst nightmare. The more he grinned, the more Nicholas wanted to punch him, and the deeper Seiji seemed to enter his fugue state. Seiji said in a determinedly calm voice, "Hello, Jesse," and continued to stare.

Seiji and Jesse seemed in a world of their own, where nobody else existed. Certainly not Nicholas. Seiji was always more affected by Jesse than he ever was by anyone else. Jesse got everything, and Nicholas couldn't help the resentful knot that formed in his stomach, even though Jesse had no idea Robert Coste was Nicholas's father, too.

Apparently, Jesse had no idea Nicholas was alive.

Coach Williams saved the situation by striding out in front of her team and offering a hand to the woman in the Camp Menton uniform. "Sally Williams, Kings Row. Thanks for having us. Sorry we're late. Our flight was delayed."

The woman shook Coach's hand. She had exciting earrings and a very sculpted hairdo, and she looked like a film star from a super-old movie, cut out and superimposed onto real life. She said, "*Je m'appelle* Colette Arquette," which Nicholas figured probably meant *My name is Colette* and not *A woman named*

Colette has stolen my apple. Colette clearly didn't care about any of the drama unfolding before her.

"*Je suis*—" Coach Arquette's gaze swept the team's expressions of polite incomprehension. "I am one of the managers at Camp Menton. Welcome, all of you. How delightful to have American teams with us for the first time."

Her voice was entirely flat.

"It will be my pleasure to show you around the camp," she continued, voice still flat. "You can leave your bags here. They will be taken to your rooms. This is Melodie Suard, who volunteered to assist with the initiation of the American teams, and this is Jesse Coste, another American."

"Jesse's been waiting here for your bus since this morning," reported the girl by Coach Arquette's side. "He says he knows one of you."

"Seiji," Jesse filled in. "Since childhood."

Without looking at the girl, Jesse continued to direct the sunlike force of his attention back on Seiji, who was still doing his impression of a statue impervious to sunshine or rain.

Nicholas looked over at Melodie. Initially, he'd been surprised to see her. Nicholas was familiar with girls, obviously. Coach was a girl. His mom was a girl. He used to go to school with girls. The guys back at his several other schools had talked, and seemed to think, about girls a lot. Nicholas didn't. He was busy thinking about fencing. Since starting at Kings Row, he'd almost forgotten about the existence of girls his own age. He wondered if she was any good at fencing. As she was at Camp Menton, he guessed she must be.

"Follow me," said Coach Arquette.

She turned and made her way up the tree-lined avenue, their coach at her side. Harvard and Assistant Coach Lewis were right behind them.

Even though he was with his teammates, Nicholas found himself feeling very alone. Seiji and Jesse were maintaining an intense silence, the air between them seeming to crackle with fraught, unspoken words. In fact, nobody was talking, except for the girl. Nicholas felt as though he might burst if he kept watching Seiji and Jesse watch each other, so he looked at her. Melodie was compact, had hair that was even lighter than Jesse's tied up in a messy bun, and wore fencing whites. She was eyeing their whole group with a disappointed air.

"I hoped," she announced with a sigh, "that one of the American teams would show signs of a real workout ethic."

Nicholas stared at her in bewilderment.

"I pictured you Americans as rugged. I thought you were all so interested in training and in, oh, what is the English word... *gains*," Melodie continued. "I'm very intrigued by the practice of using bodybuilding to enhance fencing. But you are all so skinny."

"I think of us as leanly muscular," suggested Nicholas.

Melodie scoffed.

Silence reigned among the lemon trees. The glamorous coach

named Colette was showing them the common area between the buildings, where people gathered for meals when the weather was nice. There were carved beech picnic tables set under an orchard of swaying green and gold. Nicholas already missed the fiery fall colors of the trees around Kings Row.

Apparently, rich people donated their summer houses to act as dormitories for the Camp Menton kids. Through the trees, Nicholas glimpsed rambling cottages with rose briars growing up the walls, and modern buildings the sparkling-white color of fresh laundry. They looked like houses from magazines. It was beautiful, not like anything he'd ever seen.

He glanced over at Seiji, wanting to share the wonder as he had when they were looking out on the town, but Seiji wasn't looking at Nicholas. He was still totally focused on Jesse. He seemed entirely unaware Nicholas was there.

Nicholas swallowed and tried to pay attention to the tour.

The centerpiece of Camp Menton was not the orchard cafeteria or the fancy dormitories. Coach Arquette led them to a building made of crumbling gray stone, with a peaked roof and a tower with a bell currently hanging silently. She led them through an echoing stone corridor, past the armory, where sword maintenance was carried out.

"The *salle d'armes* at Camp Menton was modeled after the Honved Fencing Club in Budapest. That was a converted synagogue, and this is a converted chapel," announced Coach Arquette with justified pride.

It was a cavernous space, white plaster walls curving to a ceiling stenciled with gold symbols against a blue sky, starting cerulean blue and ending in cobalt at the dome. The seats for the audience mimicked an amphitheater in ancient Rome, tiered benches enclosing the space rising up on every side. The converted floor had fixed metal *pistes* made of corrugated steel sheeting set into the floor, demarcated by broad swathes of smooth dark green.

"Honved also has a record number of women champions," piped up Melodie.

Nicholas was distracted by the sight in the *salle d'armes*. There were fencers doing drills along each *piste*, their masks and fencing whites making them an anonymous, undifferentiated mass, shifting along the strips with unbelievably smooth precision. These fencers moved like the sea by the cliffside roads leading to this place only reversed: Theirs were the same fluid motions as the sea, but with white beneath and the silver of their clashing swords as the crests of the waves. Nicholas noticed that many of them were using a French grip, a different type of hilt on a fencer's weapon that gave extra reach but allowed fencers less stability. Seiji was the only fencer he'd ever seen use a French grip before.

The training of the Camp Menton fencers was being overseen by a tall, stern man with gray eyes and graying brown hair. He paused snapping out commands to nod in their direction.

"That is Coach Robillard, one of our finest." Coach Arquette raised her voice. "The Kings Row team is here."

"So I see," said Coach Robillard, his sharp eyes focused on only one of their group. "I trained Seiji Katayama last year. Ice-cold mind for strategy, that boy. Can't wait to see how you've improved, Seiji. Hope the rest of you are half as good."

He didn't actually sound hopeful about that, but he'd change his mind.

The fencers moved like an ocean and like an army. Like an army of people who were better than Nicholas. For now.

Nicholas was lost in delighted amazement. It wasn't that long ago that Kings Row seemed out of reach for him, like a whole other world he couldn't hope to attain. Now here he was, part of a great team, learning that the world of fencing was vaster and more impressive than he'd ever imagined. He got to be part of this world, too.

Nicholas had thought Seiji forced him to drill constantly, but his drills clearly didn't compare to those of the Camp Menton fencers. He couldn't imagine how long it took to move with this balletic precision.

"Naturally, before we permit drills, we do all the usual exercises for speed, strength, and flexibility," Coach Arquette continued. "After drills, the students are encouraged to keep sharp by fencing each other in practice matches in their spare time. Here at Camp Menton, you have the chance to fence against opponents at the highest level."

Nicholas had read a lot of Seiji's books about the history of fencing. He cheered up. "Like a match at a competition?"

"Yes, like a competition," confirmed Melodie. "There's a judge, and the matches are scored."

Nicholas stared at the sea of fencers again, the light on their foils shining like stars. He imagined all the new people he could fence and the new skills he could pick up while he was here. "When can I fence my first match?!"

"Not until after you have completed several hours of training exercises. You will come to learn the Camp Menton ways soon enough," Coach Arquette assured Nicholas. "I'm sure your team is very disciplined," she added, addressing Coach Williams.

"Indescribably," said Coach Williams.

"That's good," Coach Arquette told them. "Because we have strict rules. Classes must be attended and not skipped, and lateness will not be tolerated. We also have a curfew. No camp attendees out after nine PM. This is what Menton expects from a serious fencer."

Aiden laughed, a shockingly loud sound in the intense, cavernous space. Several heads turned.

"Oh, sorry," drawled Aiden when Coach Arquette focused an outraged gaze on him. "I thought you were making a joke. You couldn't call me a serious fencer. I'm more the flippant type."

"He's kidding," said Harvard. "Ignore him."

Usually their captain sent Aiden a fond smile when Aiden acted out, showing Harvard wasn't really mad, and Aiden settled right down.

France must have had everybody off balance. Harvard didn't

give Aiden the smoothing-down smile, and Aiden stayed all bristly.

"Ignore me?" he asked. "With this face? Be serious. Apparently, we all have to be in this dreary place."

With that, Aiden turned and strolled out of the *salle d'armes*.

Coach Arquette cleared her throat. "Yes, perhaps it is time to show you to your rooms. You must all be exhausted."

The rest of the Kings Row team, Melodie, and Jesse Coste retraced their steps out into the light and away from the shining spectacle of all those flawless fencers. Coach Williams already looked embarrassed. Harvard and Aiden were both being weird. Bobby seemed intimidated, and Dante was hovering over Bobby. Seiji wasn't responding to anything Nicholas said or did.

He fell back to join Eugene, who was at the rear of the group, dragging his feet. That wasn't like Eugene at all.

"Bro . . . ," Eugene said slowly. "I don't . . . I don't feel super good."

Nicholas looked to Eugene, his true bro, and noticed the alarmingly gray cast to his face. Nicholas cupped Eugene's elbow and was even more concerned when a good amount of Eugene's weight hit his palm. Nicholas wasn't going to be able to hold up Eugene on his own. Eugene was all muscle. Luckily, Melodie hadn't gotten too far ahead. She noticed that Eugene and Nicholas had stopped in their tracks and trotted back to them.

"Oh no, is one of the Americans broken?"

She appeared to notice Eugene for the first time. Her eyes went wide. Nicholas was glad to see she shared his concern.

Eugene was looking more and more unwell by the moment. His face was dazed, and his eyes had gone unfocused. Nicholas, badly worried about him, patted Eugene's hand where it rested on his shoulder.

"A little help? Jesse?" called out Melodie. Seiji and Jesse were the only two people still in view. Jesse reluctantly turned away from Seiji. "This boy should go to the infirmary."

"The infirmary?" Eugene, who was drooping, raised his head and met Melodie's concerned gaze. "I'm really okay."

A look came over Jesse's face that, oddly, reminded Nicholas of Harvard. It was an *I'm the captain and I will handle this* expression. Jesse was, Nicholas recalled, captain of his team at Exton. Still not glancing at Nicholas, he took Eugene's arm from Nicholas's grasp and efficiently draped it around his own shoulders.

"You're going to the infirmary with us," Jesse informed Eugene.

"I'm not leaving Eugene!" protested Nicholas.

"Actually, bro, it's cool," said Eugene slowly. "Maybe I should get checked out. I'll just go to the infirmary with these nice blond people. Did I hear you mention something about workout ethics?" he continued, addressing Melodie. "I'm sure we all have lots to say to each other about training exercises."

Melodie lit up. "I have many thoughts."

"Obviously, me too, but infirmary first," said Jesse sternly.

"I will take care of him," Melodie promised Nicholas, while Eugene nodded. "Please go tell Coach Arquette."

Nicholas wasn't sure what was going on, but it seemed as though Melodie and Eugene would be friends. That was nice. As for Jesse, Nicholas figured Jesse thought he knew best about everything.

The three lurched away, Jesse and Melodie mostly supporting Eugene between them. Nicholas ran up the pathway to tell everyone what had happened. Coach Williams peeled off instantly to check on Eugene, and Nicholas fell into step with Seiji with a sense of relief. Yet, he still couldn't catch Seiji's eye. Seiji wandered through Camp Menton without seeming to see any of it, to all appearances lost in a private vision.

Assistant Coach Lewis stayed with them as they were shown to their sleeping quarters. Coach Arquette dropped Nicholas and Seiji at the room they would be sharing first.

Seiji remained just as quiet as he had been when Jesse was around. Nicholas couldn't help wondering if Seiji would be this absorbed with Jesse the whole time they were there. Was it not enough that he had to compete against a memory of Jesse back at Kings Row?

Nicholas couldn't worry about that. Not when he and Seiji were here in France to fence together. This was going to be awesome. He couldn't let Jesse Coste spoil it.

Shoving those thoughts to the back of his head, Nicholas pushed the door to their room open. Seiji seemed to barely register Nicholas's reaction and moved past him to enter the room while Nicholas stood openmouthed in the doorway.

The room had a circular window like a ship, as though they were going on a fantastic voyage to adventures. There was a ceiling that came to a high triangular point, and broad rafters above their heads. Through the circle of the window, Nicholas could see stars starting to appear, but there were already far more stars than he had ever seen in the city, as though someone had filled a cup to overflowing with light. A cloth-covered dressmaker's dummy stood in the corner, undressed and facing the wall, as if waiting to be dressed in Kings Row colors. There were two beds with crisp white sheets standing parallel to each other with iron bars at their heads. Nicholas loved his and Seiji's room at Kings Row. Here was another beautiful room, in a beautiful place where he could learn all he wanted about fencing.

Nicholas had no idea what Camp Menton had in store for him and Seiji, but he couldn't wait to get started.

13 HARVARD

Coach Arquette showed Harvard to a quaint cottage that Harvard's mom would've called a *bijou belle demeure,* then left him on the doorstep while she showed Nicholas and Seiji to their room. Dying roses twined up the crumbling stone cottage, nestled in among the trees. Harvard headed down a narrow hall, walking softly on the uneven flagstones of the floor so as not to disturb anyone sleeping, and trying not to wonder where Aiden had disappeared to.

He and Aiden were going to be sharing a room here. The thought made Harvard's stomach shift, a thrilled and uncomfortable flutter wanting to be born there. Harvard told himself he was being ridiculous. He'd had sleepovers with Aiden a thousand times. He and Aiden had been sharing a room for their entire

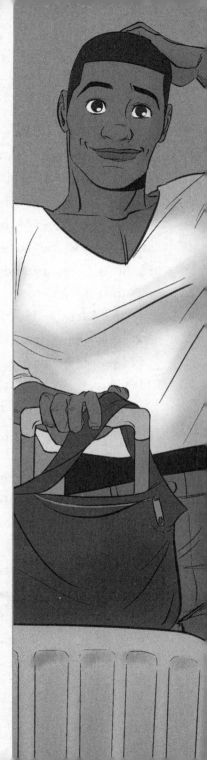

school life. This couldn't be any different. He wouldn't let it be different.

Coach Arquette had said their room was upstairs on the right. Harvard went up a narrow stone staircase with a very strange picture halfway up that portrayed several cats, several nuns, and a swing. Upstairs was a whitewashed hall with a tapestry on the farthest wall. One of the heavy oak-and-metal doors was open, and someone was hanging off the iron ring that was the door handle, a grin plastered all over his face.

A revelation came to Harvard, bright as the stars in the night sky over Menton. He'd forgotten Kings Row and Exton weren't the only Americans at Camp Menton. MLC was here as well.

Here was Arune Singh, his old friend from elementary school. They'd reconnected at the match between MLC and Kings Row and had been texting since then. Mostly memes, but friendly ones. Arune hadn't begrudged Kings Row their victory against his school. Arune was like that: a good sport and a better friend.

"Arune," breathed Harvard, and threw himself into his arms for a bro hug. Arune returned the bro hug with enthusiasm.

"Hey there, Harvard. Great to see you, too. Where's the pip-squeak?"

"Uh . . . ," said Harvard.

It had been a while since Arune had seen Aiden. Back when Aiden was ten, he was still kind of short and slight and shy and didn't get as much attention as he did now. He'd always had Harvard's attention, of course. Harvard had never seen Aiden growing up as Aiden changing, but instead as the world reacting to Aiden correctly at last. The world was finally giving Aiden his due.

Still, he knew Arune would be surprised when he saw Aiden. And for the first time in his life, Harvard wished that he and Aiden weren't sharing a room.

Aiden had made it so clear that he had far better things to do than hang out with Harvard.

"You know what? I'm beat. Let's catch up tomorrow, Arune, okay?" said Harvard. "And let's train together. I'll show you some moves."

"Maybe I'll show you some of my own," said Arune. "Can't wait."

They fist-bumped, and Harvard went into his room. It was nice, far bigger than the room he and Aiden shared back at Kings Row, with a pitched ceiling and rafters high above Harvard's head. There was a dried sprig of lavender, tied with twine, hanging in the casement window. And there were two narrow white beds with intricate iron headboards pretty close together.

On instinct, Harvard crossed the room and began to push the two beds together, the way he always would have before. Then he realized what he was doing, bit his lip hard, and began to hastily move the beds farther apart.

"Great idea," Aiden said from the doorway, and Harvard started.

Aiden's hair and face were wet, as though he'd been splashing water on them. His eyes were wide open and poison green.

"Let me help," Aiden continued, and shoved the other bed against the farthest wall, into the darkest corner of the room. "Much better."

"There's no need to be childish," Harvard told him.

Since Aiden had done it first, Harvard pushed his own bed against the opposite wall. That way, at least they were even.

"If you'd rather be farther apart, I'm sure you could share with *Arune*," Aiden bit out. "Saw that touching reunion in the hallway."

"There's no talking to you at all," Harvard said, exhausted. "Sometimes I wonder why I bother."

"I wouldn't, if I were you," Aiden agreed in a silky voice.

Aiden hadn't spent the night in his and Harvard's dorm since the night they kissed and Harvard had said he wanted it to go further before realizing they had to stop their charade. No doubt Aiden had been avoiding the awkwardness. Now the awkwardness was here in France.

Worse than feeling awkward, Harvard also felt so guity.

Normally, they would have pushed the beds together. Harvard would have invited Aiden onto his bed, or Aiden would have simply crawled onto Harvard's blankets, smug and as certain of his welcome as a much-beloved cat. They would have spent their first night in Camp Menton talking until dawn lit a path over the sea, Aiden making mean jokes that Harvard laughed at and sharp observations that Harvard used to navigate the world. Aiden would have said Harvard was a great captain, and, with

Aiden beside him, Harvard could have believed it was true. In the mornings, Harvard used to coax Aiden awake. Aiden always wanted to cuddle closer and sleep in.

Harvard sighed and unzipped his suitcase, then glanced over his shoulder and caught Aiden stripping his shirt off, a bar of moonlight across the arched line of Aiden's back. Harvard looked away fast.

They couldn't pull the covers over their heads and talk the night away, forgetting everybody else in the world. If they were under the covers, close and warm, it would be far worse than Aiden sleeping nestled against him on the plane. Now only a glimpse of Aiden by moonlight made vivid memory flash inescapably across Harvard's brain, Aiden's hair loose on a white pillow, every treacherous instinct in Harvard's body forgetting reason and only understanding desire. There had been no doubt in Harvard's mind what he'd wanted when Aiden asked if he was sure. His whole body had said: *Yes, I want to; yes, I want everything.*

He still wanted.

That was awful of him, Harvard thought miserably. Maybe it was creepy, even, to stay near Aiden when he felt that way. But they were best friends: What else was he supposed to do?

Even the bright moment of recognizing a familiar face in a new place felt spoiled somehow, turned bitter by Aiden's acid tongue. If things were different, Harvard wouldn't have been so delighted to see Arune. Harvard was secure in possession of a best friend; Aiden so supremely the best Harvard didn't truly need any others. That was how it had always been.

At least it was before Harvard ruined everything between them. He'd tried to fix things, the day after that night. He'd promised that he and Aiden would be friends as they always had been, that friendship was what he wanted. He'd done what he had to do to fix them, the unit that was Harvard-and-Aiden, the most important relationship in Harvard's life.

Only they were still broken.

Harvard slept uneasily that first night in France, with the moon's rays searchlight bright in his eyes, and when he dreamed, he dreamed that he was hiding and didn't want to be found out.

When he woke, Aiden's bed was empty. He got out of bed, forcing himself to smile and remembering his promise with Arune. Even if Aiden didn't think Harvard was worth hanging out with anymore, someone else did.

He made his way down a narrow path toward the orchard dining area. In Menton, on the border of Italy and in a pocket of ultra-Mediterranean sunshine between the mountains and the sea, the weather was almost always gorgeous.

Arune was at a table crowded with MLC students and their friends, and he waved Harvard over and introduced him to everyone. They seemed like great guys and girls. A couple were Italian, so Harvard tried out his few sentences of lousy Italian and laughed as a girl named Chiara taught him how to pronounce the words correctly.

Then Chiara's face slackened in awe, as though she'd suddenly experienced transcendence.

Said transcendence was Aiden, moving gracefully around the picnic tables toward them. Harvard willed himself to look away. Everybody in the orchard watched as Aiden went by. Harvard had promised himself that he wouldn't be just like everybody else. He failed to look away, all the same.

For a moment, with the shadow of leaves, he thought Aiden looked sad, and Harvard's heart clenched, feeling for an instant as though they were back in elementary school, when Aiden was so much smaller and Harvard always wanted to protect him. *Aiden, has something made you unhappy?*

Then Aiden reached their table. Sunlight poured gold onto his face and his hair, and it was clear there was nothing wrong with him at all.

"Well, whoa," said Arune. "Harvard wasn't kidding when he said you'd changed at our match together. This is a glow up like a supernova. Hey, Aiden. Nice to see you again. It's been a long time."

Aiden arched an eyebrow and regarded Arune without speaking. The whole table hushed as they waited for a reply that clearly wasn't coming.

Harvard dropped a pebble of conversation into the pool of awkward silence: "You remember Arune? From elementary school."

"Oh, right, Armand," drawled Aiden.

Aiden was often carelessly rude to people, while Harvard felt he should be carefully polite. Harvard didn't approve of Aiden's behavior or anything, but often it made him smile and relax a little.

Harvard didn't feel like smiling or relaxing now. No matter how often Harvard told himself that this was normal, that nothing had changed, he wasn't sure he believed it.

14 SEIJI

The dummy in the room Seiji was sharing with Nicholas looked vulnerable and lonely, standing in that dark corner. Seiji wished it wasn't there. Then he told himself he was being ridiculous. It didn't matter that the dummy was there.

It didn't matter that Jesse was at Camp Menton.

Seiji closed his eyes and there was Jesse, dominating the landscape of sea and lemon trees as he dominated everything else.

Every time Seiji saw Jesse, he felt as though he were still trapped in that single cold moment at the end of their fencing match, when Seiji had realized to his incredulous horror that Jesse had won. He felt like he was losing the match all over again.

Seiji sat on the edge of his white bed and stared down at his empty hands. He'd thought, back then, he wouldn't ever be able to bear picking up an épée again. That would have left his whole life empty.

His father had been wrong when he said Seiji could pick his battles.

There were times in your life when you were trapped and had no choice at all.

Seiji's eyes snapped open.

If he was trapped, he was going to fight. Jesse was here, and they were inevitably going to be fencing each other. He tried to imagine what it would be like, finally facing his old partner on the *piste* after so long. He tried to visualize himself winning point after point, regaining the power he'd thought he'd lost in that match, but he couldn't manage to make the vision feel real.

His thoughts were interrupted, as usual, by Nicholas.

"Isn't this the coolest room?" Nicholas asked enthusiastically. "We should dress up that dummy."

Seiji lifted his suitcase onto the bed and riffled through it, pulling out the shower curtain he had meticulously folded before they left Kings Row.

"*You're* a dummy," Seiji told Nicholas, comforted. "Help me hang the shower curtain up between our beds so I don't have to see your stupid face."

Nicholas's stupid face was grinning as he complied. Then he prowled around the room, opening his suitcase and pulling out clothes so he could dress up the dummy in his Kings Row blazer. Nothing Nicholas did ever made any sense.

While Nicholas's back was turned, Seiji took a moment to survey Nicholas, taking in his scruffy hair and the long limbs that extended from the black tank top he always wore. He was so different from Jesse, who was shiningly blond and composed at all times.

Yet Seiji couldn't shake the feeling that there was something similar about Nicholas and Jesse. Something Seiji couldn't quite place, even if it was just the way each boy drew Seiji in toward them.

Seiji clamped down viciously on that thought and drew the shower curtain closed so he couldn't see Nicholas. He refused to go there.

Earlier, in a miserable daze at being confronted with Jesse on arrival, Seiji had felt his most ferocious pang of unease when Nicholas went back for Eugene. Camp Menton would be fine, if Nicholas stayed beside Seiji.

"Were you listening to everything the Camp Mention coach was saying? All the rules and the curfew and stuff? Was it this intense in France when you were here before?" Nicholas asked as they got ready for bed, the shower curtain in between them.

"The standard of fencing is far higher in France," Seiji reminded Nicholas. "And, of course, *your* fencing is substandard, even for America."

"You're such a comforting friend," said Nicholas in a tone that informed Seiji he was being sarcastic, except for the friend part. Since the curtain was between them, Seiji let himself smile.

Seiji hesitated, reluctant to admit he hadn't heard a word the coach had uttered. "What precisely was she saying?"

"Like that we can't skip classes or be late, and that if we break curfew maybe they behead us, and they're going to train us until we drop?"

"You can't expect them to go easy on you like I do, Nicholas," said Seiji, and Nicholas snorted loudly from behind the ducks.

"I'm glad we came," Nicholas announced decisively. "And I'll take any match I get. I want to. It would be great if Jesse Coste challenged me. I hope he does."

"*Jesse?!*" Seiji exclaimed.

Once again, Seiji relived that cold, eternal moment when he realized that Jesse had beaten him at nationals. Nicholas shouldn't feel that way.

"You shouldn't fence against Jesse." Seiji's voice cut the night air. "You can't compete with him. He's better than you are."

Nicholas went silent, so Seiji must have won the argument. Seiji climbed into bed and set his alarm for four AM, Central European Standard Time, because Seiji wouldn't let jet lag tell him what to do.

When he woke, the gray dawn light was reflecting off the sea and into their room, quivering like liquid so that the ducks on their shower curtain seemed as though they were in unfamiliar waters. Seiji could hear Nicholas snoring from behind the curtain, which usually made Seiji want to smother Nicholas in his sleep.

This morning he was so desperate he wanted to shake Nicholas and ask him for company, but Nicholas wouldn't be even marginally coherent this early. Besides, in the cold light of morning, Seiji's path was clear. Seiji didn't need anyone to protect him from Jesse.

This was a training camp, and Seiji was here to train. He'd lost his fencing partner, but he hadn't lost fencing. That was why he had come to France the first time, after losing to Jesse so catastrophically. France had reminded him that no matter where he was, if there was a *piste*, Seiji was where he belonged.

That was still true. Jesse couldn't take that.

15 NICHOLAS

Nicholas dreamed of a trophy gleaming gold, which said, in Seiji's voice, "He's better than you are," and his father's newspaper clipping, which folded itself into a paper airplane so that it could fly away from Kings Row to find Jesse.

He woke up in a hopeless fight with the bedsheets, the sunlight shining through their curtains yellow as lemons or ducks, and realized he had slept through his alarm.

Oh no. Seiji.

Seiji got up every morning at four AM to train, but recently the two of them had been waking up early to train together. Nicholas had even been able to persuade Seiji to eat breakfast at a reasonable hour. He sat at Bobby and Dante's table with Nicholas and sometimes Eugene. Occasionally the captain even sat with them—and with the captain came Aiden, so it was the whole team. Those mornings were the coolest, but Seiji wasn't used to hanging out in a crowd. Nicholas had made a bargain with Seiji: Seiji would help him during practice, a hand on his shoulder or an arm correcting his form. In exchange, Nicholas would intercept any fist bumps or people talking to him when Seiji didn't want them to. Unless Nicholas was there, Seiji would eat by himself.

Nicholas leaped out of bed and hurriedly flung on clothes, then rushed out of his and Seiji's room. As Nicholas approached, he saw many people were gathered for breakfast in the common area between the buildings, enjoying their breakfasts at the carved beech picnic tables set in the orchard. A rich spread was laid out on the creaking tables. There were croissants, and pastries that were kind of like croissants but chocolate, and dozens of other pastries like cream tarts and éclairs. There were cuts of meat and slices of cheese heaped like dragons' gold. Most of all, there was an enormous amount of lemon-related foods: lemon tarts, lemon curd Danishes, lemon meringue pie, puff pastry lemon knots, lemon cake, madeleines with lemon glaze, lemon bars, lemon meringue tarts, lemon poppy-seed scones, lemon muffins, and lemon ricotta pancakes—no, crêpes— folded up into tidy triangles. There were golden apples and peaches and dusky grapes and violet, black-veined figs, with a juice bar, an espresso machine, and an urn of hot chocolate to the side.

Nicholas decided he was starving; he couldn't fence or find Seiji and the rest of the team if he was starving.

Once he'd acquired a few pastries to fend off starvation, Nicholas quested for help, but the first few groups of people he passed were speaking different languages. He recognized Spanish. He didn't recognize several more. It was as if Nicholas was lost in a sea of strangeness. A girl asked him a question, in which he discerned the words *parlez-vous français*, and since Nicholas definitely didn't *parlez* any *français*, he could only stare back at her.

Then he heard people speaking English by the juice bar.

"Hey, I'm looking for Seiji Katayama," said Nicholas to a knot of boys wearing purple-and-green school ties and speaking in British accents that seemed to be mostly coming through their noses.

One boy with straw-colored hair blinked and said, "Oh, I know who you mean. The American who can actually fence. He's over there, sitting with the Bordeaux Blades—Bastien, Marcel, and Melodie. They're three fencers who have all been training in Bordeaux with the famous Coach Robillard since they were small. Can you imagine the luck? Bastien Robillard is the coach's son, and the other two are his friends. Marcel had to go live in America, poor guy, and I don't know much about the girl, but everyone says Bastien's one of the best fencers in Europe."

The boy pointed to a table under a tree. Nicholas saw Seiji

first, the way he held himself unmistakable. Across the table from Seiji was an Exton boy, thankfully not Jesse. Nicholas recognized him as Marcel Berré, the aloof French guy who was the oldest member of the Exton fencing team. Assembled around Marcel was Melodie, the girl from yesterday, and an unfamiliar boy. The three of them didn't look anything alike—Melodie, blond and fair-skinned; Marcel, black-haired and dark-skinned; and the strange boy, brown-haired with a summer tan—but they had a similar air of confidence. Maybe that was the training. Nicholas remembered the stern-voiced coach from the *salle* yesterday.

The boy Nicholas didn't know, who must be Bastien Robillard, was talking to Seiji.

Beside Melodie sat Eugene. Nicholas was relieved that his bro looked better than he had the day before. Then his attention snapped to Seiji again. His back was to Nicholas, but he could tell that Seiji was listening intently to whatever the fencer from Bordeaux were saying to him. Seiji seemed all right. His shoulders didn't have the tension they had when he was plunged into an uncomfortable situation.

"Bastien Robillard and Seiji Katayama. That is a table of fencing geniuses," confided the boy, sounding awed. "I'm Rupert, by the way."

"Hey, Rupert, I'm Nicholas."

"Oh, I say!" exclaimed Rupert as realization dawned on his face. "You're American. Sorry about what I said before! I'm sure you're a great fencer, too."

"I'm gonna be," Nicholas told him with a wink, and departed for Seiji's table.

Nicholas approached with a weird, disoriented sensation. He'd expected to find Seiji sitting alone. Instead Seiji was paying attention to the stranger seated next to Marcel. Seiji was even having a conversation with him. *In French.* Seiji appeared to be exchanging social pleasantries. That seemed more alien than anything else.

"Nicholas, you're late," said Seiji, switching to English and narrowing his eyes in annoyance.

Nicholas relaxed at this familiar greeting in a world of strangeness under foreign trees. "I sure am."

Seiji's breakfast was always healthy and wholly unsatisfactory, so Nicholas couldn't steal from it. Nicholas had once expressed his feelings on this subject, and Seiji had told him to stop stealing food. That wasn't happening, so they had reached a compromise: Seiji would bring a single small breakfast roll for Nicholas to steal, but Nicholas had to promise to steal it, because Seiji wasn't eating it and unbalancing his lean, mean fencing-machine diet.

Nicholas checked Seiji's plate and saw his roll, snagged it, and felt prepared to face the French stranger.

"Hey, I'm Nicholas Cox," said Nicholas. "Sorry, I don't speak French."

The boy nodded in a friendly way. He looked a year or so older than Nicholas and Seiji. "Seiji was just talking about you. I hear you fence at Kings Row with Seiji."

Seiji said, "If you can call what Nicholas does fencing."

Nicholas rolled his eyes. He expected the other boy to do what the students at Kings Row did when faced with Seiji's attitude. They would back up, rebounding from Seiji as though they'd expected air and instead walked into an ice wall.

The boy smiled and winked. "Genius has its privileges, one of which is saying exactly what genius thinks. No matter how unflattering it is to those of us who are merely talented. Nice to meet you, Nicholas. I'm Bastien Robillard."

Bastien seemed cool. What was he doing hanging out with Seiji?

Nicholas personally thought Seiji was really cool, but he'd gotten used to others not sharing that opinion. Nicholas felt weirdly worried, as though he had something that might be snatched away, but he wasn't gonna be like a mean junkyard dog, growling at anyone who came near his bone.

"How do you know Seiji?" Nicholas asked.

"I lived in France for a year, how many times must I tell you?" said Seiji. "His father was my coach. Bastien and I used to train together. It's true—Bastien is talented."

Bastien seemed pleased rather than insulted by Seiji's implicit acceptance of Bastien saying that Seiji was a genius and Bastien was beneath him. Two other boys went by, calling out, "*Bonjour,* Seiji!" And they didn't look offended when Seiji only inclined his head at them in return. They took it as though they were used to it.

Nicholas figured it made sense that a lot of people at Camp Menton knew Seiji. It was just unsettling seeing Seiji be popular. What did he need Nicholas for now?

But Seiji deserved to be popular. This just meant France was an awesome place, as Nicholas had always believed. There was no reason for this gnawing sensation of unease.

At that moment, Bobby and Dante arrived at the table. Nicholas stood to greet the two of them. Bobby was wearing long, narrow ribbons in blue, white, and red, the colors of the French flag. He looked very cool. People at the training camp didn't wear uniforms, since a whole new outfit for a long weekend would be a bit much even for rich kids. They wore Camp Menton badges over their own clothes. The badge was a pewter replica of twin blades meeting in a match, with the motto *Labor omnia vincit* written beneath in flowing script.

There were a whole lot of crisp shirts and khakis going on.

"Did you hear about Eugene?" Bobby whispered.

Nicholas frowned. "I knew he was feeling kind of sick, but—"

Bobby's big brown eyes were bright with sympathy. "It's as bad as it could be!"

Nicholas almost dropped his plate. *"He's dying?"*

"He is right there, guys." Dante pointed down the table.

"He ate something with pineapple and had an allergic reaction!" exclaimed Bobby. "He fainted and had to be taken to the infirmary. They say they're not going to let him fence this weekend."

"Oh my God, that's worse than dying," Nicholas murmured.

Bobby nodded sadly. Dante shook his head wearily at both of them.

Eugene saw them staring at him in horror and said, "Abroha." He sounded quieter than usual but seemed cheerful despite dark circles under his eyes. Melodie was holding his hand. For comfort, Nicholas supposed.

"I'm so glad you're okay, I'm sorry I didn't know about the pineapples," Nicholas burst out in a flood of relief.

"Yeah, it sucks not getting to fence," said Eugene. "But I'll sit and watch with Bobby. I bet I'll learn a lot. Always keep grinding! Even with your mind. Anyway, at least I got to meet Melodie out of it. That makes it worth it."

He and Melodie smiled fondly at each other, then Melodie returned to her conversation in French.

"I'm so sorry I left you," Nicholas said in a lower voice.

Eugene gestured dismissively with a fancy bread thing with chocolate in it. "Whatever. Shame you missed me hitting the floor; I'm told it was pretty dramatic. Melodie and my Camp Menton bro had to drag me to the infirmary. It was actually all pretty amazing."

Nicholas didn't know how fainting could be amazing. Eugene must have realized this from Nicholas's expression.

"Melodie has all this je ne sais quoi."

"I don't know what you're saying, Eugene."

"I'm saying blondes are great," said Eugene. "Everybody loves blondes."

Nicholas couldn't help thinking of Jesse Coste, hair catching the sun, impossible to avoid. He frowned.

"I don't."

"It's horrible this illness will keep you from working out while you're here," Melodie said sympathetically.

"Just this once, I think the gains can wait," Eugene said.

He and Melodie smiled at each other again. Marcel, the boy from Jesse's team at Exton, gave them a cool look.

"Really, Melodie," Marcel murmured. "A Kings Row boy? On the reserves?"

"Eugene tells me his team is the greatest," Melodie returned calmly.

Marcel met Nicholas's gaze and raised an eyebrow as he settled back into his seat, as if sizing him up. Nicholas sized him up right back. Marcel was on the Exton team. One day, their teams would face off in the state championships.

Why wait? Nicholas could fence Marcel—or any of the Exton boys—at Camp Menton. Coach Arquette had said people fenced each other in practice matches here all the time. It was encouraged. Nicholas felt his pulse kick up, racing with excitement at just the idea of fencing someone from Exton. He hoped he would get to fence Marcel before camp came to an end.

"You know, Nicholas"—the sound of Bastien's voice snapped Nicholas out of his reverie—"France is the birthplace of modern fencing. Our skills have been honed for generations. Our ancestors fought duels across the Old World. We Europeans are, I'm afraid, a little prejudiced against American fencers. Seiji certainly set us straight. I'm looking forward to seeing what you can do."

Bobby looked as alarmed as Nicholas felt.

"Nicholas is fast as lightning, but he's new to fencing," Bobby said loyally.

Bastien smiled at Bobby, and Bobby went as red as his ribbon.

"But that's marvelous," said Bastien. "That's what all the stories are about, are they not? The raw, natural talent who comes late to the sport and dazzles everyone set in their ways. Don't you agree, Seiji?"

"No," said Seiji. "People need to train. That's how sports work." Seiji surveyed Nicholas's plate with an air of extreme distaste. "*Cheese Danish* shouldn't mean *Danish with eight different types of cheese piled on top of it.*"

"Quit blighting my cultural experience," said Nicholas, grinning at Seiji and eating his Danish. The Comté cheese was delicious.

Bobby was talking for two and Dante for none as usual. Seiji was smiling in that way that used neither his eyes nor his mouth but was simply a relaxing of the usual frown. Bastien was a nice dude, and Melodie and Eugene were getting on like a house on fire. It seemed for a moment that everything was going to be okay.

Then Jesse Coste strolled up, French sunlight turning his hair into a fancy gold helmet. The day went dim around him. He and Marcel nodded at each other in Exton solidarity.

"Hello, Jesse," said Bastien. "Jesse goes to Exton with my friend Marcel. Your schools are close, aren't they? Do you all know each other?"

Jesse looked at Nicholas with polite blankness. "Do I know you?"

"I'm on the team that's going to beat you at state," Nicholas shot back.

"In any case, I do know Seiji. He and I have been fencing partners since we were small," announced Jesse. He gave Seiji a possessive look, as though Seiji were an épée or a trophy.

Bastien frowned. "How strange he never mentioned you."

"That *is* strange," said Jesse with supreme composure. "Hello again, Seiji."

"Hello," said Seiji in a wooden voice.

All light now seemed leeched from the orchard.

"Is it nice being back in France?" Bobby asked Marcel brightly, covering the brief pause.

Marcel unbent slightly. Bobby had that effect on people. "I've been looking forward to coming home all year."

"But you're on the best team in America, so it's not all bad," Jesse said with his sunny smile.

The table full of Kings Row students bristled.

Bobby tried again. "I love your hair. What kind of shampoo do you use?" he asked Melodie valiantly.

"I don't know..." Melodie seemed faintly perplexed. "The kind in the showers of my *salle*?"

Bastien laughed, looping an arm around Melodie's waist. "Melodie learned footwork when she was three. Fencing is all she thinks about. She's very good."

Melodie beamed at him. "Bastien's coached me almost as much as his father."

Sometimes Nicholas imagined having learned fencing from early childhood. Having the same time-polished skills as Jesse so that Seiji wouldn't ever look down on him.

"I know the Robillards are a famous fencing family," Jesse said with his super-bright smile that made Nicholas's head hurt. Bastien smiled back.

"The Costes are no slouches themselves. Like father, like son, from all I hear."

"People do say that," Jesse admitted modestly. He glanced sharply over at Nicholas as though he could feel the weight of Nicholas's stare on him and wished to remove an irritant. "Do you have any family to speak of?"

"No. Not to speak of," said Nicholas distantly.

He knew his voice sounded weird. He was saved by Bastien addressing Dante in Italian, speaking chattily at length and finishing a sentence on an upward tilt, as though asking a friendly question. Dante glanced up from his plate and answered briefly. Bastien appeared taken aback.

"What did Dante say?" Nicholas whispered.

Bobby whispered back, "He said, *I hate fencing.*"

"Right," said Nicholas. "Classic Dante."

Marcel, Bastien, and Melodie stared at Dante. They seemed too well-mannered to point out that this was a training camp for fencers.

"This is a training camp for fencers," said Jesse Coste.

Dante shrugged. Jesse returned to staring at the back of Seiji's head with the focused air of someone attempting mind control, as though Jesse thought his force of will gave him superpowers.

"It's really great to see so many Americans here," Bastien continued with determination. "Usually it's the same people over and over. Fencers come to the Camp Menton from France of course, and from Italy and Germany and England, but never before from America. We're all looking forward to seeing your skills."

From what the English boy at the buffet table was saying, they didn't seem to be expecting much. Nicholas felt a jolt of horror at the thought of living down to everyone's expectations.

"Americans don't take the sport seriously," remarked Marcel.

"I take everything seriously," said Seiji.

That was so undeniably true, it silenced the whole table. Nicholas wished the captain were here. Harvard was so steady; he anchored their whole team.

Harvard was sitting at another table and talking to a guy Nicholas thought he recognized from their match with MLC. Maybe he was wrong, though, and Harvard had struck up a friendship with a random person. Their captain had a winning personality. Even Aiden liked him, and Aiden didn't like anybody. Sometimes Nicholas got the feeling Aiden didn't even like *Aiden* much.

Where *was* Aiden? He was always late to everything these days. He said he was sleeping in, but he didn't look as though he was sleeping much. Nicholas couldn't figure it out.

The silence that had fallen on their table seemed to spread until the only sound was the leaves rustling in a rippling warm breeze. Nicholas gazed around to see why and noted that Aiden had come to breakfast at last.

Aiden didn't look as though he'd slept much, but that was the norm these days, so maybe it wasn't jet lag but his party lifestyle that was affecting him. Being tired actually suited Aiden, turning his face mysterious with angles and hollows in it. Leaves from the lemon trees fluttered down, seemingly in slow motion, and got caught in his fancy bedhead. People paused with forks frozen halfway to their fallen-open mouths as Aiden passed by.

But Aiden was still annoying, so what was the big deal?

Bastien had taken hold of the edge of the picnic table as though he were clinging to the edge of a cliff. "Oh, and I say this with feeling, *mon Dieu.*"

Nicholas wasn't sure what that meant.

Bobby leaned in to whisper to Nicholas. "Do you see the way Bastien's staring at Aiden? And Bastien's incredibly good-looking, isn't he?"

"Is he?" Nicholas checked.

French sunshine seemed different from American sunshine, at once brighter and paler, primrose colored. The sunlight was splashing through the leaves of the boughs above the picnic table. Bastien's shoulders were broad beneath his white polo shirt, and his brown curly hair was untidy in an on-purpose way. He had a cleft chin.

"Almost as good-looking as Seiji," Bobby confirmed in a very low voice.

"What? No way," said Nicholas.

"Do you think Bastien and Aiden will date?"

Nicholas shrugged. "Probably. Aiden dates everybody, right?"

Aiden had even dated the captain, but that hadn't lasted long. Nicholas felt another prickle of unease. Harvard and Aiden had seemed really happy when they were dating. Would the captain feel okay about seeing Aiden go off with other guys the way he used to?

Even familiar things felt strange in France.

The hush that had fallen over the table was broken by Melodie opining that Aiden was too skinny for her taste, and Jesse asking imperiously what everyone was staring at.

"Your captain, though, his shoulders have great potential." Melodie sneaked a glance at Eugene. "So many men neglect their delts."

"That's what I'm always saying!" Eugene exclaimed.

Bastien was still staring over at Aiden, but with a mighty effort to be polite, he wrenched his attention back to their table.

"Your pardon." Bastien turned to Nicholas with an apologetic smile. "Got distracted for a second there. Nicholas, before you came, Seiji was telling me you're his fencing partner."

Jesse's sunny expression went into an eclipse.

"Fencing with Seiji was always such a revelation," Bastien said. "I'd be thrilled to fence with his partner. After drills, what do you say you and I have a match, Nicholas? Everybody enjoys watching a good match."

His first practice bout! Nicholas's heart raced with excitement. "Yeah, totally!"

Sometimes people remarked that Nicholas ran recklessly toward disaster. Nicholas didn't see their point.

"Wonderful," Bastien said happily. "Well, I want to go introduce myself to someone. Catch you later, Nicholas. Excited to find out what you can do."

He swung easily up off the bench and launched himself toward Aiden's retreating back.

Nicholas's heart was pounding, his body was alive with nerves and anticipation. It felt like pins and needles, but in a pleasant way. His first bout. His first match with everyone watching! Nicholas couldn't wait, but he had a full day of training ahead of him, the sort of training that had forged fencers like Seiji and Jesse. The sort of training that prepared people for the Olympics.

Bastien had called this the Old World, with an inflection that suggested Nicholas's world could not compare. With its ancient stone buildings and system of rules inflexible as the stone, it did seem like an entirely different world. But Nicholas felt at home in Kings Row now. He could prove himself at Camp Menton, as well.

When Nicholas looked up from his plate, he found Jesse watching him. Jesse, who Seiji had said Nicholas couldn't compete with.

"What?" Nicholas asked.

Jesse opened his blue eyes very wide. "I'm just looking forward to watching your match," Jesse answered innocently. "So excited for everybody to find out exactly what you can do."

16 AIDEN

Aiden was exhausted before the training drills at Camp Menton even started. He worried the drills might actually kill him. He hadn't slept well in the bed Harvard had exiled him to, as far away from Harvard as he could be. He got up early to walk the cliffs restlessly, staring out at the sea, and when he finally came to breakfast, he discovered Harvard eating with his new best friend, Arune. Great. Good for Harvard. Aiden resisted the urge to storm off and sauntered away casually instead.

Some guys tried to talk to Aiden, as usual, but he was busy. Aiden had to find his own new best friend, coffee.

"You're late," observed a coach with steely gray eyes when Aiden eventually wandered into the *salle d'armes* clutching his cup of coffee. "That incurs penalties for your whole team."

Aiden cast a look at his team, huddling close together in the dense chill that only gathered in old stone buildings.

Aiden, refusing to draw closer to them or show the least apprehension, drawled, "What penalties?"

"Can't be worse than suicides," muttered Nicholas.

"Suicides," replied the coach succinctly.

Ah. The only thing worse than suicides. *More* suicides. Aiden and Nicholas shared an eye roll, united in disapproval of the camp rules in general and suicides in particular. Nicholas gave Aiden a little grin afterward.

"You have already missed part of the drills," said the coach. "It's essential you give your best efforts to the remaining portion."

Aiden wasn't in a *best efforts* frame of mind. He wasn't in an *efforts* frame of mind.

"What is our aim?" shouted the coach. Aiden dimly recalled from yesterday that his name was Robillard.

"Speed, strength, technique!" shouted the other teams.

"You missed orientation," mumbled Nicholas.

"I'll be honest with you, Nicholas, I wouldn't have listened anyway," muttered Aiden.

They started with fencing-specific exercises in which they executed moves similar to fencing moves. Once perfected, they would then move on to fencing-transferable exercises, in which they did nonfencing moves in order to increase strength and flexibility. For fencing. Then, and only then, would they be allowed to pick up blades.

So this was hell.

Aiden probably deserved to be there, but Harvard did not.

They started with lateral broad jumps, five sets of fifteen repetitions. Halfway into the first set, Aiden felt dizzy. Maybe he should've eaten breakfast. Maybe he should've eaten yesterday.

Nicholas looked like he was going to throw up. Harvard left his own strip to see to Nicholas, murmuring advice. He hesitated by Aiden for a fraction of an instant, but Aiden clearly wasn't worth the bother. Harvard moved on.

Coach Robillard penalized Harvard for pausing. They were assigned more suicides.

Standing long jumps were a little better, but the last week was really catching up to Aiden, and honestly, why bother? Why love fencing? Why love anything?

When they were made to do five sets of reverse long jumps, Aiden started idly fluttering his eyelashes at random boys in the *salle d'armes*, in order to see which ones he could make stumble. The answer was...most of them.

"Mr. Kane!" snapped Coach Robillard.

"Don't make me run suicides because I'm beautiful," said Aiden.

The Kings Row team was assigned more suicides.

Pistol squats, vertical jumps, band thrusts, and anterior

planks followed. The Kings Row team sucked. It would have been embarrassing if Aiden had cared at all.

He didn't dare let his eyes linger on Harvard, muscles moving, sleek under the dancing colors shed by the stained-glass windows. He couldn't watch Harvard move, or watch his constant attentive kindness for everyone but Aiden. But Aiden himself was terrible, and Nicholas was flailing. He clearly hadn't done half these exercises before.

Only Seiji moved with absolute, elegant precision. He should have been drawing looks of admiration. Instead, due to the company he was in, he was drawing looks of pity.

Seiji kept his gaze focused straight ahead, his expression neutral. With each pitying glance Seiji got, Nicholas's face clouded with misery and fury. Nicholas was making more and more mistakes.

Exton and MLC were keeping up far better. The MLC fencers weren't up to the standards of the European fencers, but they looked good compared to Kings Row. Exton was miles ahead, smooth and polished. Led by their captain, Jesse, a shining figure who moved smoothly on the *piste* as though he were skating on ice, Exton looked like winners.

As the captain of the Kings Row team, Aiden knew Harvard had been so hoping to win the state championships this year. Aiden had been hoping a little himself. But clearly, if you asked anyone at Camp Menton, they would tell you Kings Row had no chance at the championship.

Luckily, Aiden had decided to stop hoping for anything before he arrived.

The coach wrapped up the drills and said, "Excellent work, everyone. Kings Row, I expect more from you. Mr. Kane, you will not be late to our classes again."

With that, it was time for a break.

"Where's Eugene?" Aiden asked idly as Harvard encouraged the others to hydrate. "Did he fake sick? I suspect Eugene is a secret genius."

Harvard frowned in Aiden's direction, which was the first time he'd really looked at Aiden all day. "Eugene fainted, and he had to go to the infirmary."

Aiden felt confirmed in his belief Eugene was a secret genius.

"I should try fainting to get out of these classes, too," he drawled. "You can catch me."

It was a joke. It was how Aiden always talked to Harvard. It made them both freeze. Aiden felt like someone had stabbed him with an icicle that shattered, leaving cold shards working their way through his heart. He wondered if Harvard remembered the time during trust falls when Aiden had been the one who caught Harvard. Aiden had relived that moment far too often. He'd thought continually of how it had been to hold Harvard, warm in his arms, and feel as if he could keep him. Harvard probably didn't remember anything at all.

Harvard glanced at Aiden, then glanced away. "Look. I've been thinking. What if we, uh, do something together tonight after fencing?" Before Aiden could respond, Harvard added swiftly, "You know, as friends."

The brief bright hope that had winked into light in Aiden's chest became a black hole. "Sorry, buddy. Busy later," Aiden lied breezily. "Got a date."

He left the *salle d'armes*, left Harvard's disappointed dark eyes, and went out into the daylight. It was too bright here. It made Aiden's exhausted eyes sting. He leaned against the cool stone wall, tipping his head back and wishing for peace.

"Oh, hello. There you are. I'm Bastien," said some French boy.

Aiden opened his eyes and made himself smile.

"Aiden Kane. They post about me on the fencing message boards. The warnings are true."

The French boy seemed intrigued. Apparently, people at Camp Menton had no sense of self-preservation. Aiden glanced back over his shoulder at Harvard, who was laughing with stupid Arune again. Aiden hadn't seen Arune since elementary school, when Arune had laughed—gently enough, but it still stung—at Aiden for being Harvard's small, devoted shadow. Humiliation had a particular charred taste at the back of Aiden's mouth that he was very familiar with at this point. Had Harvard been in touch with Arune this whole time and just never mentioned it?

Seeing Arune made Aiden feel as if he were still that kid who used to cling to Harvard, when Arune and Harvard were friends and Aiden felt like the hanger-on of the group. But Aiden had changed since then. Arune didn't seem to have changed much. He still seemed cool.

Arune was as tall as Harvard, and as good at sports, and he was kind in the same way Harvard was, without even having to think about it. Aiden had worried all through elementary school that Harvard would trade up for a better best friend.

There was more to Aiden's feelings about Arune than petty jealousy, though. Aiden couldn't set eyes on Arune without flashing back to that incident when they were nine, and feeling his insides curl up hot with shame.

No, Aiden wouldn't think about it.

The French boy—Blaise?—was talking about welcoming Americans to Camp Menton and some match he had later on. Apparently, it was the first Camp Menton bout of the year.

"I can see you're difficult to impress," the French boy was prattling on. "But if you let me try, I think I can manage it."

"Who knows what I might let you do," Aiden murmured.

Bernard, or whoever, smiled. "If I win my match, it's tradition for me to get a reward. So . . . do you think I could get a date?"

The impulse toward cruelty stirred, the same way it had with the last nameless, faceless boy at Kings Row. Aiden smiled, and it wasn't a pleasant smile, but the French boy looked fascinated.

"Only if you absolutely crush him," Aiden purred.

Perhaps Aiden would feel better if he saw someone else feel worse.

The empty motions of flirtation came easy, thank God. The

rays of sunlight in France seemed particularly piercing, bouncing off white mountains and azure sea to stab Aiden in the eyeballs. He'd wanted to go to France, but wherever he went, there he was. There seemed no hope of rescue.

Except then Coach Williams said, "A word with you, if you please, Aiden Kane."

Aiden meandered over to where Coach stood, with a brief feeling of relief. Coach's vacation clothes appeared to be a blue-and-white hoodie, slightly fancier than the red-and-white hoodie she wore at Kings Row.

The relief dissipated as Aiden grew closer. The way Coach looked at him, reproach in her direct dark eyes, made Aiden want to flinch. So he flung up his head and sneered instead.

"What was today's performance about? I'm surprised by you."

"At this point, I can't imagine why," said Aiden. "Seems like totally on-brand behavior for me."

He wondered how Eugene was.

"Are you going to ask me how Eugene is?"

"That didn't occur to me," said Aiden. "No."

"Your teammate's fine," Coach told him briskly, and Aiden let out a small sigh of relief. Coach caught him. Her eyes sharpened. "Why are you trying so hard to mess up your life, Aiden?"

He wasn't trying to mess up his life. He was just trying to be someone who could be content with what he had. He was tired of wanting what he couldn't have. He'd done it for years. Once he'd started dating around, there'd at least been the relief of distraction, the pleasure of being the one desired. He'd still wanted what he couldn't have, it had still hurt, but Aiden could think about it less.

Then Harvard had started dating, and Aiden was wretchedly and blazingly miserable, and when Harvard was feeling unsure about how dating went, they'd tried their ill-fated dating experiment. And Aiden was suddenly aware of exactly what he was missing out on—in vivid and soul-destroying detail. He kept thinking if only he'd done it right, if only he'd been better in some way, then Harvard would have wanted to date him for real. Only Aiden hadn't been good enough.

He had to accept that he wasn't good enough.

That seemed long and embarrassing to explain, and Aiden had an allergy to being emotionally vulnerable.

"I don't know what you mean, Coach," Aiden answered. "My dad? Rich. My face? Beautiful. My personal life? Thrilling. What's the problem?"

"The problem is, Aiden, that if you keep going on the way you are, you could get in real trouble. Watch yourself. Imagine the worst-case scenario here: If you get expelled from Camp Menton, your father will pull you out of Kings Row rather than have you face any consequences."

He'd never wanted to be like his father, but perhaps he was anyway. Time to put childhood dreams up on a shelf where he should've put his childhood teddy bear years ago, along with those old childish longings to be good and to be loved.

"*C'est la vie*," said Aiden.

Coach let out an explosive breath. "You can always make up for any mistakes, Aiden, no matter how bad they are. It's not too late. All you have to do is try."

"Sorry, are you a fencing coach or a life coach?" asked Aiden.

"I wish you'd try at fencing!" Coach snapped. "I really thought you were turning things around, Aiden. You were finally attempting teamwork. You were talking to your stepmother again. What went wrong?"

Rosina hadn't been Aiden's stepmother. She'd left Aiden's father—and Aiden—before they'd married. Nobody stayed, except Harvard. Aiden had never trusted anyone to stay and care...except Harvard.

Aiden remembered Harvard standing at their dormitory window back at Kings Row. The only person Aiden had ever really loved, telling Aiden that falling in love with him was the worst thing he could imagine.

"I guess I'm a hopeless case," he said lightly.

Coach was massaging the space between her eyebrows. Aiden left her so that he could experience existential despair among the lemon trees.

After a time, he wandered back toward the sound of murmurs and a ripple of laughter. There seemed to be some excitement going on. Aiden drew closer, wandering down the corridor toward the *salle d'armes*, listening to the voices. Apparently, people were looking forward with prurient glee to seeing one of the French champions trounce an American kid.

At the edges of the *salle d'armes*, there was a crowd gathering, finding seats on the circular benches, or places to stand. Harvard was easy to spot, Aiden's eyes long accustomed to searching for and finding him in every crowd. His shoulders were broad beneath a white shirt, and he was standing beside Arune, wearing his most attentive and supportive expression. Harvard had embraced Arune on sight; he hadn't touched Aiden, other than grabbing his arm, in over a week. Aiden listened more carefully to the surrounding whispers to figure out who the American fencing was.

A cold needle of misgiving pricked when he saw the too-confident French boy loping across to the *piste* toward a smaller figure, who made whites look like being badly dressed. Who, Aiden realized, was Nicholas Cox.

Aiden often made fun of Nicholas. He couldn't understand the way Nicholas lived or did his hair, but that didn't change the fact Nicholas was his teammate.

Aiden had asked for him to be crushed.

Coach said Aiden could make up for his mistakes, but Aiden kept making new ones instead.

17 SEIJI

It was soothing to be around fencers of his own caliber again. Seiji loved seeing other fencers' strengths that he could replicate and improve upon. He liked the hard work and intense rhythms of the fencing drills, the sense of pushing himself and his body over and over again. He relished that drills created muscle memory, so that movements could be perfected and then made effortless.

But Seiji was, of course, aware of the looks and stares Kings Row got every time they were singled out and sent to run suicides.

"Sorry," panted Nicholas.

Seiji blinked. "For what?"

"Because we have to run all these suicides," said Nicholas.

Seiji didn't particularly enjoy running suicides, but he saw their value.

They improved speed, stamina, and—most important for a fencer—explosiveness, the ability to harness muscle power in a burst, which was essential for lunges. That was what he told himself as he felt Jesse's eyes on him. He forced his mind back to the task at hand.

The first lap of suicides, on the tracks marked out through the lemon trees, was a race among all the fencers at Camp Menton. To Seiji's total lack of surprise, Kings Row came last.

Then they had to run more suicides. Their team had a record number of suicides to run. From this day forth, Seiji had the suspicion Kings Row would be considered unforgettable at Camp Menton.

It was better to run suicides at a steady pace and not make them a race, but Nicholas never listened when Seiji told him this.

"I won!" Nicholas panted when they finally finished.

"You can't win at suicides," Seiji replied.

"Well, I just did!" Nicholas leaned against a lemon tree and gulped for air.

Seiji regulated his own breathing. "You did not. If anyone won, *I* won, because I did it correctly and paced myself."

"I beat you at suicides, and now I'm going to rock this match with Bastien."

"You did not beat me, and now you must hydrate."

He produced the extra water he carried for Nicholas and forced it on him, flicking a few drops of water at Nicholas to emphasize his point. Nicholas tipped the water bottle over his own head.

When they headed back toward the *salle d'armes*, the Exton team was standing outside the chapel door: Jesse; Marcel; and the Leventis twins, Thomas and Aster, who made up the rest of the team. Aster was on the team and Thomas the reserve, which was surprising to Seiji as last year Thomas had been by far the stronger fencer, but Seiji didn't have much attention to spare for the twins. Jesse was already staring in their direction, and from Jesse's expression, something had upset him terribly.

Seiji had no idea what that could be. Jesse wasn't running suicides. Jesse wasn't about to watch his fencing partner be decimated in front of the entire training camp.

Seiji had to witness Nicholas's match despite the reluctant feeling in his chest, as if there were a stone inside his rib cage that he had to drag around. Friends had to watch other friends' matches. Nicholas had taught him that. Even though Jesse would be there.

To Seiji's relief, Nicholas went through the chapel doors without a word to Jesse. Seiji had noticed Nicholas was strange around Jesse. Perhaps Nicholas was intimidated by him.

Nicholas went to change into his whites, and Seiji went to join the audience. He decided not to sit with the rest of the Kings Row people, because Bobby disliked Seiji and would go all quiet and not enjoy himself. Instead, he stood alone, ready to watch the disaster.

His heart sank as Nicholas and Bastien moved into position on the *piste*. Jesse entered the *salle d'armes* without his Exton teammates, making a beeline for Seiji immediately. Seiji stared straight ahead at Nicholas and Bastien. The sky through the stained-glass windows was the same bright, pale blue as the sea past the trees, and the sunlight transformed the steel strips into a molten yellow. Nicholas and Bastien, *en garde* facing each other, looked like the illustrated tableau from a storybook. Seiji knew how this story would end.

"Care to do some training together later?" Jesse asked carelessly.

"No," said Seiji.

He didn't know how Jesse could bear to think of training when they were watching a tragedy unfold before their very eyes. Bastien was being showy to what Seiji considered an unnecessary degree, his flawlessly displayed technique highlighting how rough Nicholas's technique was in contrast.

There were particular idiosyncrasies displayed in fencing techniques that could be distinguished by nationality, reflecting the prevailing training in those countries. Seiji found this a fascinating area of study. Each strength he observed provided him an opportunity to learn and excel. Italians favored saber work, and Hungarians foils. Korean teams were trained for speed, each move lightning fast, and the generally superb French teams relied on a strong parry.

Seiji recalled that Bastien's parry was especially strong. That was why Seiji used to train with him.

Seiji had never accepted an inadequate fencing partner until Nicholas.

For Nicholas, whose training was so scanty and whose only chance was to strike fast and get past someone's guard, fencing someone whose main strategy focused on defending against a strike was a disaster.

Seiji winced as Bastien blocked Nicholas without even having to try.

"Wow," murmured Jesse, sounding almost awed. "He is *terrible*."

"He wasn't trained!" Seiji snapped.

Jesse's eyes narrowed, like shutters snapping shut on blue sky. "I don't care about *why* he's terrible. I only care that he's terrible."

Nicholas, fearless as usual, tried an attack by disengage. Bastien hesitated for an instant, caught off guard by how quickly Nicholas could move, but it was only an instant. The next moment, Bastien used a parry one, and Nicholas was blocked and blinking as though not sure what Bastien had done.

Nicholas had the nerve and he had the speed, but athletes were made, not born. If he'd had a trainer from the age of seven like Seiji had, it might have been different. But nobody had shaped Nicholas's potential.

Jesse was right. Facts were facts. You had to accept them, no matter how sad they might be. Seiji was used to accepting Jesse's evaluation of fencers, and Jesse could see Nicholas's every weakness in the same way Seiji could.

At that moment, Bastien deflected Nicholas's blade with a strong, sharp grazing movement along it, beat and pressure at once. Nicholas actually dropped his épée on the ground, totally disarmed. A scandalized, horror-struck murmur rose from the crowd. They'd come to see the American get beaten, but they hadn't realized he would be destroyed like this.

The memory of losing his final point to Jesse made Seiji close his eyes in a brief cold flash of shame.

"Poor kid," said Bastien, stopping by Seiji once the match was concluded, and speaking too low for Nicholas to hear. "Nicholas is nowhere near your level."

"This isn't like you, Seiji," added Jesse, loud enough for Nicholas to hear. "You know you're a better fencer than everyone at Kings Row. You don't belong there. You belong at Exton. With me."

His eyes were clear and cool blue, the eyes Seiji had measured himself in all his life. Seiji kept telling himself to endure and win, but what if Jesse was right?

Seiji turned on his heel and left the *salle d'armes*. He caught up with Nicholas by the door to the armory.

Before Nicholas could speak, Seiji snapped, "You think that you can win just by wanting to. You can't. The only way to win is to be better than your opponent. If you can't do that, you're just embarrassing yourself."

Under his fading summer tan, Nicholas went pale.

18 NICHOLAS

At the end of training on their first day, Nicholas lay flat on his back in the grass and in a state of despair.

"Wow, your match did not go well," murmured Bobby. "Even Dante could tell it went badly."

Dante nodded.

"Yep, Bobby. Thanks, I know," said Nicholas.

"The whole camp saw you drop your épée on the floor."

"I know that, too," said Nicholas.

Far worse than the whole camp seeing, Seiji had seen. Jesse Coste had seen while standing beside Seiji. And Seiji had been embarrassed by Nicholas.

That hurt to think about, far worse than Nicholas feeling embarrassed himself. Nicholas would never have made it to Kings Row if he'd let embarrassment stop him. The

157

phrase *like water off a duck's back* suited Nicholas, he thought. Water fell on you, and you shook it off, and that was that.

If Seiji had expectations of Nicholas, and Nicholas had let him down, then that wasn't water. That burned.

His mom had never been impressed with him. She'd always been disappointed. His dad probably would be, too. It was pretty clear what someone used to Jesse would think of Nicholas.

Today Nicholas was being forced to confront a lot of truths he hadn't wanted to admit to himself. Watching the drills he'd realized with a sinking feeling how much better Exton was than Kings Row. Exton had outperformed them on every level. Even MLC, who they'd beaten before, hadn't made a show of themselves like Kings Row had. The overall level of the Camp Menton trainees was far higher than any of the American teams. Nicholas knew good fencing when he saw it. From the moment he'd seen Seiji fence, Nicholas had known what real excellence looked like.

These fencers were Seiji's natural companions, with skill so finely honed their movements seemed like instincts. Seiji belonged among them, in a way he didn't at Kings Row.

Admitting this burned like fire, but of all the Americans, only Seiji and Jesse could compare to the best at Camp Menton. That boy Bastien, who'd taken him apart on the *piste*, called this the Old World, but defeat had felt like realizing the real world was huge and terrifying beyond Nicholas's dreams. It was as though he'd believed he was climbing a mountain, that he could see the peak far above him but within his reach someday, then the dark clouds parted, and Nicholas realized he had a sheer, towering cliff to scale.

He levered himself up on one elbow in determination and stopped contemplating the lemons of despair. Instead, he looked at his friends. Bobby and Dante were here for him. Well, Dante was probably just here for Bobby, but it was still so nice.

"This is actually great," he told Bobby energetically.

Bobby blinked at him. "Um . . . how?"

"It's only up from here. Every fencer that I face here gets me one step closer to being able to beat Exton."

Nicholas nodded to himself with resolve. He was at a training camp, so this was clearly the ideal time to train.

Bobby nodded, too. "All the fencers here are so good. I'd love to be able to fence like them someday."

Bobby's attitude was the only possible attitude to have. Sure, Kings Row didn't do great today, but the team could use the opportunity of this training camp to get better. Thinking of the team made Nicholas look around.

"Where's Eugene?" he asked.

"He had to stop by the infirmary for a checkup after he saw your match," Bobby explained. "Um! I'm sure it wasn't that he felt ill after seeing your match. Tell him, Dante!"

Dante shrugged.

"I'm sure he only wanted to have Melodie, like, smooth his pillow and pat his hand." Bobby laughed.

Nicholas stared off into the hazy blue among the trees. "Yeah, they seem like very good friends."

Dante was suddenly struck by a violent coughing fit. Nothing was going right today.

Nicholas, Bobby, and Dante picked themselves up off the ground and wandered over toward the infirmary to see if they could help out Eugene, but the nurse told them Eugene already had guests and that they should come back later. The infirmary was a small brown brick building beneath the shadow of an olive tree. One of Nicholas's few allies was in there.

Unfriendly strangers were all around. Somebody snickered as they went by, and mimed Nicholas dropping his épée. Whatever. Nicholas didn't know why they had to point out what everybody had seen.

Bobby took hold of Nicholas's arm so that he could be the bright link between Nicholas and Dante. Nicholas grinned down at Bobby's beribboned head.

Nicholas couldn't spot Seiji anywhere, but at least he was with his next-most-favorite person. Bobby could always cheer him up.

"Listen, I have an idea for an activity before dinner. And after dinner, Melodie says people hang out in the orchard," Bobby said. "Everyone says the French are a fashionable people. Let's try to look cool."

Normally, Nicholas felt pretty fancy if he tucked in his shirt. But perhaps Bobby was right. They were in France.

Time to look cool.

19 HARVARD

Harvard had given a lot of thought to what made someone a good captain. A captain had to lead by example. A captain had to be the first person to laugh when things weren't going well. Sometimes you were losing so badly, you had to lean into it and make light of the disaster.

Above all else, a captain had to be there for his team. So Harvard swung by the infirmary to check in on Eugene. He found Eugene being fussed over by the blond girl who had first greeted the Kings Row team, and looking delighted about life.

"Hey, Labao, I was worried about you," said Harvard. "But I see there was no reason to be."

"Hey, Captain!" Eugene beamed. "Nah, I'm beasting it up as usual. And yourself?"

"Can't complain."

A captain shouldn't.

Harvard laid out his offerings, fruit and chocolate and—since this was Eugene—protein bars and energy drinks. Eugene murmured thanks, then nodded, not subtly, toward the door. Harvard cast an amused eye toward the hovering girl.

"Just came to bring gifts and go."

"Thank you!" Eugene told him. "You're a man of discernment and good judgment, Captain. Unlike some, naming no names, obviously I'm talking about Nicholas."

"Tact and good shoulders," confirmed the blonde. "Exactly what one wishes for in a captain."

"Ah, thanks," said Harvard. "And thank you for taking care of our Eugene."

"I have a beautiful, giving nature," announced Melodie. "Many have remarked upon it."

"Also, you lift." Eugene beamed again as he bestowed this accolade, and Melodie beamed back at him.

"Free weights are such an essential part of fitness."

Harvard had noticed Melodie hanging out with her friends yesterday. Melodie, Marcel from Exton, and the boy who'd just humiliated Nicholas in front of the whole camp.

"Your friend Bastien won a match against our teammate earlier." Harvard frowned. "He made quite a show of it."

Melodie bristled in defense of her friend. "Bastien was led astray. That boy Aiden told him to achieve a crushing victory and win a date!"

A date. Harvard forced away the familiar and horrible idea of Aiden on a date with someone else, and focused on Melodie's accusation. It couldn't be true. Aiden wouldn't ask a stranger to crush Nicholas. He would never be that cruel. Bastien must've been overly dazzled by Aiden's presence, just as everyone else was. Just as Harvard was. Bastien was another in a long line of boys who fell all over themselves trying to please Aiden, who Aiden casually picked up and as casually threw aside. Because it amused Aiden to play around with other people.

But Aiden wouldn't do this.

Against all the evidence Harvard's heart said, *Aiden couldn't possibly.*

Harvard didn't want to listen to his stupid, treacherous heart anymore. It was always wanting to soften toward Aiden, believe the best of him, tricking Harvard by going uneven in his chest when Aiden was near. Harvard resented his heart more than Aiden, and then resented Aiden for that, too.

Aiden could sometimes be cruel when he was hurt. But why would Aiden want to humiliate Nicholas, who was one of his teammates?

Harvard felt that the more he tried to hold on to Aiden, the more Aiden was slipping away. He was hiding behind his facade, his smiles, the version of Aiden everyone else saw. Harvard had always believed he had the key to the secret door, to Aiden's true self, but now it was as if that door had closed forever.

Eugene, a born team player, looked torn between his impulse to be loyal to a teammate—and his impulse to be loyal to a teammate.

"I'm sure Aiden was only messing around. He didn't mean any harm." He hesitated. "Aren't you sure of Aiden, Captain?"

Harvard paused for too long, then spoke at last, to drown out the protesting thumps of his own treacherous, hopeful heart.

"I always was."

Eugene, who truly was a brocean, frowned. "And now?"

Harvard hesitated. They were interrupted by a nurse, who informed them Eugene appeared to be doing great and had a strong constitution. Harvard translated the French to Eugene, and they fist-bumped, then Harvard tactfully left Eugene and Melodie alone.

He had the impulse to pull out his phone and text Aiden. No matter what he was doing, Aiden would always drop everything to come cheer Harvard up. But he couldn't do that anymore.

He'd always been sure of Aiden before. It was different now. He could barely look at Aiden, doing drills under the blue dome of the Camp Menton *salle d'armes* with easy grace, as if Aiden were wind or light made flesh. When he did look, he was torn between these new intense feelings and the urge to shout at Aiden because he wasn't trying.

Harvard shouldn't let his heart get in the way of his responsibilities.

This hadn't been a great day for the Kings Row team. Harvard was the captain. It was his job to keep up morale. He had to find his team and find the right words to cheer them. He had to make things right with Aiden.

This was all such a mess. He didn't know how to get back to normal. But he had to keep trying.

20 SEIJI

The rules of Camp Menton forbade the younger trainees going off grounds, so Seiji went to the farthest point that was permitted, at the edge of the trees by the sea. He stood there alone for a while. Once it got dark, Seiji trailed back through the lemon trees. Then Seiji's first stroke of luck of the day occurred, and he ran into his captain.

Harvard was walking and staring at the ground, with his hands stuffed in the pockets of his hoodie, but when he saw Seiji, he smiled. The captain had a nice smile, steadying as a hand on your elbow.

"Are you looking for someone, Captain?"

"I was looking for my team," said Harvard. "How's camp so far, Seiji?"

"It's fine," said Seiji.

It wasn't a lie. Seiji had enjoyed practice bouts against fencers who were on his level. Camp Menton itself was fine. The problem wasn't the camp; it was that Seiji was in the worst group, and Jesse was a witness to Seiji's humiliation.

He wasn't going to complain to Harvard about that. They were a team, and his captain had done nothing wrong.

"How's Nicholas?"

"I assume he's fine," said Seiji. "I haven't spoken to him since he lost the match against Bastien. I told him he'd embarrassed himself, and I left."

Seiji was familiar with the type of pause that followed. It was the type of pause that happened when someone wanted badly to tell you that you'd made a social error.

"Uh…maybe you hurt Nicholas's feelings by telling him he was embarrassing. Nobody feels good right after losing a match."

Seiji frowned. "*I* hurt Nicholas's feelings?"

When Seiji risked a glance up at Harvard, he didn't look as if he were judging Seiji. He looked earnest, in the same way Harvard did back in the Kings Row *salle* when he was instructing Nicholas on a move and very much wanted him to listen.

Seiji was glad to have Harvard as his captain, even though Harvard needed to work on his low lines. He would rather have Harvard as his captain than anybody else.

"Sometimes our friends can hurt us worse than anybody," the captain said, his voice very soft. "Your opinion matters to Nicholas. He doesn't want to embarrass you."

"Then he needs to get better at fencing!"

Harvard sighed. "He's getting better every day. And you're helping him get better. But when you lose a match or—or something else important to you—sometimes you feel bad, and you want your friends to be there for you."

When you lose a match, sometimes you feel bad. In Seiji's experience, that wasn't true. Usually, when Seiji lost a match, even if he was frustrated by failure, he could appreciate the opportunity to learn by fencing a worthy opponent.

Except...there had been that one match, when he'd lost against Jesse. He hadn't felt frustration or appreciation then. What he'd felt had been too many emotions, too tangled and hot and terrible to name, tangled like a ball of live wires in Seiji's chest.

Would he have wanted Nicholas to be there for him, the day he lost to Jesse? Obviously not at the time, as he hadn't known Nicholas, and he didn't enjoy strangers.

But if he *had* known Nicholas, perhaps that might have been all right. He wouldn't have been by himself in the empty hall afterward, still in his fencing whites, staring down at his empty hands.

"Just something to think about," said Harvard, then he guided Seiji toward one of the picnic tables, where Nicholas, Bobby, and Dante were all assembled, even though it wasn't a mealtime. "Hey, here you all are. Looking good, everyone."

Seiji was thankful the captain had complimented the others. Seiji couldn't have done it. Bobby was dressed in a top adorned with red-apple and white-star sequin patterns, which was very colorful, but colors generally suited Bobby. Dante looked much the same as usual, though he'd tamed his dark wavy hair a little.

Nicholas was the problem. He looked extremely strange. He was wearing a black T-shirt with a non-uniform blazer over it, and he was holding his body stiffly as if he wasn't sure if he wanted the blazer to touch him. Worse than that, he'd turned his hair into a bizarre, rigid sculpture. Usually, Nicholas's hair fell into his face in a soft brown messy swoop, but now it was pushed off his face in a flat shape. This made him not seem like Nicholas at all.

If Seiji had hurt Nicholas's feelings when Nicholas lost his match, immediately telling Nicholas he looked awful was probably not the move. He sat down silently on the bench beside Nicholas instead. Dante and Bobby were on the other side of the table, so maybe Nicholas had saved this seat for him.

Bobby beamed at the compliment. "Thanks, Harvard! We heard the trainees mingle after dinner and got dressed up to make a good impression."

Seiji glanced uneasily down at his own clothes. Perhaps he was the one who'd gotten things wrong.

"I look the same as usual."

Nobody had told him this was a formal gathering. He could go and put on one of his suits if it was required, as it was with certain drinks receptions, but nobody else was wearing a suit.

"Yeah, so you look cool already," said Nicholas.

"*Mmm,*" said Bobby, going bright red.

Seiji edged closer to Nicholas. He wished Bobby didn't dislike him so much. It made everything very awkward.

"We're making get-well cards for Eugene," Nicholas told him, nudging pencils and paper Seiji's way. "Wanna draw one?"

Seiji gave some thought to what Eugene would like best on his card, and he drew a careful picture of protein shake ingredients, with a list by the side to show that the drawing was accurate. He folded the picture and wrote, *Recover soon.* Then he considered the matter some more and added *Bro*, because Eugene would like that.

Bobby and Dante squinted doubtfully as though they thought Seiji's card was weird.

"Oh, cool card," said Nicholas, hanging all over him in the way Nicholas did, which Seiji didn't dislike. "Eugene will be into it."

"That's what I thought." Seiji was pleased to be vindicated.

Harvard had sat down to make a card as well. "Good effort earlier, Nicholas."

"I lost, like, really badly," said Nicholas with a touch of gloom. "Everyone's laughing at me."

"They're stupid, then," said Harvard. "So what if you lost? I'm sure I'd lose against Bastien, too. You were brave enough to try."

Bobby and Dante admired the card Harvard was making Eugene. "That's such a nice message!" Bobby told Harvard.

So Seiji took this opportunity to talk quietly to Nicholas.

"When you lost the match earlier today...," said Seiji, "was that—bad?"

"It wasn't good," said Nicholas. "Like, literally nobody thought I did well."

"No, I mean...what I said. I was thinking, I should have offered more constructive criticism. I might have started by explaining to you what you did wrong."

Nicholas shrugged. "Yeah, you could've done that."

"You did practically everything wrong," Seiji explained. "I wasn't sure where to start."

"Yup, total disaster," Nicholas agreed easily. "Still, I'll do better next time. Every match is an opportunity to learn."

Seiji nodded. "I think so, too."

"Right," said Nicholas. "It's chill."

They were both chill. That was good. Beyond the safety of the picnic table, though, there were twinkly lights being turned on. The air was filled with the scent of garlic bread and the rich savory smells of beef bourguignonne and chicken chasseur. After dinner the gathering would begin, and soon Jesse would come.

"Since you don't speak French"—Seiji cleared his throat—"you should stay beside me."

"Yeah, I will."

Seiji hesitated. "Promise you'll do that."

"Sure," said Nicholas. "I promise."

21 AIDEN

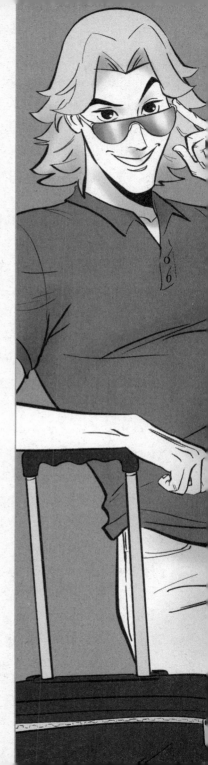

"Aren't you sure of Aiden, Captain?" Eugene asked from within the infirmary.

Harvard's silence in response to that question echoed throughout the hall. Anyone who happened to be walking by might learn of Harvard's lack of confidence in his best friend.

Aiden's hand stilled on the handle of the infirmary door. Whatever. He shouldn't check up on Eugene, because Eugene didn't need him. Eugene had Harvard to comfort him. Nobody was better at that than Harvard, so Aiden didn't even have to try. Aiden turned around and shoved the ghastly handful of weight-lifting magazines he'd collected at a startled nurse. Then he showed himself out.

Nobody else had much confidence in Aiden, but he'd always

thought Harvard saw him differently. Saw him less the way he was and more the way he hoped to be. Only, of course, Harvard didn't see him differently at all. That was why Harvard had turned him down.

It was fine, Aiden told himself. It was nothing he didn't know already.

"Oh, hello there," said some French guy, strolling up to Aiden. "You look nice."

"Yes, that isn't a new thing for me," Aiden said absently.

The boy smiled. "Ready for our date?"

"Our what?" Aiden demanded irritably. "Who are you?"

The boy smiled wider as though he understood Aiden was playing a game, and he enjoyed the game, too. "I'm Bastien. I beat Nicholas Cox for you this morning. I'm thinking we could get dinner?"

Oh yes. He had offered that date. One more in a long list of terrible decisions Aiden had made.

Aiden said in a silky voice, "I'm thinking you should get lost."

The cute French guy blinked.

"Seems we have a lot in common," said Aiden. "I, too, think it's hilarious to make a show of beating someone younger and considerably less skilled than me."

The boy licked his lips. "I didn't think about it that way. If you're mad about that . . ."

"Oh no," said Aiden. "I'm a terrible bully myself. But I didn't enjoy seeing *my teammate* get mocked by European fencers."

"Let me make it up to you."

"Go make it up to Nicholas," Aiden snapped. "If I want to be with someone nasty and pretty, I can look in a mirror. I have no interest in wasting time with a second-rate copy of me. And I've already forgotten your name."

He stormed off. Harvard was being the perfect captain and looking after his teammates, so it was safe for Aiden to go back to their room and retrieve Harvard Paw. It was a comfort to hold on to him. Also, perhaps if he walked around holding on to a stuffed animal, people would stop bothering him.

When he came down to dinner, people still bothered him.

It was absurd what people would let you get away with, just because you were ridiculously good-looking.

"You're a true original," some guy told him.

No, Aiden thought, *I am a clearly disturbed individual carrying a stuffed animal through France.*

Aiden shrugged. "Well, I'm not a reproduction. People have tried and failed to make copies."

He fussed around with his teddy bear, propping it up against a water glass, then realized his mistake when Harvard came to find him. He wished he could hide the bear. It was fine if everyone at Camp Menton thought he was weird, but he didn't want Harvard to know he was pathetic.

"Hey, Aiden. I was looking for you."

"I can't have dinner with the team," Aiden told him hastily. "I'm having too much fun with Vlad from Hungary here."

"Victor," said the guy. "From Holland."

"Don't be difficult, Viggo," said Aiden.

Unfortunately, the guy chose this moment to have some self-respect. He rose and stomped off, leaving Aiden alone with his best friend. Of all the nerve.

"This is why it would never have worked between us, Valentino," Aiden called after him.

When he glanced up at Harvard, he found Harvard already gazing down at him. Harvard was probably thinking about Aiden's worthless ways.

"I've already had dinner with the team. The older trainees are allowed down into the town," Harvard said. "Wanna come with me?"

Yes.

"Sorry, I have a date," Aiden bit out.

"With who?"

Aiden made a dismissive gesture. "You know I never remember their names."

Harvard took a deep breath, then said, "Cancel it."

Aiden closed his hand on the bear's stuffed arm, unobtrusively, behind his plastic water glass. Harvard didn't mean that the way it sounded.

"I think it would be good for us," said Harvard, heartbreakingly earnest. "A chance to—get back to being best friends."

"Don't you think our bond is unbreakable, buddy?" Aiden made himself laugh.

Harvard didn't laugh. He stood there looking steadily down at him, as sincere as Aiden was insincere.

"Yeah, I do," he said, making Aiden's joke serious. "Come with me, Aiden. Please."

Aiden went. He didn't stand a chance against Harvard. He never had.

It was a beautiful evening on the Riviera. Aiden was walking down the Esplanade des Sablettes with the boy he loved, trying desperately to think of a way out of this situation.

The issue was, Aiden thought with gathering unease, their surroundings were picturesque and romantic. The sun was low in the sky, turning the Mediterranean into a wash of gold and tinting the mountains beyond purple, and happy couples seemed to be decorating the esplanade like the palm trees that lined the walkway. People were holding hands, all in love.

He'd held Harvard's hand a few times when they were pretending to date. Harvard had reached out and held his hand first, and it had felt as if nobody had ever done it before.

Now the back of Aiden's hand brushed against Harvard's, and Harvard jerked back as if Aiden were a scorpion who'd stung him.

Aiden clung to Harvard Paw, lifted his free hand, and pointed desperately at a stall. "Ice cream!" he said. "Let's get ice cream."

Once they were at the front of the line, Aiden put on his

reading glasses to study the menu. He didn't wear reading glasses on dates, only when he was comfortable and didn't care about being more attractive than usual. Then Aiden proceeded to be disgusting and inconsiderate.

"I will have the lemon sorbet, and he will have"—Aiden searched among the ice creams and found the obvious winner—"the fig and foie gras ice cream," Aiden declared grandly in French.

Harvard rolled his eyes, fond. "My friend's joking. I'll have the blood orange sorbet."

Spoken in Harvard's low serious voice, French was sexy, Aiden thought with horror. Aiden hadn't heard Harvard speak French before. How could his best friend betray him by speaking French in France?

They'd always planned to go together. Aiden had been to France before, obviously—he was a spoiled rich kid whose dad had a yacht in Menton—but he'd never been to France with Harvard before. He'd last visited France with...some guy? Aiden didn't recall. Last summer Harvard had cruelly abandoned Aiden to go to France with his parents and learned to ride a motorcycle.

No, Aiden told his treacherous brain. Do not think about the motorcycle.

They ate their ice cream in an awkward silence. He and Harvard had never had an awkward silence before. Aiden didn't even dare look at him.

Aiden had always known that if he ever pursued anything with Harvard, he would ruin the best thing in his life. Well, here was ruin.

Aiden searched his mind frantically for some way to prove to his own disordered mind that this wasn't a date. Flirting with other people! If he flirted with other people, everything would work out.

He heard a click of high heels behind him and whipped around to give his latest pursuer a melting look.

He went for maximum purr. "Mademoiselle?"

"Madame," corrected the woman of around fifty, who was wearing a gray power suit. "Very flattered, but happily married, and you're a touch young for me. What I wanted to say was, I'm a scout for a modeling agency. May I give you my card? You're a stunning young man, and don't let anyone ever tell you otherwise."

"They don't," said Aiden morosely.

Well, that was a disaster. Harvard was laughing as Aiden threw the card in the trash. Aiden shoved Harvard's shoulder, then pulled back his hand and stuffed it into the back pocket of his own jeans. Harvard's shoulders weren't safe.

"Wow, don't sulk. The nice lady thought you were a *stunning young man*," Harvard said, his voice sweet and affectionate. Aiden wished Harvard would just stab him.

Instead, Aiden tried to keep up the joke. He batted his lashes. "What do you think?"

Oh yes, Aiden. What a good joke. Extremely hilarious.

Had Aiden teasing Harvard *always* sounded like flirting? Was he being pathetic now, or had he been pathetic this whole time?

Maybe Harvard was just noticing how pathetic Aiden was now. Harvard went conspicuously silent. Aiden bit down on his lip hard.

Someone tugged on Aiden's sleeve and said, in a small shy voice, "Pretty."

"I *know*," Aiden snarled, whipping around. That was no use to him at all. Harvard didn't care, so why did everyone keep bothering him about it?

A small child of indeterminate gender in a sailor suit, with curling brown lovelocks, was holding up a black-and-white stuffed toy for Aiden's inspection. Guilt struck Aiden down with a terrible and relentless hand.

"I have a bear, too," said the little kid.

Overcome by remorse, Aiden went down on one knee so that he could properly admire the bear. "I see," he said. "Very handsome."

"My mom gave me him," confided the kid, glancing up at the woman with bold red lipstick, who was holding their hand.

Aiden flashed her a grin. "That was nice of her."

"Who gave you your bear?" asked the kid, studying Harvard Paw's beret with fascination. Aiden had wanted Harvard to be dressed for the occasion.

"My best friend, Harvard," Aiden told the kid, slanting his grin Harvard's way.

Except Harvard wasn't looking at him. He was looking in entirely the opposite direction. He'd caught sight of Arune and a couple of MLC boys and was waving determinedly to get their attention.

Aiden's stomach curdled, sour. Great. Arune was here.

"That was nice of your friend," said the kid.

It had been. Everything about Harvard was nice. Harvard had been the tallest boy in class then, the same way he was now, and Aiden had been small and pathetic. He'd just wanted to follow Harvard around and had used the bear as an excuse, but then Harvard had smiled so warmly it made Aiden forget all the cold echoes of his vast empty home, and he offered Aiden the bear to keep for his own.

"Yeah." Aiden's smile returned, charmed by the memory. "It was. That's why I called the bear Harvard Paw after him. The name is also a pun."

After deep thought, the kid offered, "My bear is a panda. He is called Mr. Bear."

"Well, that's a good name, too," said Aiden, standing. "Nice to meet you."

"Nice to meet you, Harvard Paw!" the kid called after him, using their panda's paw to wave after him.

The paw-waving operation was too intricate and met with immediate failure. The stuffed bear rolled right off the esplanade.

The kid burst into tears. Aiden went to the edge of the walkway, to see if he could retrieve the toy from the sandy shore, but this was one of the points in the esplanade where there were only stone steps leading down into the sea. A black-and-white paw surfaced, buffeted by the tides, as though Mr. Bear were appealing for help.

Harvard was absorbed in his conversation with Arune and had noticed nothing, but Aiden knew what Harvard would have done, if a kid was crying.

So Aiden dropped Harvard Paw, pulled off his shirt and kicked off his shoes, then dove into the sea.

He submerged for only a moment before surfacing. In the gathering dark of evening, it was difficult to find a single stuffed animal in an ocean of shadows. He snatched at a moving shape, ending up with a fistful of seaweed.

At the edge of the esplanade, a crowd was gathering, their whispering becoming another sea of murmurs. Aiden was able to distinguish, in French, the words "Did a child fall in?" "Is it a puppy?" and "Who is that beautiful merman?"

Then, always singular and distinct to Aiden no matter how many other voices there might be around him, one particular voice said, "Aiden, over there!"

Aiden had gone on a class hunt for Easter eggs when he was eight. He and Harvard had a whole system worked out, so they could find the most chocolate eggs. Aiden was smaller and could wiggle into little places or climb trees, and Harvard could run fast and reach up high. They made a good team.

A light shone on the waters, cast by the flashlight on Harvard's phone. Aiden followed the beam trustingly, snatched at another dark shape, and found himself holding a sodden panda toy. Then he looked around for the source of light.

Harvard called in his captain's voice, "Now over here!"

Aiden threw the bear. Then he had his hands free, and with the help of the flashlight, he found the stone steps leading out of the water.

His hair had gone loose, his hair tie lost to the waves. He had to shake the wet mass back as he climbed the stone steps out of the dark sea into the glittering lights of the esplanade.

Someone in the crowd said faintly, *"Mon Dieu."*

Arune was holding Harvard Paw. Aiden snatched him back. That was Aiden's bear, and Arune couldn't have him.

"How many teddy bears are involved in this situation?" Arune asked.

Harvard, always to be relied upon, had already restored the wet panda toy to his owner. The kid was now clutching the panda, looking up at Harvard, and sniffling.

"Don't cry, there's a good boy," said Harvard.

Oh, was the kid a boy? Okay.

The kid was still crying, but he stopped when Harvard kneeled down, enfolded him in his arms, and patted his back.

Aiden glared down at his tiny head. Stupid, lucky children who couldn't even keep hold of their toys.

"Where's my shirt?" Aiden demanded.

Apparently, Arune had that, too. Aiden grabbed it back and put it on without thanking him.

The shirt was very little help. The material was soaked through and plastered to Aiden's wet skin as soon as he shrugged it on. It was warm in Menton, between the Mediterranean and the mountains, but it was still October at night. Aiden shivered and hated the world.

"Oh, hey," said Harvard, and unzipped his Kings Row hoodie.

Harvard always dressed sensibly for the weather, Aiden thought miserably, and then started when Harvard draped the hoodie around Aiden's shoulders. Aiden clutched on to it by reflex.

"Come here," Harvard continued.

"I won't give it back, I need it," protested Aiden, still clutching. "I'll get a chill. I'll die. How can you be so cruel and unfeeling? Don't take it away."

Harvard rolled his eyes. "I'm not taking it away. I'm doing it up, so the night air won't get inside it. Idiot," he added affectionately, and cuffed gently at Aiden's head.

He bullied Aiden into putting his arms in the hoodie sleeves and then zipped it up. Aiden moved in closer. They had gone on exactly one date outside Kings Row, a practice date to the county fair. He and Harvard had gone on the Ferris wheel, and

Harvard had put his arm around him. It felt like he might do the same thing now.

He could feel Harvard's warmth through his wet clothes. Later that night, they had been caught in a rainstorm and kissed frantically up against the door of their dormitory.

I love your hair, Harvard had murmured in Aiden's ear. For a couple of days after, whenever Aiden looked in the mirror, he'd thought of Harvard saying that, touched his own hair, and smiled.

He wasn't smiling now. Harvard's knuckles were resting against Aiden's stomach. Aiden's mind was filled with suddenly crucial math. Four points of contact. Two layers of fabric between them. Aiden's heartbeats, gone too fast and wild to count. Harvard swallowed once.

Aiden startled back, in a movement like a wild bird held in someone's hands. He couldn't let himself be held when he wasn't going to be kept.

"So, uh…you were in the ocean, Aiden?" asked Arune. "We all thought you'd be out on a date with that guy Bastien. He said you'd promised him a date if he won his match."

"I hardly call beating Nicholas Cox a victory," Aiden drawled.

"Didn't Nicholas once beat you?" Harvard asked.

Aiden gave up on drawling and shoved him. "I've told you that was a fluke!"

They had discussed this extensively, and Harvard could quit teasing him about it anytime. Harvard *knew* Aiden had simply been caught off guard by Nicholas's total imperviousness to psychological warfare. Usually Aiden could win a match, even against people who were technically better than he was, by zeroing in on their weak points. Nicholas was almost all weak points, but he didn't seem to care about having that remarked on.

"It wasn't a fluke. Nicholas is a great kid and has huge potential as a fencer," Harvard told Arune earnestly.

"Ugh, I've told you to stop having whole-hearted belief in people," complained Aiden, shoving him again. "You're so gross."

"Cool, okay, give me back my hoodie," Harvard teased, and he reached out and pulled the zipper of the hoodie down.

Then Harvard froze.

Joking around was ruined, standing close was ruined, touching was ruined. Aiden stood on the edge of the sea, in the ruin of their friendship, staring up at Harvard with wide, desperate eyes.

"Sorry, I have to ask," said Arune. "People had bets on it, even back in middle school. Did you guys *ever* date?"

Aiden had always hated Arune, and he'd been so right.

What the hell, Arune?! Why would someone ask that out of the blue, for literally no reason? After shooting Arune a single desperately enraged look, Aiden assumed an air of complete indifference.

Harvard coughed then receded like the tide, leaving Aiden alone.

"Uh, guys," said Arune. "Is that a no?"

They'd agreed they would pass off their weekend of practice dating as just another one of Aiden's flings.

"Yes, we did date briefly, but as you can imagine—" began Aiden in a breezy tone.

"No," said Harvard loudly. "We didn't date. Not really. It was nothing. Right, Aiden?"

He met Aiden's gaze. The reflections of electric lights on the water were growing brighter as the sea and sky grew darker, absinthe green and yellow, and dangerous red. The lights stretched onto the horizon, which was now very distant and very dark.

Aiden said, "You're right, Harvard. It was nothing at all."

22 NICHOLAS

Nicholas wasn't exactly used to large gatherings. Plus, this was a *French* gathering, so it was super classy. Nicholas had gone to get-togethers at his old schools, held in beat-up gyms where Nicholas would much rather have been fencing. Loud, obnoxious music would play, and everyone would look sweaty without having exercised at all. The boys would stand on one side of the room, and the girls on the other. "How do we ask the girls to dance?" one guy had whispered in Nicholas's ear. Nicholas had stared blankly and asked, "Why would we want to do that?"

Tonight, the music playing was tinkly but somehow sweet, as if someone had put big wind chimes up in the sky among the white clusters of stars. People were dressed up and mingling as though it was simple, with the graceful ease of adults.

It was still awkward. Nicholas would still much rather have been fencing. There were a lot fewer girls than at Nicholas's old schools, but there were still some, and a couple of them were dancing with a few boys. Some boys were also dancing with other boys, and one girl with another girl. None of the Kings Row boys were dancing with anyone.

"Dancing under the stars would be fun," Bobby said wistfully, hopping from foot to foot.

There were strings of white light threaded through the lemon trees, mirroring the stars and making curves like tiny galaxies captured in a net of leaves. The lights in the lemon trees caught red and white sparks off the sequins on Bobby's shirt as he hopped.

Dante cleared his throat. "Let's."

Surprise touched Bobby's face. "Really, will you? Aw, what a pal. Are you sure you don't mind?"

Dante didn't answer in words, since that wasn't Dante's way. He led Bobby out onto the cleared space that was the dance floor and leaned back and forth like a tall tree bending slightly in a storm, while Bobby danced enthusiastically around him in a circle.

They left Nicholas and Seiji standing side by side in total silence.

"I dislike dancing," Seiji offered eventually. "Sometimes I have to do it at my father's parties."

"Yeah, dancing sucks," said Nicholas.

Faint satisfaction touched Seiji's face, since they were in agreement. Seiji was a shade taller than Nicholas, which Nicholas kind of liked for some reason he couldn't pin down. Nicholas tilted a grin up at him. It was far better to be silent and awkward with Seiji than to do anything else with anyone else.

Seiji had asked Nicholas to stick with him so Nicholas wouldn't embarrass him any more than he'd already done. Nicholas was happy to do that. A few times people approached them and talked in French about fencing, and Seiji translated for Nicholas, which was helpful. The others seemed startled that Nicholas-of-the-dropped-épée was included in the conversation, but because Seiji was there, they were polite enough. This Seiji-the-social-butterfly stuff took some getting used to. Nicholas hoped it wasn't too much of a nuisance for Seiji, having Nicholas around. Normally, he didn't worry about bothering Seiji—he just went ahead and did it—but at Kings Row Seiji didn't have all these glamorous European companions.

At Kings Row, there was no Jesse. The threat of Jesse Coste's presence lurked behind the strings of light and the whispers of leaves, and what could have been a nice, awkward evening.

Just then, a silhouette appeared, moving soft-footed across the leaf-strewn ground, light slipping through the leaves to find his bright hair.

Nicholas went tense with dread, but it wasn't Jesse. It was Aiden, wearing very fitted rich-person jeans and a dark crimson shirt with a scoop neck and long sleeves. Aiden, Nicholas reflected, fit in among French people. Nicholas unconsciously tugged on the blazer Dante had loaned him and tried to push a hand through his newly styled hair.

Nothing could go wrong for Aiden's hair. It was bulletproof. Right now, it was loose and a bit ripply around his face, as though he'd gotten it wet and let it dry by itself, but that was probably on purpose. He pushed it back with a languid hand.

"Hello, freshmen. Why have you done your hair like Seiji does his hair, Nicholas?" Aiden inquired.

"To look cool, 'cause we're in France," Nicholas explained.

That was when Seiji turned to face Nicholas with his black eyes gone wide.

"Is that what I look like?" Seiji demanded.

"Nah, I look way better," Nicholas replied.

A mischievous smile leaped onto Aiden's face, reflecting the amusement Nicholas felt. Nicholas was expert enough in Seiji expressions to know by now that the tic at the side of Seiji's mouth meant he was quietly appalled.

The French guy who'd beaten Nicholas, Bastien, approached their group.

Bastien glanced at Aiden, then at Nicholas, then back at Aiden, but Aiden was studying the trees as though he found them fascinating. Bastien opened his mouth but ultimately didn't speak, only shrugged and slid back into the crowd. Nicholas wondered what his deal was. Other Camp Menton trainees glanced Nicholas's way and snickered, no doubt imagining that Bastien had come over to taunt Nicholas for sucking. Maybe Bastien had. Everyone at Camp Menton seemed to find Nicholas's ineptitude deeply humorous.

"I told that guy I'd go on a date with him if he won his match," Aiden confessed.

Nicholas blinked. He guessed there was a bright side to losing the match after all. He didn't want that prize.

"I...didn't know Bastien's match was against you," said Aiden, eyes still on the trees.

"'Course not," said Nicholas. "Why would you want to see me lose in front of everybody? You're on my team."

Aiden made a complicated little hook shape with his mouth. It was like Eugene was allergic to pineapples, and Aiden was allergic to being believed in.

Nicholas had no idea why Aiden got so many dates. He seemed like a lot to handle, honestly.

Yet at that moment, another admirer approached, blushing under his freckles. "I'm Colm," he said in an Irish accent. "Aiden, isn't it? You look amazing."

Aiden rolled his eyes. "Every moment's radiant o'clock for me. Get used to it."

"I'd like to," said the boy. "Will you dance with me?"

Wow, everyone was obsessed with dancing. Nicholas sneaked a look over at Seiji to share their dancing-related distaste and saw the captain approaching out of the corner of his eye. Nicholas perked up.

"Look, there's Harvard. With his friend Arune. Do you know him, Aiden? Arune's super nice."

Aiden's attention slid abruptly away from the trees. Something shifted in his demeanor, like a light being flipped on a stage to indicate, *Everyone, look over here!* though his expression didn't change. He stepped forward and slipped an arm around Colm's waist. Colm jumped and then relaxed, turning his head so their faces were very close together.

"I'd love to dance," Aiden murmured.

They moved onto the dance floor before Harvard reached them, Aiden turning rather pointedly away. Harvard wasn't looking at the dance floor. He was smiling at the rest of them, so clearly, he was fine with whoever Aiden was dating. Nicholas grinned back, and Eugene joined the group.

Nicholas and Eugene hugged, Eugene thumping Nicholas's back with almost his usual terrifying strength.

"Thanks for the card, Seiji, my guy," Eugene told him. "Really liked it. Very you."

"You're welcome," said Seiji, clearly pleased.

Eugene turned to the rest of his teammates. "Hey, guys, I have a huge problem. Melodie says she loves to waltz."

Nicholas shook his head in commiseration. "Why does everyone like dancing?"

Eugene stared. "Dancing sounds awesome, bro! I'd love to waltz with her! But I don't know how."

That was a problem Nicholas couldn't help him with. He wasn't entirely sure what waltzing even looked like.

Then Seiji's arm, set against Nicholas's, went tense as sprung steel.

Through lemon trees and starlight walked Jesse Coste and Marcel Berré, the Leventis twins behind them. Jesse's curling golden hair was swept back in a way that Nicholas thought of as a rich-boy style, but it suited him. Slightly dressed up with his hair done that way, Jesse looked indefinably more grown-up. He resembled their father even more than usual.

"Hello, Seiji," he said.

The Leventis twins, Thomas and Aster, exchanged a look. Nicholas wasn't sure which of the twins, with their identical brown mops of hair and mirror-bright blue eyes, was which. The only difference between them was that one twin usually frowned while the other usually wore a smile. The smiling one, surprisingly, was the one who led the way into the crowd and away from the Kings Row team.

Maybe they didn't want to be near the Kings Row team, in case the other Camp Menton trainees would think they were losers, too.

"Hi, Jesse," said Harvard. "There are other people here, you know."

His voice was warm and not judgmental, but faint color stole into Jesse's face. "Hello, everyone," he said with a smile too sudden to be at all sincere. His gaze skipped over Nicholas.

Arune snorted with amusement. "Hey, Jesse. Hi, Marcel. Fun match we had against Exton the other day."

"You're still overextending when you lunge," murmured Marcel.

Nicholas thought it sounded like constructive criticism—like Coach would give him. Or like Seiji would give him. He honestly didn't think it was a mean comment. The Exton boys just knew what was best when it came to fencing and let everyone know they knew best.

Eugene eyed Jesse in the manner of a lion spotting a fresh antelope. "Hey, bro."

Jesse stared, clearly finding it impossible to believe anyone would ever address him that way.

Eugene persisted. "Can *you* waltz?"

Jesse regarded Eugene with suspicion. "I can waltz."

"Can you teach me how, bro, real quick?"

"Do you not know how?" Jesse seemed so deeply startled by this information that, for a moment, Nicholas thought he might switch into coaching mode and waltz with Eugene. Instead, Jesse said disapprovingly, "Your captain should be the one to fill the gaps in your expertise."

Harvard looked taken aback, but willing. "Well...if you like, Eugene, I could..."

"Oh wow!" exclaimed Eugene, totally oblivious to Harvard offering to waltz with him under the lemon trees. "She's coming! She's beautiful! Everybody, act normal!"

"Not sure you're playing to this group's strengths," muttered Arune. "Hey, Harvard, c'mon. Let me introduce you to some fun German fencers I know."

As Harvard and Arune moved off, Melodie Suard drifted in from another building that provided accommodation for Camp Menton, this one a whitewashed farmhouse with a painted wheel in the window. She had her long hair down, which would get in her eyes if she fenced, Nicholas thought critically. Eugene sighed.

Melodie fluttered her eyelashes. "You look dashing tonight, Eugene."

"You too!" said Eugene. An expression of extreme mortification crossed his face an instant later.

Melodie smiled at the compliment, then held out a hand, fingers circled with silver rings, and placed it on Eugene's arm. "Would you care to dance?"

"Um," said Eugene. "Great that you asked. Let me tell you, I can totally dance. But maybe later? I'm . . . not feeling well."

Melodie's face softened with concern. "Ah, of course. You should rest a while. Shall we go talk down by the brook?"

"I would *love* to go talk down by the brook," said Eugene enthusiastically.

"On our last night, that's when we have the proper party," Melodie continued. "We shall waltz then."

"Oh . . . ," Eugene said. "Great. . . ."

Melodie glided off to the brook, Eugene following close

behind. Another pair of fencers stopped by Seiji, speaking to him in a language Nicholas didn't even recognize but with an admiring intonation. Clearly, people had been watching Seiji train all day. Before Jesse came, Seiji had been careful about introducing Nicholas to people, but this time he seemed to forget Nicholas completely and turned his back on Jesse with alacrity.

That left Nicholas alone, in the cold spotlight of the Exton boys' gaze.

"Were you expecting to be introduced as Seiji's fencing partner all night?" Jesse asked. All the warmth and charm was gone from his voice.

"What's it to you?" Nicholas asked.

Jesse's eyes were frozen lakes. "Who are you, exactly?"

Nicholas stared at the contempt on the face of his father's son.

Jesse continued, "I know the truth about you."

Nicholas's heart felt stuck in his throat. His voice had to scrape past it to come through. "You do?"

"Everything I care to know," said Jesse. "You're some scholarship boy from nowhere, who's all over someone immeasurably more talented like a rash. What, you expect me to believe you wanna be pals because you enjoy Seiji's sparkling personality? You want to be close to him because you want to steal some of his glory. Seiji doesn't need users like you around him. He needs *me*."

Marcel coughed. "I hear a social acquaintance calling, I

think...," he said. "I should see what they want. Since they're an acquaintance. Who I know socially."

Neither Jesse nor Nicholas acknowledged his departure. Nicholas was watching Jesse too closely for that, as though he were observing Jesse through the mesh of a face mask, waiting for Jesse to make a sudden move. Jesse, who had all Nicholas's speed and everything Nicholas would never have. Jesse, who was dismissing Nicholas in the way Seiji had dismissed him once. Except Jesse, unlike Seiji, was always charming people. Jesse was being cutting to Nicholas on purpose.

Nicholas bristled. "You don't know anything about me."

Except perhaps that wasn't true. How Seiji fenced was the first thing Nicholas had noticed about Seiji. He didn't care about glory, but he cared about seeing how Seiji fenced, being part of a perfect whirlwind of precisely honed skill. He cared about having the diamond intensity of Seiji's focus trained on Nicholas alone. Sometimes it was all he thought about.

Maybe that wasn't a great way to think about your friend. Maybe Nicholas wasn't a great friend. Standing here, facing Jesse, he felt once more as if it were his father telling him all the ways in which Nicholas couldn't measure up. Being disappointed in him and embarrassed by him.

Ice-blue eyes narrowing, Jesse said quietly, "Give it up and leave Seiji alone. It's no use. You're never going to be good enough to get what you want."

It was very clear to Nicholas that he should punch Jesse in

199

the face. Nicholas could picture doing so with vivid clarity, could already feel the grind of his fist connecting with Jesse's teeth, the hot blood spurting onto his knuckles. But Camp Menton had strict rules. If Nicholas got thrown out for punching people, he would be letting down his team. He would embarrass Seiji.

So Nicholas clenched his fists, turned around, and stormed out of the party.

23 SEIJI

Certain people only wanted to be seen with Seiji after they realized what he could do on the *piste*. Seiji could always tell and always found it tiresome to endure their company. He couldn't stand the pretending.

When a pair of German fencers cornered Seiji at the party, though, he let them. The alternative was facing Jesse. They talked about plans for the Olympics until the Germans left and Seiji had to brace himself and turn back to the group. His one comfort was that when he turned, Nicholas would be there.

He turned around, and Nicholas was gone.

"Where's Nicholas?" Seiji asked sharply, instead of the casual, party-conversation remark he'd been planning to make.

"He left," said Jesse, his eyes

glinting, catching silver on blue in the party lights. "Which gives us an opportunity to talk. I think we should."

"I should find Nicholas," said Seiji.

He wanted an explanation. Nicholas had promised Seiji he would stay. But he hadn't.

"I don't get it," Jesse told him. "You *never* had any use for the hangers-on."

"Who are you talking about?" Seiji snapped.

Surely not Nicholas.

"Who else?" Jesse's mouth twisted. "That boy. The one who's always with you."

Nicholas, a hanger-on? How odd. Seiji had taken people at Jesse's valuation for years. It had never occurred to him before that Jesse could be comically wrong.

Seiji's lip curled.

Jesse's voice rose with outrage. "Why are you looking at me like that?"

"Sorry. I'll stop looking at you. I'll start looking for Nicholas," Seiji said in a level voice. "I don't think there's any need for us to talk."

"You're right," said Jesse unexpectedly, voice still confident, and Seiji blinked in surprise.

Jesse was like that. Always the same, golden and sure of himself, no matter what country they were in or what age they were. Seiji had always watched him, trying to learn that golden certainty the same way he learned fencing moves.

But Seiji had never been able to learn how Jesse could turn any situation to his advantage. He was always caught off guard when Jesse turned the tables on him.

Jesse put a hand on his arm. Seiji went still.

"Do you fence with that boy because he's left-handed like me?" Jesse asked intently.

That made Seiji remember one fencing match in particular, where Nicholas had moved like Jesse, left-handed and lightning fast. It made Seiji recall, too vividly, how it felt to have a fencing partner who was a mirror of yourself turned quicksilver.

How it felt to have such a partner, and how it felt to lose one.

"Nicholas is nothing like you," snapped Seiji.

"I know. *I* can fence. Which is what I came here to do. With you. Fence a match with me," Jesse replied.

Seiji felt his insides twist with panic.

"I'm not going to fence you," Seiji answered, keeping his voice even.

"Why not?" Jesse pursued. "Afraid you'll lose to me? Again?"

Seiji's answer was as fast, and as badly thought out, as one of Nicholas's fencing moves. *"No."*

"So you'll fence with me." Jesse smiled, a little relieved and a great deal triumphant. He was used to winning faster than this, but he was seeing victory in view now.

"Why do you want to fence with me, Jesse?" Seiji asked distantly. "So you can humiliate me in front of everyone? Again?"

Like Nicholas had been humiliated today. Seiji's hand closed, as though on the hilt of a sword that was slipping from his grasp.

"No!" Jesse snapped. "That wasn't—I didn't—look. We don't have to do it in front of anyone. We can sneak into the *salle d'armes* at night. Nobody will see."

That was against the rules, Seiji wanted to protest, but then he thought of losing again in front of an uncaring audience. He wouldn't argue for that.

"If nobody would see," said Seiji, "why do you want to do it?"

"If you win a match," Jesse responded, "you can ask for a reward."

He knew that look. Seiji had seen Jesse close to victory a thousand times.

"What do you want, Jesse?" Seiji asked, feeling too much to show any of it.

"The same thing I've wanted all this time," said Jesse. "I want you. If I win, you leave Kings Row. You come back with me and join the team at Exton."

Seiji looked around for Nicholas, but he was nowhere to be found. Seiji felt extremely betrayed. Nicholas had offered to help Seiji in social situations. This was the worst possible social situation Seiji could imagine, yet Nicholas wasn't helping him at all.

"You can't force me to go to Exton."

"I'm *helping* you!" Jesse told him. "I'm giving you the perfect excuse to leave. You were embarrassed when you lost to me? I saw you today. Nobody at Kings Row is on your level, and you know it. Kings Row is dragging you down, and I want to save you. I think you want it, too. Your pride just won't let you admit it. So let me do you a favor, Seiji. You can keep your pride this time. You can have what you want. You can be on the winning team. You can even blame me. If you come back and be my partner again."

"All right." Seiji pulled his arm free of Jesse's grasp. "I'll fence with you. And if *I* win, I want something, too."

Jesse drew closer. "Tell me."

"If I win, you never suggest me coming to Exton again. I stay at Kings Row, and we fence you at the state championships. And that's how it is between us."

"That's what you want?" Jesse blinked. "Fine!"

"Fine," Seiji said in a tight voice. "Excuse me."

"Seiji," Jesse called. Seiji glanced over his shoulder to see Jesse shining golden by moonlight, as though no harsh words had been spoken between them. Serenely confident, Jesse said, "I'm looking forward to winning."

Seiji wanted to snarl back that *he* would win, but that felt like committing himself to yet another match, this time with words. That would feel like letting Jesse win over and over again.

"Do you know something, Jesse?" Seiji asked. "You talk too much."

Then he turned and left the party. He made for the house where he and Nicholas were staying, but he didn't have to go that far. Nicholas was leaning against the fence that served as a perimeter for the training grounds, hands stuffed in the pockets of his ripped black jeans, his face moody.

"Why did you go?" Seiji asked coldly. "You said you wouldn't."

He wanted Nicholas to explain himself, but as soon as he spoke, he felt like he'd said too much. He wasn't like Jesse, who could use conversational feints. Whenever Seiji spoke, he left himself open for attack. Showing he cared was like begging to be disarmed.

"I don't see how leaving could embarrass you, Seiji," said Nicholas mystifyingly. "Your old pal Jesse was being a jerk, and I didn't want to stay at the stupid party. So I left. What's the big deal?"

"Why would you care what Jesse says to you? You never care what other people say to you!" Seiji exclaimed. "Is there some reason that Jesse's different?"

A strange silence followed, broken only by the sigh of the sea wind. There was an expression on Nicholas's face that Seiji found disturbing. Nicholas never looked that way. It was like seeing an open book slammed shut.

"Is there a reason, Nicholas?" Seiji asked, much more quietly. "If there is, tell me."

It might have been the closed-off look on Nicholas's face, changing it so much from the face Seiji was used to, or the way his hair was swept back tonight. It might have been simply an effect of how disturbed Seiji was. For a moment, it was like seeing Jesse's face superimposed over Nicholas's. The coloring was different, but the determined tilt of the jaw, the shape of the furious mouth, seemed for an instant exactly the same.

Nicholas couldn't be like Jesse. If Nicholas was like Jesse, Seiji would have to stay away from him. Seiji's stomach turned over, sick and unsettled, and he found himself scared of what Nicholas might say.

"No," said Nicholas at last. "There's no reason."

Only it sounded to Seiji as though Nicholas was lying. There was the same bitter resentment in Nicholas's brown eyes as there had been the day they had actually come to blows. Seiji wanted, with sudden ferocity, to hit Nicholas again.

"Then why did you go?" Seiji demanded.

"Why do you *care* if I went away?" Nicholas riposted.

Panic filled Seiji's ears with the roar of the sea. He thought again of losing that match to Jesse, being alone after and staring down at his empty hands.

"I don't care," he said desperately. "I don't. It's just, you said you would stay."

"Why should I? You were busy talking to those fancy European fencers. You turned away and left me to get insulted by those Exton boys."

Had Jesse hurt Nicholas? Jesse could do that sometimes, unthinking and confident in his own superiority in a way that crushed the people around him. But surely Nicholas wouldn't let himself be crushed by anything. Seiji found he'd come to rely on that.

Seiji said, low, "I didn't mean to turn away from you. I was thinking of Jesse."

"You were thinking about Jesse?" Nicholas's voice was bitter. "Yeah, that fits. You always are. Why are you even at Kings Row?"

"What?" Seiji whispered.

"What happened that made you decide not to go to Exton?" Nicholas asked. "If that's where you actually want to be, why aren't you at Exton with Jesse already?"

Seiji couldn't talk about it. He wouldn't talk about it. He didn't know why Nicholas would ask. He didn't know why Nicholas made him so angry, even angrier than Jesse did. *Fool me once, shame on you. Fool me twice . . .* Seiji didn't want to be a fool again. He didn't want to be disarmed.

"Great question," Seiji snarled. He pushed past Nicholas and walked on into the dark.

24 AIDEN

Aiden watched in fascinated horror as a beautiful blond girl gently encouraged Eugene out onto the dance floor. Eugene clearly didn't know how to dance, even an informal dance, and was even more clearly in the grip of self-consciousness that was making him clumsy in a way Eugene normally wasn't. His moves were indescribable. Aiden hoped nobody knew Eugene was on the same fencing team he was.

The blonde began to look alarmed for her safety as Eugene's own face began to fill with panic. Aiden took pity on his teammate and kicked him hard in the ankle. Eugene went down to the ground on one knee, relief spreading across his face.

"Aiden, how could you?!" exclaimed the blonde. She seemed vaguely familiar, but Aiden had no idea what her name was. "I saw you! *J'accuse!* You did that on purpose to brave Eugene, who is recovering from sickness!"

"Yes, I'm a wicked bully," claimed Aiden. "Better go see to him."

Eugene glanced over his shoulder, mouthing *thank you* to Aiden as he limped off. The girl had her arm protectively around her wounded dove Eugene's waist as she helped him to a chair.

Aiden smirked to himself.

Aiden slid his arm around his dance partner's neck, with a flirty sidelong smile, so he could draw in close and observe things of actual interest to him over the guy's shoulder. Tiny Bobby Rodriguez was dancing up a storm, with his faithful suitor in attendance. Poor Dante. Aiden couldn't believe Dante had come all this way to attend a fencing camp he had no interest in, purely to be with Bobby. Who, to add insult to injury, only had eyes for Seiji Katayama.

Which was why Aiden had decided to remember Dante's name. Aiden had a lot of empathy for someone who made a fool of themselves over a big crush. Aiden had been there, done that, bought the HELPLESSLY PINING FOR HARVARD LEE T-shirt.

Harvard was in a knot of people as usual. He didn't call them like moths to a flame, something bright and useless and ultimately destructive. Harvard was a hearth fire, promising real warmth, drawing everyone in. Arune was with Harvard, too, laughing at one of his jokes. Whatever, Arune. Many people thought Harvard was funny. Arune wasn't special.

The memory of why Aiden had always resented Arune kept creeping back.

Harvard and the others had been sitting under the trees making Eugene get-well cards earlier, but Aiden wouldn't make a get-well card for anyone. Not after the last time.

When they were nine, Harvard had gotten sick, and the teacher had suggested they make him get-well cards. In those days, Aiden lived mostly in daydreams. It was preferable to being at home, hoping someone would pay attention to you. In the bright visions Aiden spun in his mind, he was the star of every show, the most important one, who everybody wanted to be with. In every daydream, Harvard was really impressed with him.

Nine-year-old Aiden was making his get-well card for Harvard, which depicted Harvard and Aiden in a rowboat off on an adventure. It was a beautiful pea-green boat, like the boat that the owl and the cat from Harvard's storybook went to sea in. Aiden's mind wandered. He found himself staring out the window, worrying about whether Harvard would get well soon and thinking of how nice it would be to sail away with Harvard for a year and a day, and never go back home at all.

Harvard and Aiden paired up to share a desk, and Arune sat at the next desk over. Arune had always been nice to Aiden, but sometimes—like all the other boys, except Harvard—Arune teased Aiden for being short and shy. It was done in a nice-enough way. Aiden didn't usually mind.

That day, though, Arune leaned over the space between their desks, laughed, and said, "Let's see what you're drawing." Before Aiden could react, Arune had tugged the card out from under Aiden's sheltering arm as Aiden sighed and stared out the window.

That day Aiden minded very much.

"Quit it, Arune!" he shouted, stunningly loud for quiet mouse Aiden. "That's not funny. Give it back to me now!"

Arune was laughing, but he stopped laughing as he unfolded the card and saw—Aiden's chest felt like it might collapse in on itself—the little pink heart Aiden had doodled, hardly even conscious of what he was doing. A heart floating like a bubble on the surface of the blue waters, where the pea-green boat sailed.

A heart with *Aiden Loves Harvard* scrawled inside it.

Arune's eyes met Aiden's. Aiden froze, going quiet and still, feeling every bit the mouse they all called him. He felt like a mouse caught in a trap.

Arune stared. Aiden stared. Time froze. Then a teacher snatched the card.

"What's happening here?"

"He took my card," Aiden whispered, and when the card was safely delivered back into his hands, Aiden crumpled it at once. He twisted the card viciously, as his heart twisted in terror at the thought Arune *knew*.

He understood, for the first time, why his father was always talking about being strong. He didn't want to be weak and afraid. He didn't want to rely on someone else's mercy to be saved.

Aiden never wanted to be the one in a vulnerable position ever again. And he never had been, except with Harvard. He'd put his heart in Harvard's hands when he was too young to know it wasn't safe to give your heart to anyone. They were the best hands Aiden knew. He trusted Harvard not to crush his heart or throw it away, to be careful with it.

Even now, his heart was in Harvard's hands. He didn't want it back. He wasn't planning to use it. Honestly, if it were anywhere else, it wouldn't feel like Aiden's heart at all.

He just wished he could cut the strings connecting himself to his heart, constantly tugging Aiden in Harvard's direction, making Aiden long to be wherever Harvard was. Once the connection was cut, Aiden could live perfectly well without his heart. His father would like him better that way. He'd do better that way. Everyone knew he was born to be the heartless type.

"So, there's a goodbye party on the last night at Camp Menton," Aiden said lightly, returning his attention to his dance partner. "There are two parties for a camp that lasts only three full days? The French know how to live. But have you considered the most important kind of party?"

"One that's just you and me?" his dance partner murmured in his ear.

Aiden thought the guy's name was Colin? He was pretty sure Colin was from Iceland.

"I meant the after-party," said Aiden. "A more exclusive event, in which one can get into a lot more trouble, and thus have a lot more fun. And I know just the place to hold an after-party. My father's yacht is in the harbor."

Colin from Iceland blinked at him. "Your father has a yacht in Menton harbor?"

"My father keeps several yachts along the Riviera," said Aiden. "What's the alternative, rent a yacht every time you need one? We're not peasants."

Colin from Iceland laughed. *Don't laugh*, Aiden thought. *What I'm saying is obnoxious. Harvard wouldn't let me get away with this.*

Across a space of swaying lights and warm air, Harvard was laughing at something Arune was saying.

Every time Aiden had to see Arune, he had to face that Arune *knew* how pathetic Aiden was. That Arune could tell Harvard at any time.

A murderous expression might have flitted across Aiden's face, because Colin from Iceland sounded slightly nervous when he asked, "Are you all right?"

"Better than all right," Aiden lied through his teeth.

Nobody was more expert than Aiden at seeming like he was having the best time when he was having the worst time. If other people didn't know Aiden was unhappy, maybe it wasn't true.

He just wanted Harvard to stop paying attention to Arune. He wanted Harvard to look at *him*.

Aiden backed himself up against a tree and beckoned to the Icelandic guy. "Come ravish me," he commanded.

Naturally, his dance partner came, mouth and hands eager, no more personal to Aiden than the tree he was arching his back against.

The hanging lanterns and the stars were a swinging blur in Aiden's tired vision, curves of light becoming glittering scythes that might cut, the whole party scene transformed into a brightly menacing fever dream. The only relief was the steady dark of Harvard's eyes, turning to him at last.

The trees were golden and dying back home, but in this town the leaves were still green, pretending to be summer. Aiden would have kissed anyone to draw Harvard's dark, steady eyes to him like they were now.

Aiden laced his fingers in his dance partner's hair—why did anyone have stupid long hair anyway—and drew him in tight against his own body, kissing harder, trying to kiss right through him.

When Aiden started undoing the buttons on his partner's shirt, Harvard left the group he was dancing with and came over.

"Could I have a word?"

"We're kind of busy," began Colin, but Aiden shoved him back, giving Harvard enough space to step in and take hold of Aiden's wrist.

When Harvard pulled him deeper into the orchard and toward the sounding sea, Aiden went.

"Hey," Harvard said. "Maybe tone down the public displays of affection a little there, buddy. The . . . the coaches were looking at you."

Right, and the team couldn't get in trouble at Camp Menton. Harvard was just being a good captain.

It was probably a relief for Harvard to see Aiden with someone else. Push his best friend off on the nearest guy, consider Aiden's inconvenient crush over and done with. Problem solved.

For years Aiden had dated guys, and Harvard hadn't cared. It wasn't fair for Aiden to be furious that Harvard still didn't care now.

Harvard had to stop being gentle and reasonable. Aiden had to make him stop.

Aiden said, with breathless malice, "Don't be so boring. It was just a kiss. Air, lips. A kiss is nothing."

He watched Harvard's mouth with the fascination of a hunter watching prey. Frustration flexed the corners of that mouth, but then Harvard's mouth went soft once again as he let out a sigh and tried to sound patient.

"I know a kiss is nothing to you, Aiden, but there are people out there for whom a kiss *does* mean something. They might be confused or think it means more than—" Harvard cut himself off. "And you might get into trouble with the teachers. If you and Colm want to take it elsewhere, then you should, but—"

Aiden couldn't listen to Harvard making it clear that as long as Harvard wasn't forced to witness the offending spectacle, Harvard didn't care what Aiden did.

"Oh, Captain," Aiden said, fluttering his eyelashes but

speaking savagely. "I don't actually remember asking for your wise advice. Try to recall we're not in elementary school, and you're not getting a sticker for being such a good boy. I'm not a little kid anymore. I didn't ask for you to interfere."

Even Harvard's tolerance wasn't infinite, Aiden thought as Harvard's dark eyes kindled. Harvard losing patience felt like taking Harvard's sword in a fencing match. Having Harvard finally react to him sang through Aiden like a victory.

"Fine! Do whatever you want, then!" Harvard shouted.

"I *will*," said Aiden.

Harvard had never looked at Aiden this way before, as if he was truly disappointed in him. It made Aiden want to run. It made Aiden want to live down to all of Harvard's apparently low expectations.

"Aiden," Harvard almost growled, sounding at the very end of his patience. "Why are you acting like this? You're skipping training, you're blowing off the team—"

Aiden raised an eyebrow. "That's just what I'm like, isn't it? Selfish, unreliable, uncaring."

He wanted Harvard to contradict him, say no, that's not who you are. Harvard always had before. Harvard's eyes were always warm when they looked at Aiden, always saw the best in him.

Now Harvard's eyes were a cold mirror, and perhaps there was no good in Aiden to be found. "You know, I made excuses for you for so long. I really thought that if you had someone who believed in you, a real friend, that you might..."

Each word twisted, cold and sharp, in Aiden's chest. "What? That I might change? Turn into a good little boy like you are? Well, you were wrong."

"Obviously," Harvard said. "You've made yourself very clear. I get it now, Aiden. I should never have believed in you at all."

Both went still, but that only lasted for a moment. Harvard opened his mouth, and Aiden moved. Before Harvard could say anything, before he could be kind, lie, and take it back, Aiden pushed past him and ran toward the camp gates.

"Aiden?" Coach Williams called. "Where are you going?"

Without stopping, Aiden shouted back, "Breaking curfew."

Aiden walked away from the party and from his team, then out toward the town. It was already past curfew. He had no destination in mind. If you didn't care where you were going, it didn't matter where you wound up.

Aiden wandered the streets of Menton by night, Harvard's furious words echoing dully in his mind. A warm breeze ran through Aiden's hair and got in his eyes. That made his eyes sting and his sight blur, so the stars seemed to be scattering wildly, loose and unmoored across the sky. The sea was singing a soothing lullaby to the shore, the multicolored houses had all gone silver in the dark, and there were lovers and friends mingling together under the electric lights. It was a beautiful night.

Aiden always tried not to be alone. He found it ironic that now he was alone in one of the most romantic places on earth.

"Oh hello," murmured a passing stranger in French. "I'd love to get to know you better."

"Trust me," Aiden said shortly, "You wouldn't."

Aiden considered what his father might think of this predicament. He'd always known how easy it would be, to let go of everything that was important and become like his father. Maybe it would be better to lose Harvard and be heartless. Maybe this was where he was always meant to end up. If you didn't care about anything, nothing ever mattered.

When Aiden finally headed back to camp, he found Coach Robillard waiting for him at the gate, gray eyes narrowed. Before Aiden could decide whether to even bother offering an explanation, the coach snapped, "You were warned what would happen if you broke curfew, Mr. Kane. You're expelled."

He remembered Coach's warning. If he was expelled from here, he had to leave Kings Row.

Aiden gave a hollow laugh, lost on a sea breeze. "Perfect."

25 HARVARD

This evening was supposed to be about fixing things!

"So, what's wrong with Aiden?" Arune asked when Harvard came back. Harvard was worried he looked shaken. He *felt* beyond shaken. He felt wrecked.

He couldn't show it.

"That's the question everybody's asking," said Harvard. "Honestly, I think he's just ... bored."

That was what Aiden kept telling Harvard. Maybe it was time to believe him.

Bored with Kings Row, bored with his best friend. Ready for a new adventure. Coach Williams had believed Harvard could keep Aiden's behavior in check. But Aiden had made it more than clear he was no longer interested in listening to Harvard.

"I saw Aiden kick some other

guy on the dance floor!" said Arune. "What's next, puppies? Is it true that he breaks so many hearts your coach has forbidden guys to use the excuse 'Aiden dumped me' when they drop out of fencing?"

Harvard was silent.

Arune whistled. "Guess it's true."

"Come on," said Harvard. "He's not like that. He can be thoughtless, but he's not mean."

Harvard worried that he was being unfair, wanting to excuse everything Aiden did just because of how Harvard felt about him. Aiden dancing, loose and easy, moving through a hundred spotlights as if someone had poured out all the stars in the sky just for him. Aiden kissing someone else, his hands in someone else's hair, running along someone else's jaw, smoothing down someone else's shirt. Harvard had a terribly distinct memory of Aiden's hands as he touched someone else, the dark crimson edges of his sleeves flirting with his graceful fingers. Aiden wearing his reading glasses, looking adorable. Aiden being so sweet with a little kid that Harvard had been forced to look away with a lump in his throat. Aiden coming out of the sea, limned in light, skin gleaming and hair sparkling with seawater.

"Whatever you say, Harvard," Arune said doubtfully. "At some point, though, I don't know if it matters whether you're thoughtless or mean. The results stay the same. I'm just worried he'll hurt you. Like he hurts everyone else."

It hurt Harvard that he knew what it was like to kiss Aiden.

Back at Kings Row, Aiden had kissed Harvard until his senses reeled and the world tipped into nonsense. Harvard had never kissed anyone but Aiden, and to Aiden, a kiss meant nothing. His best friend hurting him on purpose had never seemed like a possibility...until now. But now Harvard was hurt and Arune was right; Harvard was just like everyone else.

Looking back on it, Aiden had been careful when they'd embarked on their ill-advised fake-dating plan. He'd made sure to check in that everything was okay with Harvard, that Harvard wouldn't be alarmed when everything was new to him. He hadn't acted as if Harvard were an idiot for being overwhelmed by Aiden and not knowing what to do. Even though Aiden must have thought the whole plan was stupid and pathetic, he'd been kind.

Well. Harvard knew what Aiden really thought now.

A kiss is nothing.

That wasn't true for Harvard. Still, he had to accept it was true for Aiden, no matter how much of a lie it seemed. He felt as if he'd lost sight of his best friend somehow, but perhaps he'd never seen him clearly in the first place. He shouldn't be angry with Aiden for being the person he'd always been. It wasn't Aiden's fault if Harvard had imagined Aiden as someone he wasn't. It wasn't Aiden's problem if Harvard had made up someone to fall in love with. That was Harvard's responsibility.

Another thing Harvard was responsible for was his team, and he could see Eugene wilting with tiredness across the way.

"Sorry, I see something I should take care of," he told Arune.

"Classic Harvard," said Arune as Harvard walked off.

Eugene was sitting in a chair, swaying slightly with fatigue as Melodie, Bastien, and Marcel danced around the chair in a circle. Even aloof Marcel was looking cheerful. Bastien spun Melodie around so that her long blond hair spun out like ribbons and she laughed. Harvard liked Bastien well enough when he was with his friends. When Harvard thought of Bastien humiliating Nicholas, though, or Bastien with Aiden, it was different.

With an effort, he smiled at everyone as he said he'd come to force Eugene to bed.

Bastien didn't smile back. "Did you and your friend Aiden disappear into the trees earlier?"

Harvard raised an eyebrow. "That's none of your business."

Aiden was none of *this* guy's business. Harvard had always hated the guys who got jealous and possessive about Aiden. He'd never wanted to be like them. But he was the one who had been jealous earlier. He was no better than Bastien.

"Did you see my match earlier?" asked Bastien with a slight sneer. "What did you think of it?"

Maybe he was a little better than Bastien.

"I did see your match," said Harvard. "I didn't think much of it."

He let his tone say, very clearly, *I don't think much of you.*

Bastien's lip curled. "Nicholas wasn't much of a challenge. None of you Kings Row boys would be, besides Seiji. That's clear."

"Excuse me?" said Harvard.

Bastien's voice was loud enough that others were listening by now. Even the coaches and trainers, talking in a knot over in the far corner, turned around to see the source of the dispute. "I heard you're the captain of the Kings Row team. The worst team Camp Menton has ever seen. Must be pretty embarrassing."

Harvard folded his arms.

"I guess if the captain of the team kicked your ass," he said, "that would be pretty embarrassing for you. Let's have a match on the last day of camp. Let's make it the *last* match. The one everybody goes home talking about."

Bastien shrugged. "Why not? Is there anything you want as a reward?"

"There's nothing I want from you," said Harvard. "Just quit badmouthing my team."

"I'll put fifty dollars on my captain to win," announced Coach Williams from the group of coaches and trainers. "Now scram, everybody. It's almost curfew."

Harvard escorted Eugene to his room. Melodie came along. She and Eugene were holding hands.

"Eugene, *mon petit chou*, my friend is going to duel your captain," said Melodie. "We are star-crossed."

"I'm sorry, babe, but team above all," said Eugene. "Bros before . . . I can't call you that—I respect you and your awesome fencing prowess."

"I've known Bastien most of my life," murmured Melodie sadly. "I must support him. Age before beauties."

Eugene grinned at being called a beauty, then concentrated on the problem. "What if Bastien ate something he was allergic to? It happens all the time by total accident, Captain...."

Harvard pretended to cuff Eugene, but then had a shockingly vivid memory of pretending to cuff Aiden and having his fingers graze Aiden's silk-soft hair. There were so many ways of being best friends, ways he was desperate to get back to. Everything they had been seemed tangled inextricably around this new awareness. Their past was all tangled up with their present, and he felt like something indescribably precious was being dragged away with the tide, to sink past saving.

When Melodie left them, Eugene leaned back against his bedroom door and sighed dreamily. "Do you think she likes me?"

"She called you her little cabbage just now," said Harvard. "So, I'm gonna go with yes."

"Did you have your first kiss when you were way younger than me, Captain?" Eugene asked wistfully.

"No," said Harvard, who'd had his first kiss less than two weeks ago.

Eugene beamed. He looked tired but so happy, and Harvard remembered feeling that delighted and that radiantly certain, tangled up on a bed with Aiden before he had to pull away. Eugene clocked the expression on Harvard's face. "You okay, Captain?"

"I'm okay. Go in and rest, that's an order!"

I'm not okay, Harvard admitted to himself. *I'm lying to everyone.* He didn't want to. He just didn't see how he could stop.

Harvard's mom called him a late bloomer, and Harvard had always believed that was true. Now Harvard thought it was just that it had always been Aiden, and some part of his mind had been protecting himself, knowing it would be no good.

He was exhausted, and he had a match tomorrow. He should go to bed.

Instead, Harvard waited up for Aiden to get back, but Aiden didn't. He was probably out with some guy. Harvard didn't sleep for hours, but he must have fallen asleep at some point during the long night before Aiden got back, because Harvard never heard him come in.

26 NICHOLAS

The next morning, Seiji didn't sit with the team at breakfast. Nicholas looked around for him, but he was nowhere to be found.

"Maybe Seiji's doing extra training," Bobby suggested. "He's so disciplined."

Maybe he was having breakfast with Jesse Coste, discussing how much fun they would have at Exton together.

"I'm going to Ventimiglia today," said Dante, and Nicholas was arrested by the unusual spectacle of Dante being voluntarily verbal. "See my cousins. Don't suppose you want to come with?"

Nicholas understood the question wasn't for him. Dante's eyes were fixed on Bobby, who seemed disconcerted.

"Oh...no, Dante. I mean, I would,

but we're here to watch the fencing and learn. I can't just skip a day. I hope you understand?"

"Yep." Dante lapsed back into monosyllables.

Bobby's small face was crumpled with worry. "You're having fun here, right? You were watching the fencing all yesterday, and it was cool, right?"

Dante shrugged.

After breakfast, Dante headed off. Assistant Coach Lewis offered to take him, but he said he'd get a bus and his cousin would pick him up. With Seiji still nowhere to be found, Nicholas went with Bobby to see Dante off. Bobby stood waving forlornly at the bus stop until even the cloud of dust left by the bus's departure had settled in the warm air.

"Well!" said Nicholas. "Time to train!"

Bobby looked behind him expectantly, mouth opening, as though he wanted to consult his shadow about training. Then he bit his lip.

"Yeah," muttered Bobby.

Even Bobby was being weird today, Nicholas thought as they wound back toward the *salle*. He kept beginning sentences and then trailing off as though he'd forgotten why he was talking. Yesterday he'd bounced around Camp Menton, but today he was wilted, head drooping, like a colorful flower someone had forgotten to water.

Nicholas gave him a one-armed hug. "C'mon. Watching the fencing will cheer you up."

Fencing always cheered up Nicholas. Today it was more important than ever. Nicholas had never refused a challenge in his life, and today was a vital challenge. He had to get better fast, so Seiji would want to stay at Kings Row.

Maybe it was impossible to get better that fast, but so what? Nicholas would try.

After the terrible, terrible exercises, they were told to partner up. Nicholas gazed around hopefully. Seiji was already surrounded by aspiring partners. So was that guy Bastien. Nicholas had been hoping Bastien would teach him some of his moves.

Nicholas noticed that Melodie wasn't besieged by partners. He thought she'd be a pretty good partner. She and her friends moved in a similar way, as though they guided one another.

Nicholas wove hopefully over to where Melodie stood, with her hair now in braids wrapped around her head as she slid on her fencing mask.

"Want to do drills?"

"Sure!" Melodie seemed pleased to be asked. "Let's get these drills down."

"You bet." Nicholas nodded with conviction and pulled on his own mask.

Melodie and Nicholas moved on their strips, passing through the motions over and over again. Coach Arquette stopped and watched them.

"You're very straightforward in your attacks," she observed

crisply as she surveyed Nicholas's movement. "Have you not considered further utilizing your speed for feinting?"

Nicholas blinked.

"Making a false movement so the opponent will not know in what line you will finish your attack," she explained.

"I know what feinting is," said Nicholas. "I just don't know what you mean by using my speed."

"Play to your strengths. Commit more fully to a false move, deceive your opponent's eye, and still have enough speed to change your line of attack at the last moment."

"Okay," Nicholas said.

"I see a big improvement from last year, Melodie."

"Wow, thank you, Coach Arquette!"

Coach Arquette nodded. "Keep training hard, and don't let your focus be shifted by a handsome face."

"Wow, thanks, Coach Arquette," said Nicholas.

Coach Arquette snorted and moved on. Nicholas and Melodie continued by focusing on footwork and nothing else. Every time Nicholas suggested a quick bout, Melodie sternly refused. Usually Nicholas could coax Seiji to do one or two, but though this wasn't fun like a match, the afternoon wore on and he did start to see a slight improvement. Not long ago, he'd promised himself and Coach Williams that he would put in the work to improve his basics. It was true he had to do the long, arduous labor of building a foundation, brick by brick, no matter how frustrating.

It was tough, but it wasn't as bad as Seiji or anyone else from Kings Row being let down by him.

"Good work, you two," suggested Coach Williams, passing by with a nod of conditional approval.

"Is that your coach?" Melodie asked. "She trained a cousin of mine in Switzerland. He said she's *fantastique*."

Nicholas glowed with pride. "Yeah. Hey, show me how Bastien beat me. In slow motion."

After deep concentration on Melodie's demonstration, Nicholas announced, "I think I have it."

"I do not think you have it," said Melodie. "Fencing takes long years of study to perfect. Also, you must do many training exercises to build up your musculature. I cannot stress that enough. You are so skinny."

"Leanly muscled," Nicholas insisted.

When the lunch bell rang, Nicholas dropped his épée.

"You dropped your épée again," said Melodie in a teasing voice. "Is that a signature move of yours, constantly dropping your épée?"

She took off her fencing mask to reveal a grin. If her older friends Bastien and Marcel often helped her with moves, maybe it was a nice change for Melodie to be on the other side of training.

"Let's do this again," suggested Nicholas.

"*Hmm*, maybe," said Melodie.

"Cool, thanks," Nicholas said.

"If you are thankful," said Melodie, "tell me some gossip. Did your captain, Harvard, and that boy Aiden ever date or not? I hear conflicting reports."

"Yep, they did, but for, like, a minute. Maybe the captain got tired of all the talking? Aiden talks a lot."

"Some people like that," Melodie informed him wisely.

Nicholas stared. There was no accounting for taste. If Nicholas were looking for someone to date, he didn't think he'd pick someone super chatty.

After considering for a while, Nicholas shrugged. "Maybe Aiden got tired of dating just one guy? Aiden's always, like, breaking hearts and moving onto the next. Like a dating shark. Sharks don't sleep, did you know that? They just keep swimming. Anyway, I guess Aiden was a shark toward the captain. Personally, I don't get it."

To Nicholas, it seemed a bit like wasting your time playing table tennis and volleyball when you could be focused on fencing. He didn't really see the point in going after anything but what you really wanted.

He'd spent a lot of nights in narrow rooms listening to his mom stumble in drunk, watching neon lights play on cracked walls and thinking of everything he wanted. Desperation taught you to be sure.

He wanted to be great. He wanted to be a fencer his dad could be proud of. He wanted Seiji to stay.

Seiji didn't eat with him again. Still, Harvard was there, and the captain complimented Nicholas on how fast he was catching on to new moves. Nicholas preened, and he and Harvard had a good chat about the camp and Harvard's upcoming match with Bastien Robillard—exciting and cool, the captain would definitely win!—but it would've been better if Seiji had been there.

"Did anyone happen to see Seiji around?" Nicholas asked the table casually. In a nonchalant way.

Everyone shook their heads.

"Seiji?" Bobby lifted his eyes from the table and gazed around in what appeared to be mild surprise. "Oh, right, he's still not here."

"No, he is not!" said Nicholas. He wondered how Bobby could possibly have missed that. Bobby was still in a weird mood.

Bobby stayed in a weird mood all day. He didn't even really watch the afternoon training, just sat in the stands and stared into space while Melodie and Nicholas trained together again. Bobby was talking a lot less than usual.

After afternoon training and dinner, Bobby and Nicholas went on a walk that looped back around to the bus stop where they'd left Dante. They emerged from the trees to a path that ran along a low green hedge, beyond which were botanical gardens, a dozen different shades of green going muted silver with evening. As they walked down the winding road, a bus went by them, pebbles grinding beneath its wheels and the bus's square windows yellow postage stamps against a black background. A tall figure stepped, with no fuss, off the bus.

"*Dante!*" Bobby shrieked, dashing down the road. He hurled himself like a brightly decorated cannonball against Dante's chest.

Dante's arms went around Bobby, catching him on reflex, but then he stared at Nicholas in alarm over Bobby's head. "Did something happen?"

There! This was what they'd come to. Bobby was being so weird that Dante was speaking in complete sentences.

"I'm just really glad you're back," Bobby said into Dante's shirt.

"I'm glad you're back, too," contributed Nicholas.

And he was glad. He was a normal amount of glad.

Dante didn't even glance at him. He was concentrating on the top of Bobby's brown, beribboned head as Bobby poured his heart out.

"I told myself all day I should've gone with you. I know you came to Camp Menton just to hang out with me, and I was only thinking about fencing and not about you. I figured it didn't make sense to skip a day, but I would've liked going to Italy and meeting your cousins. I've been feeling like I was so mean, ever since you went."

"I missed you, too," said Dante.

Neither was paying any attention to Nicholas, and oddly Nicholas felt this was a moment he shouldn't be part of. Probably a best friends thing.

He sneaked away. People said he wasn't subtle, but Nicholas could do subtle when it was important.

27 AIDEN

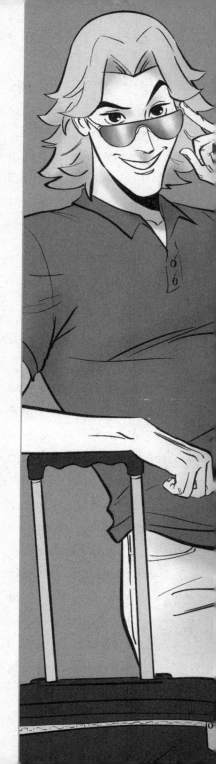

Aiden woke to a morning that was still dark and the sound of his phone buzzing beneath his pillow.

He answered with a yawn. "Hello, Aiden's house of repartee and recreation, please leave a tale of heartbroken love and longing after the beep."

There was a startled cough. "Aiden?"

Aiden sat up in bed. "Claudine?"

"No," said the woman's voice on the other end of the line. "It's your father's fiancée!"

"Right," said Aiden slowly. "So—Claudine?"

"My name is Brianna!"

"Is it?" Aiden could've sworn Claudine was the latest. This one sounded worryingly young. Aiden hoped his father wasn't having a midlife crisis. "Are you calling to invite me to the wedding?"

He slid into his jeans and walked

out the door, so he wouldn't wake Harvard. The misty, awful memory of last night loomed in his mind, too much for him to deal with right now. He scooped up Harvard Paw into the crook of his arm for comfort in these dark times.

Brianna gave a tinkling, tight laugh. "Gosh, no, we're planning a long engagement. No rush!"

"Finally, the man learns caution," murmured Aiden.

"Sorry?"

"Oh, nothing."

"Aiden, as your *new mother figure*, your father asked me to give you a call."

"His genius at delegation is a vital part of his business empire," mused Aiden.

Brianna's airy, youthful, television-presenter voice went shrewd. "So, you keep getting into trouble, don't you?"

Well, his father liked them to be smart. That was how he'd ended up with a beautiful, brilliant son. Aiden presumed his mother had been beautiful and brilliant, too. He had no clear memory of the woman. She looked good in magazines, but perhaps that was airbrushing.

"Couldn't comment," said Aiden. "This maternal support is very touching. Out of curiosity, are you in your *early* twenties?"

He wondered if Coach Williams had called his dad, or if it was the French coach who'd caught him when he crept in last night. He'd been sent to his room, and his body had been aching with exhaustion, but he couldn't face Harvard after being expelled. In the terribly cold light of this terrible day, Aiden experienced a moment of out-of-body horror as the full impact of what had happened last night sank in.

"We received the call you were expelled from Camp Menton. They're letting you stay and leave with your fellow students, though you are barred from training, and you would face discipline at Kings Row if you were remaining there. But of course, you're not. Your father says you're not to worry," Brianna continued. "He was never certain Kings Row was a good fit for you, but you did insist on going there because of your little friend. He thinks there will be more scope for your talents at a different school. He thinks that boy was holding you back from what you were truly meant to be."

So it was official. He was out of Kings Row forever.

Aiden laughed, almost hysterically. "Think about that phrase, *holding you back*. Aren't we all looking for someone who will hold us back? But we hardly ever find them. What does dear old Dad think I am meant to be?"

"You could grow up to be a great man," said Brianna. "You could grow up to be like him."

She sounded as if she meant it. That was sad. In a year, his father wouldn't remember this girl's name. Nor would Aiden.

"The worst thing is," Aiden said, "I really might."

The morning breeze was soft as gentle fingers in Aiden's hair. Aiden turned his face up to the sun and tried not to feel as if a trap was closing in on him.

Aiden hung up the phone in shock. He realized that he was

going to be late for training, and then further realized that he was no longer welcome at training. He was really, truly out. Aiden felt weirdly empty about it and wandered aimlessly back into his and Harvard's room, where Harvard had awoken and was getting ready for the day ahead. Aiden sat down silently on his bed.

"Aren't you going to get ready?" Harvard asked in a measured voice.

It would ruin Harvard's day, to hear his team was down a member. Aiden snapped on his charm in an instant.

"I don't feel like fencing today." Aiden winked. "Big night last night. Sorry!"

Harvard stood there, stunned, and Aiden knew he deserved the disgust on Harvard's face. Aiden always had.

Maybe this was for the best. Aiden shrugged, took a last look at Harvard, and left the building.

Once he was out, he realized he was holding his épée, as if he were going to training. For lack of anything better to do, he walked into the lemon trees and began to do the drills.

It was long past time to stop lying to himself, Aiden realized as he spun through the movements. Fencing had always been a joy to him, something he'd learned when he was going through his growth spurt, turning the movements of his new body from startled awkwardness to smooth grace, turning growing pains into grown pleasure. Fencing was something he'd done with Harvard, the best game they'd ever been good at together.

Pretending reluctance, being dragged by Harvard to matches, was part of the joy. It meant being on Harvard's team, getting Harvard's attention. Fencing meant that even though they were no longer children, they were always playing together.

Until now.

The sea breeze carried to Aiden the sound of measured foot-falls on the earth. Aiden paused his drills and lowered his épée. Curious, he meandered toward the noise and spotted a boy in fencing whites with mussed golden hair and obnoxiously good posture who was running drills just as he had been doing. Jesse Coste.

What was Jesse doing, training at the very outskirts of camp? Aiden supposed the real question was, why would Jesse not want people to see him training? This Exton freshman was up to something.

Aiden couldn't help recalling Seiji's expression lately, the bleak blankness that was all Seiji let show when he was hurt. Aiden knew who was responsible.

Nicholas was a clumsy idiot, but he would rather cut off his left hand—his fencing hand—than hurt Seiji. However, one thing had been made very clear by the fencing match Seiji had lost to Jesse Coste, the match Aiden had seen. *Jesse* would hurt Seiji.

"Jesse," Aiden purred.

Jesse paused his drills and raised a golden eyebrow as though it were a scepter. "Aiden?"

"Good news. As your elder, I've decided to share my wisdom with you."

Jesse made a face. "I don't want you to share your wisdom with me. You carry a teddy bear around with you wherever you go. You appear to have deep-seated emotional problems."

"One day I'll make some lucky therapist very happy," Aiden confirmed. "For now, let's not talk about the fascinating subject of me! Shall we discuss the much less interesting, and notably less attractive, subject of Seiji Katayama?"

Jesse went still and quiet. He was far more pleasant company that way.

"You know," Aiden continued carelessly, "here's a fun detail about Seiji! There are very few fun details about Seiji, so you might remember this one. When we were doing our fencing trials at Kings Row, I beat Seiji in a fencing match."

Jesse raked his blue eyes down Aiden's body, which was not a new experience for Aiden. Usually, when guys looked at him, Aiden knew what was on their mind. He also knew what was on Jesse's mind.

Because Jesse was a tragic individual, Aiden was aware Jesse was definitely thinking about fencing.

"*You?*" said Jesse. "I've seen you during training. You're nothing special. How could *you* beat Seiji?"

"Want to know?" Aiden gestured with his épée at Jesse. "Let's have a match."

He turned and headed for a grove amid the lemon trees. He didn't look back and see if Jesse was following. Boys always did.

Jesse had his mask, so he slid it on. Jesse and Aiden inclined their heads to each other, assuming *en garde* position, acting precisely as though they were on a regular *piste*. Then Jesse sailed right into a lunge made with double disengage.

There was no way to stop Jesse from scoring a point. Aiden only just stopped himself from whistling. Jesse was as fast as the fastest fencer Aiden had ever seen; Jesse was as fast as Nicholas, but he had the same cut-glass, polished-to-perfection technique as Seiji.

Oh well. Aiden had his own skills.

He offered Jesse a dazzling smile. Jesse looked perturbed, as though he wasn't used to his opponents radiating charm in his direction. "I beat Seiji the same way I beat all of them," Aiden informed the younger boy. "I don't beat them by being good. I beat them by making them feel bad about themselves. Would you know anything about that, Jesse?"

Jesse parried Aiden's lunge, but only just. "No. I win through skill."

"Funny," said Aiden. "I had another match with Seiji later. He told me, *I don't employ cheap tricks. I'll just beat you because I'm better than you.* And he did. How about you?"

"It's the same for me."

"Is it?" asked Aiden. "That's how you beat Seiji? You were

absolutely confident that you were better than him? You weren't even tempted to employ a cheap trick?"

Aiden scored a point. Jesse's blue eyes flared indignation behind the mask. Aiden kept smiling.

"Of course not!"

"Peculiar," Aiden remarked nonchalantly. "Seiji's lost matches before. He didn't even bear a grudge against me when I won, and plenty of people would have. He's not a sore loser. Yet after losing a match to you, he leaves for France, then he goes to Kings Row. I wonder why Seiji thinks he lost to you?"

Their épées clashed, exchanging glancing blows, then Jesse came in hard.

"So what?" Jesse spat. "You think I hurt his *feelings* so much that he decided to throw away his whole future and go fence at Kings Row? That's why now whenever I see him he's in the company of that other boy, which I *know* he's doing to punish me—"

"It's all about you, isn't it, Jesse?" asked Aiden. "Not sure that's a great quality for a captain to have. I know what a great captain looks like . . . and it's nothing like you."

Jesse wasn't listening. He scored another point with Aiden, using his speed but very little finesse. Now that Aiden was watching him more closely, Aiden wasn't sure that Jesse *was* as fast as Nicholas. Maybe close, but not quite.

Seiji would know.

Jesse sounded a little short of breath. "Maybe *you* have to employ tricks to win, but not me. I'm the best."

244

He stated it as if it was an undeniable fact, the one absolute truth in the universe.

"You seem very invested in that, Jesse," said Aiden. "What happens if you're not the best? Ever think of that? Or wait, let me guess. You think about that all the time, don't you?"

Jesse said, "Shut up."

Aiden won another point and pursued his advantage. "Was it worth winning, Jesse? Are you happy all by yourself?"

"How am I all by myself? Exton's a big school," said Jesse, who appeared to have caught fatal pragmatism from Seiji Katayama, like a fencing partner–transmitted disease. "Far bigger than yours."

"Has it occurred to you that Seiji's *not* punishing you?" Aiden asked. "It doesn't matter what you think about how that match went. It doesn't matter what I think—"

Jesse scoffed. "It certainly doesn't."

Luckily, Jesse had charm, because the kid was not tactful.

"It matters what Seiji thinks," Aiden finished. "He's distanced himself from you as far as he could. You used to be inseparable, but maybe that's all over. Maybe he's realized you aren't worth the trouble. Maybe he's realized he should never have believed in you. Maybe he's just done with you."

He saw Jesse flinch, and he sympathized.

"He's not," said Jesse. "He's coming to Exton. I'll make it happen. And I'm going to beat you."

In the end, Jesse was too good to defeat, and Jesse cared

far too much about winning to let any other feelings interfere. Aiden lost, but by a narrower margin than anyone else would've expected.

Jesse cast Aiden a look of triumph.

Aiden asked solicitously, "Does it feel like you won?"

"*Yes*, it feels like I won," Jesse snapped. "Because I won! Did you miss that?"

Aiden shook his head, running a hand through his hair. "It's like looking into a mirror, kid. Or it would be, but you're not as cute or as smart as me. Don't beat yourself up about it. Nobody is."

He shook his head as he walked off, leaving Jesse alone. Harvard and Seiji weren't similar people. Harvard was the single best person in the universe, and Seiji was extremely annoying and uptight, but they were both *good* people. They wouldn't hurt people on purpose, and they didn't understand when someone hurt them.

Seiji's better off without you, Aiden thought as he left Jesse behind. *And Harvard's better off without me.*

28 SEIJI

Coach had said Camp Menton was a place where they could learn new skills, including that of international cooperation. Seiji and Nicholas were in a fight. Just as Jesse's friends had always preferred Jesse, obviously all of Nicholas's friends preferred Nicholas, so it made sense for Seiji to stay away and work on international cooperation. Many of the other trainees wanted practice bouts with Seiji, so on the morning of the second day at camp, Seiji agreed to have a match with everyone who asked.

Seiji didn't have to make small talk at Camp Menton. It was natural for everyone to talk about fencing. Seiji fit right in.

"You don't remember me, do you?" asked his latest partner. "You beat me at a match in Marseille, more than a year ago."

247

Well, almost.

"I beat a lot of people," Seiji said truthfully.

The boy ground his teeth, clearly taking offense at simple honesty. "You won't beat me again. What do you have to say to that?"

One of those, Seiji thought wearily. He'd forgotten, with Nicholas at Kings Row, where *rival* meant something different.

These boys thought of beating Seiji like winning a trophy. It would never occur to them to loyally attend Seiji's other matches or take pleasure in watching Seiji fence. They wanted the victory. They didn't want the game.

The boy didn't get the victory he wanted. Once they started fencing, Seiji remembered his moves, and remembered that his opponent was mediocre at best. Seiji won fifteen to zero, and the other boy stormed off. People said that Seiji's face was expressionless. They didn't realize how carefully he'd trained himself not to constantly roll his eyes.

It relieved Seiji's temper somewhat to beat everyone in camp who approached him for a match, but it certainly didn't win him any friends. That was fine. Seiji was used to it. Seiji surveyed the stone walls of the Camp Menton *salle*, eyes narrowed, and he knew his every look was a challenge.

Once he'd won every match, people stopped making so many jokes about his team.

When he was done beating all comers, Seiji ate sitting at a picnic table by himself in the comforting shade provided by the trees. Eating alone was fine. He'd eaten alone plenty of times before, in France and at tournaments when he'd put people's backs up, or when Jesse was annoyed with him, or at Kings Row before Nicholas had made them be friends. That hadn't been Seiji's suggestion. Seiji didn't need or want friends.

He got up and headed for his room, then remembered Nicholas might be there.

Seiji turned and ran toward the crash of the sea. He stumbled over tree roots and loose stones. The air was heavy with salt and scented like citrus, slipping through Seiji's lips and tasting bitter.

He ended up on a rocky outcrop looking onto the sea, under an olive tree shaking in the rising wind. Aiden was there. He was curled up near the edge of the outcrop. Aiden seemed to like being in dangerous places. He was shivering in his thin dark crimson top, sleeves pulled down over his hands and hair whipped around by the wind. His mouth looked bruised, and the skin around his eyes did, too, as though he'd been biting his lips and not sleeping.

Aiden didn't take his gaze off the horizon, where the blue of the sea met the blue of the sky and the only difference between the two was that, in the sea, the reflection of the sun wavered. He didn't evince any surprise Seiji was there. "Hey, Katayama."

"Hey," Seiji answered in a small voice.

"You want to be alone?" Aiden sounded almost kind.

Seiji hesitated, then shook his head.

Aiden had once beaten Seiji in a fencing match, throwing

Seiji off by mentioning Jesse to him. Yet on a different occasion, Aiden had stood between Seiji and Jesse, and used the shining shield of his own assurance to give Seiji some confidence, too.

In some ways, Aiden was like Jesse. But he was on Seiji's team.

"Can I tell you something?" Seiji asked.

"Yes, freshman, I am the ideal sympathetic ear."

"Thank you. Nicholas left me with Jesse at the gathering, but Nicholas doesn't know—"

"Oh, Seiji, please learn about sarcasm—" Aiden began, but the words were tumbling out now, and Seiji knew no way to stop them.

"Jesse challenged me to a fencing match. If I lose, I said I'd go to Exton with him. It makes sense for me to go. I know I don't fit in at Kings Row," Seiji confessed. "I've never—I don't make friends easily. I get so much wrong. People don't like me. In Europe, at least the other trainees care about how I fence. Before, there was always Jesse. There's nothing like that at Kings Row. I'm never certain of anything there."

"You're doing fine at Kings Row," said Aiden. "Everybody on the team likes you. One of your little friends has such a big crush on you that he can barely open his mouth when you're around."

"I—what?" asked Seiji. "Who?"

Nicholas? Seiji thought. Extremely strangely, his body temperature seemed to drop, and he had the impression there was less air around than there should be. No, it couldn't be Nicholas. Nicholas talked all the time.

"Be kind to him if you can," advised Aiden. "That stuff hurts."

"Are you...hurt?" Seiji saw Aiden's body coiling as though to spring, and added hastily, "I get up early. I heard Coach Robillard ask you to leave this morning. I know you were in trouble in school, too. Will something happen to you?"

Aiden's body uncoiled, relaxing ever so slightly.

"I'm expelled. I guess it's the same for me as it is for you." Aiden stared out at the sea. "It makes sense for me to leave Kings Row. Maybe it would be better for me to go. But...now that it comes to it, I don't want to."

Aiden's voice was low, almost lost beneath the rush of waves. If they were telling secrets, Seiji could tell his, too.

"I don't want to go, either," Seiji confessed.

"Then don't go. Don't play Jesse's game, Seiji."

Seiji stared. "Don't fence?"

"No...." Aiden sounded at a loss. "That's not what I meant, no."

"That's the game Jesse plays," Seiji pointed out, and Aiden only shrugged, lapsing back into silence.

For so many years of his life, fencing had meant Jesse to Seiji. He'd learned to associate the two things, in the same way he'd learned the steps of his drills. The moves were instinct to him now. Seiji *had* to fence. And perhaps that meant he had to be with Jesse. Perhaps that meant he was going to lose to Jesse. Just like before.

There was nothing Aiden could do to help Seiji. When it came to fencing, Seiji was on his own.

"I wish we could both stay at Kings Row," Seiji said.

Aiden didn't respond, but he didn't have to. Seiji was only telling his wish to the sea. Finally, Seiji rose to his feet and made his way back toward the camp.

As soon as he reached the path through the trees, he saw Nicholas. There was no chance of retreating back to the trees. Nicholas was staring right at him...and smiling. Seiji glanced suspiciously over his shoulder to see if there was anyone behind him. There wasn't.

"There you are," said Nicholas. "I've been looking for you all day."

Seiji was somewhat at a loss. "But aren't we..." He paused. "Aren't we in a fight?"

"Since when?"

"Yesterday we—"

"Oh, yesterday," said Nicholas. And then, "Are you still mad?"

"...No?"

"Good," Nicholas told him. "Friends have fights. If we get really mad, we can punch each other. It's whatever. If you keep feeling lousy over every bad thing that happens, seems to me like you'll feel lousy forever. Is this why you didn't save me my breakfast roll this morning? Don't be petty. Give me it tomorrow."

Seiji had simply eaten breakfast alone and early, as usual in life before Nicholas. He'd actually picked up Nicholas's breakfast roll automatically, then noticed what he'd done and resentfully eaten it himself, but he had no intention of telling Nicholas that.

Seiji didn't know how to deal with emotions, other than shutting them up within himself and staying silent. He found himself amazed by how Nicholas seemed to feel things as strongly as he did, but then be able to open a door on those feelings and let them go. It was true that after they'd punched each other, Nicholas hadn't seemed to bear a grudge.

It was slightly worrying, to think of how many bad experiences Nicholas must have had to be able to dismiss them so easily. Seiji didn't enjoy thinking about that. It would be better if Nicholas had no bad experiences in the future.

Seiji cleared his throat. "I don't think you should have said you wouldn't leave me at a party, then gone away."

"You had all those cool European fencers to talk to, though. I was just standing around looking dumb."

I wanted you to stay with me, Seiji thought, *I didn't want to be alone with Jesse*. But he couldn't tell Nicholas that, couldn't risk having to explain why. Instead he said, "I prefer it when you are standing around looking dumb."

Nicholas grinned. "I didn't know you'd mind if I left. I won't do it again. I'm sorry."

That didn't seem fair. Nicholas hadn't been entirely at fault.

"An apology is...not necessary," said Seiji. "I was in a bad temper because of a deal I made with Jesse."

Nicholas frowned. "What deal?"

He probably shouldn't talk about his and Jesse's rule-breaking plan out in the open.

"Come with me to our room. I will explain," said Seiji, and led the way into their stone cottage.

There was a worn carpet covered in fleurs-de-lis on the stairs, which muffled their footsteps.

"I hope you didn't waste the day and paid careful attention to your training," Seiji told Nicholas.

"Yeah, I'm learning a lot," claimed Nicholas, scrambling onto his bed. He didn't even seem to notice he was messing up the covers. "Coach and I talked back at Kings Row, about how I needed to work to learn the basics all over again, and I've really started putting in the work now. I think I...haven't admitted to myself, for a while...you know, how far behind everyone else I was. I knew it, but I didn't wanna know it. The thing is, I had a coach before our coach. He was named Coach Joe. He wasn't a great coach, but he was nice to me. I, uh...loved him, you know?"

It was bizarre how Nicholas could just say something like that, talking about a man who wasn't even his father.

"I know," admitted Seiji.

"I didn't want to think badly of him. But he taught me some stuff that was wrong, and I have to unlearn it," said Nicholas. "Learning moves isn't easy, but unlearning what you thought you knew is the toughest. Still, I think I'm getting the hang of it. I'll show you tomorrow. Now, tell me what you've been doing at training camp! What's all this talk about a deal with Jesse Coste?"

Seiji told him. How Jesse had challenged him to a match, and the bargain they'd made. He told Nicholas what he had to lose.

"If I lose the match, I said I'd leave Kings Row and go to Exton," Seiji explained. "And I don't want to go to Exton."

Nicholas's face lit like a sunrise over the sea. "You don't?"

"Maybe I should," said Seiji. "Their fencing team *is* better. It makes sense to go to Exton. But... I don't want to."

Nicholas leaned forward eagerly. "Because deep down you know we can win the state championships, and that you and I are going to be great fencing partners?"

"No," said Seiji. "You're *bad* at *fencing*."

"I'm getting better—"

"That's not the issue right now, Nicholas! I made this deal. I had to, or Jesse would have thought I was scared of facing him."

"So, okay, here's the plan. You're gonna beat him."

Nicholas spoke with total confidence. Certainty came easily to Nicholas. Seiji wasn't sure how. Seiji didn't even like talking to strangers, but Nicholas could swagger through a whole strange world and face it down. Seiji wished he could be that way, but he wasn't.

Like the captain had said, Nicholas was brave.

"It's not that simple," Seiji said, speaking with a sharpness Nicholas didn't deserve, in an effort to hide his doubts. "How are we even going to get into the *salle d'armes* at night to have the match?"

Perhaps that was a way out, having the coaches catch and stop them. That didn't seem fair, though. It didn't seem brave. Seiji should try his best to keep his word.

"Huh," said Nicholas. "I think I can help you out there."

Seiji frowned. "How?"

"Well. You might've heard some guys at Kings Row hinting that I'm a delinquent."

"I would never think you were a delinquent just because you're socioeconomically disadvantaged, Nicholas," Seiji assured him.

"Yeah, I appreciate that, Seiji," said Nicholas, shoving Seiji's shoulder gently with his own in the way Nicholas did when he was pleased. "But I actually am kind of a delinquent?"

"Are you?" Seiji asked, alarmed.

"Well, I don't steal cars or anything!"

"I should hope not!" Seiji exclaimed.

There could not be any grand theft auto. If Nicholas needed a car, Seiji could get him one.

Nicholas shrugged. "I've only done, like, small delinquent things. Tiny bit of shoplifting. Slight vandalism."

"Nicholas!"

"Just, like, spray-painting walls. It's artistic, in a way—"

"Nicholas, you deface public *property*? I cannot believe my ears—"

"One fire, but it was small and accidental—"

"There must be no more fires!"

"And trespassing," admitted Nicholas. "I may have broken into Coach Joe's gym one time . . . or twenty."

"I thought you said you were fond of the man!"

Seiji wouldn't have been fond of any trainer who taught him badly, but Nicholas had an affectionate nature. He even liked Seiji, and nobody else did. Seiji wished Nicholas would stop being a criminal with a heart of gold, though. If Nicholas was arrested for committing crimes, it would make international travel for fencing tournaments complicated.

"See, sometimes Coach Joe would get tired in the mornings, or sleep the whole day away with a hangover, you know?" said Nicholas, as if it was normal for adults to be wildly irresponsible around him. "And I wanted to fence. So I'd have to find a way inside the gym."

Seiji relaxed. "If it's for fencing then it's all right."

"Yeah, exactly," said Nicholas. "My criminal skills are, like, at your service. If you need to fence Jesse tomorrow night, I'll sneak you out."

It made no real difference to Seiji's circumstances that he and Nicholas were no longer in a fight. Seiji would still have to leave Kings Row if he lost to Jesse again. He was disproportionally pleased about not being in a fight with Nicholas anymore, just the same.

"Thank you, Nicholas."

Seiji meant everything he said, but he meant that particularly.

Nicholas settled, cross-legged on the bed and grinning, face bright with mischief as night drew in over the Riviera. "Sure. I'm a delinquent, and I've heard you've got an ice-cold mind for strategy. We're a team."

29 HARVARD

Harvard had to be reasonable and keep it together. He chatted with some new fencers, trained with them, and tried to make Coach proud. Several people mentioned the match against Bastien with pitying looks that said it was obvious Harvard had no chance.

That was so intimidating that Harvard gave up on international cooperation and went to sit and eat with his team. Bobby was pining because Dante had gone somewhere. Nicholas seemed in a state of consternation about Seiji's absence. Harvard wondered if Nicholas and Seiji'd had another fistfight.

Melodie, the French blonde who'd taken such a shine to Eugene, was sitting with them so that she and Eugene could have an intense, passionate discussion about the protein content of their meal and the delicious sacrifices that had to be made to conform with work-out plans. Melodie delivered a speech about macro calculations.

"No pain, no gains," Eugene declared in a wise voice, then made grabby hands across the table. "La bread garlique!"

La bread garlique? Melodie must really like Eugene, because she only gave a small shudder. Nicholas passed the garlic bread with the air of one pleased to have understood a snippet of French.

Melodie turned her attention away from this painful subject and toward Harvard. "So, you and Bastien are going to have a match. I am rooting for Bastien out of personal loyalty and patriotism. Also, Bastien is very skilled, so I have placed a small bet. *Maman* wishes to buy herself a new plastron."

"I think you're gonna win, Captain," spoke up Nicholas. "I'd bet on you if I had any money. Scholarship kid," he added in an explanatory fashion to Melodie.

"Thanks, Nicholas," said Harvard. "Melodie's right, though. Bastien's really good. I'm just hoping we have a great match. Wouldn't want to let my team down, right?"

"You could never," said Eugene, leaning over the table to give Harvard a fist bump.

When Harvard turned back to the table at large, he found Nicholas looking troubled.

"What's up, Cox?"

"I was just thinking....You give really good motivational speeches, Captain," Nicholas said a little shyly. "Like, you tell us we're the best, and it seems as though you really mean it."

"I do really mean it," said Harvard. "You guys are the best."

Those were just facts. Harvard went to the greatest school, had the most awesome coach, had the most superlatively excellent team, had the most amazing best friend in the wide world. He'd never doubted any of those things until this week. He only wanted to live up to them and worried that he wouldn't succeed.

"Better than Exton?" Nicholas prompted, and Harvard felt light was shed on the issue of why Nicholas looked so worried and Seiji wasn't here at all.

"Way better than Exton," Harvard told him. "Their team has nothing on mine."

Nicholas nodded earnestly. "You told me once that you know whether or not someone is a loser when you see how they lose."

"Did I?" asked Harvard. "I'm so wise. Pay more attention to me when I correct your stance during drills."

That didn't make Nicholas laugh. He was still looking worried, for some reason.

"Here's the problem, Captain. You always say great stuff about all of us. Aiden always has to say *you're* the best captain. And anyone can tell he really means it. But since he's not around . . . We all think so, too. *I* think so, too. You shouldn't count yourself out against this Bastien guy."

"I'm just being realistic," said Harvard.

"When I had my first match against Seiji," said Nicholas in the tones of one sharing a highly personal and thrilling memory, "I totally thought I could win. But I lost real bad. Everyone called me Zero for a while. Seiji was a jerk about it, too. Seemed like the whole world wanted me to feel dumb for being overconfident. I get that it was dumb. But I'm not sorry, and I wasn't wrong. I mean, I was wrong about that one match, obviously. But one day, I'm going to beat Seiji in a match. Then he'll beat me in another one. Then I'll beat him twice in a row. It's gonna be great. I don't care how many times I lose. Well...I care, but it doesn't matter. I know I'll win a match against him one day."

"That's a great attitude," said Harvard. "You're always right to believe in yourself."

"What am I gonna do, give up?" Nicholas asked.

"Not you, Nicholas Cox," Harvard said, amused and touched in equal measure. "Never you."

"So, you believe in yourself, too, Captain," said Nicholas.

"I'll try," Harvard told him.

"Good. Remember, my nonexistent money's on you." Nicholas winked.

"When do you think Dante is getting back?" Bobby burst out. "Does nobody miss him at all?"

Nicholas stared. "Uh, no. I like Dante and all, but it's been one day."

Harvard couldn't help thinking Aiden would've made a sarcastic remark at this point.

As Aiden wasn't there, Harvard said mildly, "Seems like we all miss our friends."

The sentence had slipped out without Harvard thinking

to apply it to himself, but once he said it he was struck silent, thinking about how much he missed his friend.

At afternoon training, Harvard couldn't even take pride in how much better Nicholas was doing, or even how much he himself was learning. Aiden wasn't there, and what should have been a shining experience was ashes without him.

As the sun slid down and dyed the white mountains the color of flame, Harvard didn't have the heart to spend time with Arune and his new friends or even with his team. He walked into his room and started when he found Aiden already there. Aiden had his hair in a messy bun and was wearing his own Kings Row hoodie with jeans. He was as dressed down as Aiden ever got.

Far more alarmingly, his bags were packed, fencing equipment in one bag, open suitcase showing clothes folded within.

"Hey, Harvard," Aiden said quietly. "Can we talk?"

"Oh! Yeah, of course."

He went over to Aiden immediately, without even thinking. Then panic at the thought of getting close hit Harvard like a bird hitting a windowpane. Harvard slammed to a halt and chewed on his lip. Aiden patted the bed beside him. Harvard sat with care on the very edge of Aiden's bed.

Aiden watched him sit, his mouth twisting. "Right. I wanted to say—sorry, for last night."

Which part of it? Harvard would have asked…if things had been normal between them. He made it a policy not to let

Aiden get away with everything, but things were a long way from normal.

"No big deal," said Harvard, and watched Aiden's mouth twist again.

What was he supposed to say? *Oh, it's fine that you kissed another boy to punish me for interfering in your life. Even though it was mean and made me suspect you're aware I have feelings for you that you don't return?*

No. No way. If Aiden knew, Harvard didn't want to know.

"You were right," Aiden continued. "You said if I didn't stop acting out, there would be real consequences. I'm out of Camp Menton, and I'm out of Kings Row. You probably don't care, since you're done believing in me and all, but I thought you should know."

For a moment, the wash of horror and loss was so profound, Harvard couldn't see. But then his vision cleared, and he saw Aiden's face. Once again, he had the strongest, strangest impression that Aiden was suffering.

He couldn't make it harder for Aiden to go.

He could give Aiden this much truth, at least.

"Hey," offered Harvard. "I'm so sorry for what I said."

"For what?" Aiden sounded lost.

"I was mad about the way you've been acting lately. I didn't mean it. I could never stop believing in you, Aiden. I wouldn't know how. Even if you do leave Kings Row, you'll still be my best friend."

Aiden didn't even seem pleased to hear it. He only nodded, as if he were accepting a truth he was well aware of, wayward locks of hair tumbling down into his eyes. He blinked and looked through the casement window at the darkness over the lemon trees.

"Even if I do leave Kings Row," Aiden said, "I'll still be your best friend. If that's what you want me to be."

"What do you want, Aiden?" asked Harvard, and saw Aiden startle slightly. "Do you want to leave Kings Row?"

"I think it might be for the best," said Aiden. "Even if it hurts right now. Like when I had my growth spurt, and I used to get those pains in my legs. Maybe me going will be like growing up."

So Aiden did want to go. Aiden thought it would be for the best.

Harvard said, "I only want the best for you."

Aiden burst out, "My father has a yacht in Menton harbor. I'm staying until camp's over and am holding an after-party on the yacht. Come. If—if you want."

The memory of yesterday, of watching Aiden kiss someone else with slow, thorough abandon up against a tree, came flooding back. Harvard wasn't signing up for that again. He really might lose his mind and do something unforgivable.

"Doesn't really sound like my scene," said Harvard. "I hope you have fun."

The strange smile on Aiden's face made Harvard feel sick. "I'm sure I will."

And Harvard knew what that meant, but he had no right to be bothered by Aiden messing around with guys. He'd never had the right. It didn't matter how much he hated the very thought. It would have been massively unfair to Aiden to show that Harvard minded.

"So—we're okay," continued Aiden, still in that soft, worn voice. "I didn't want to leave Kings Row...without us being okay."

"We're okay," said Harvard. "We're whatever you want."

Aiden's mouth twisted for a single sharp moment, then he curled his lips into a smile and scoffed slightly. "Sure."

"I mean it," said Harvard. "Come here."

He'd never been great with words, no matter what Nicholas thought. He wasn't witty like Aiden or wise like Coach. He'd always reached out, taken comforting hold of his teammates' shoulders, hugged his mom or his dad so each of them could be sure of the other's warmth. He'd thrown an arm around Aiden's shoulders, close and protective and above all else affectionate, a thousand times. Once he had hold of Aiden, the world seemed a better and brighter place. Holding Aiden had been one of his favorite things.

But everything was different now.

He put an arm around Aiden, drew in his body, and instantly realized what a mistake he'd made. What used to feel warm and safe now felt like a lightning strike along Harvard's spine rather than in the sky. Aiden's eyes met his own, startled, eyes gone wide and lashes flickering, almost as though he was afraid. They were both leaning into each other already, and both turned their heads slightly, and their lips met. Almost by accident.

The kiss was gentle as light on water, and it felt like light itself turned solid, radiance becoming something Harvard could touch.

Nearly as soon as it began, Harvard jerked back. "Sorry!"

It was his fault. He was the one who had screwed up their friendship, and who couldn't seem to make it right. And now he was running out of chances.

"I—no, I'm sorry," muttered Aiden, to whom kisses meant nothing, who might have just been offering out of pity what Harvard so obviously and pathetically wanted. Harvard didn't want to hear it.

"You know what?" Harvard said. "Nobody needs to be sorry. Nothing happened."

Aiden offered Harvard a strained smile. "Right. Nothing."

The two separated and silently got ready for bed. Harvard tried to put the kiss out of his mind, but it swam to the front of his brain as he lay in the dark. Nothing happened, he repeated to himself once again. Harvard couldn't sleep, because he kept thinking about what hadn't happened.

He'd never been the one who had trouble sleeping before.

Other people believed everything Aiden did was graceful, but Harvard knew Aiden was graceless in slumber. He had insomnia. He was always pestering Harvard to bore him to sleep, would complain without cease when Harvard woke him in the mornings, and yet never set an alarm to wake himself up. Aiden in the morning was cranky and high-maintenance and too sleepy to be charming about it.

Harvard used to love watching Aiden wake up in the mornings and not know why he loved it. Now he rolled over and looked at Aiden sleeping in his narrow, distant bed against the farthest wall, arm outflung from under rumpled sheets, hair bright chaos, and everything about the sight made Harvard's chest ache. It had been better not to know.

He realized now why people said *at sea* to express feeling bewildered and lost, nothing but mysterious distance all around them with nobody else in sight and only fear of what might be to come.

Aiden was only across the room, a brief expanse of moon-silvered floor all that separated them, but it seemed like the Mediterranean.

30 SEIJI

Seiji woke in the early morning, resisted the eternal temptation to use the shower curtain to smother Nicholas in his sleep for snoring, and walked outside. The sky had paled from dark gray to almost white, still nowhere close to blue. Seiji took his phone out of his pocket, frowned at the screen, and thought about calling his father.

Jesse's parents and Seiji's parents had been friends once, in the way Seiji had heard many parents were friends. They got together and talked about their children. Whenever they met, Jesse's mother and Seiji's mother would play a game of who could be most coldly polite. Seiji's mother always won. She was very gifted in that way.

She is undoubtedly a genius in the boardroom, but when it comes to social situations, a moment in that woman's company is like being stabbed in the heart with an icicle, someone had said in the society pages once. Seiji's father had read it aloud to his mother, and she'd smiled. Seiji's father was the only one who could make her smile.

At first, Seiji believed his father and Robert Coste would be real friends. Robert Coste had his son's effortless charm. Robert Coste would speak extensively of Jesse's and Seiji's progress in fencing. Seiji was sure that if his father listened, he would come to like fencing more. Why would his father keep meeting with Mr. Coste if he wasn't beginning to be interested? And Mr. Coste seemed to enjoy the meetings with Seiji's father.

Seiji believed it was progress when his father made time to attend an important fencing tournament, but that had ended in disaster. All through the match, Seiji kept thinking about how his father was watching, and he let nerves overcome him and made mistakes. He threw off Jesse with his odd behavior. It was Seiji's fault that Jesse and Seiji got bronze and silver medals, respectively, and another fencer with far less polished technique had a good day and got the gold.

Robert Coste took them to a side room afterward and delivered to them a detailed and helpful accounting of where they'd gone wrong. Like Jesse, Mr. Coste was wholly focused on fencing.

Seiji and Jesse listened attentively with their heads bowed while Jesse's father outlined their mistakes.

Seiji's father took a seat and listened quietly, too. For a while.

Then he lifted his head and said, "Shut the hell *up*, Robert."

Seiji and Jesse were shocked, but nobody looked more shocked than Jesse's dad.

"They won't improve if—"

Seiji's soft-spoken father cut Mr. Coste off with a flat, "I really don't care. Don't you ever talk to my kid that way again. Can I have a word in private?"

Through the door, Jesse and Seiji listened to the sound of a low, grown-up fight.

"We won't ever fight, will we?" Jesse had murmured.

And Seiji had replied, "Never."

Seiji had made sure to win the gold at the next tournament, but his father was at a business meeting and couldn't come to the match, so it didn't matter the same way the last tournament had. Robert Coste was there, though, and he praised them both.

He wished he hadn't messed up that tournament his father had attended. Everything would have been all right if he hadn't done that.

Seiji's father said Seiji should tell him if Robert Coste spoke to him in a way that made Seiji uncomfortable, but his father didn't understand how important fencing was. He thought Robert was obsessed and intense about fencing. He didn't understand that *Seiji* was obsessed and intense about fencing. That was what it took to be a champion.

So Seiji didn't tell his father anything about his matches again. Since Seiji's whole life was fencing and the Costes, that meant Seiji and his father talked even less than before. Seiji told himself it was perfectly natural and nothing to be upset about. They were both busy people with little in common. Why should they talk much?

It would do no good to call his father, but for some reason, Seiji did it anyway. His father answered on the third ring.

Without planning to say it, Seiji burst out, "Jesse challenged me to a fencing match. He said that if I won then I had to leave Kings Row and go to Exton and be his fencing partner. We made a bargain."

"So what?" Seiji's father asked. "You didn't sign anything. Even if you signed something, I have lawyers on retainer. Many lawyers."

"I keep my word," said Seiji.

He heard his father sigh over the phone. "I know you always try to play fair. But what if the other person doesn't play fair?"

"I still do," Seiji answered.

"Oh, Seiji," said his dad.

He sounded sad. Seiji was sorry to make his father sad, but he couldn't give way on this matter.

"Also, Nicholas and I had a fight," he added. "I assumed we wouldn't be talking after our fight, but he says he's not angry anymore and he is talking to me. Actually, there seems no way to stop him doing it. I've grown accustomed. But I don't understand why we had the fight and so I don't know how to stop it happening again."

"What was the fight about?" his father asked.

"Jesse," said Seiji.

"Can't express the depths of my surprise," muttered his father.

Seiji sympathized with his father. He found it difficult to talk about emotions, too.

"Nicholas keeps getting angry with Jesse, and there's no reason for him to get angry. The other students at Kings Row are sometimes cruel to Nicholas because of him being poor, but he doesn't get angry with them, and he doesn't get angry with me when I beat him at fencing or when I say the things that make other people angry. But he gets mad at Jesse, and I can't figure out why. I hate it when it seems as though there's a secret reason people act the way they do."

So many social situations were opaque and distressing, but Nicholas was always transparent. Seiji didn't want to be confused about Nicholas. He didn't want Nicholas to be like everybody else.

"Have you considered that perhaps Nicholas is angry for your sake? Maybe he doesn't like the way Jesse treats you."

That hadn't occurred to Seiji at all. He paused to consider the idea of Nicholas being angry *for* him, rather than angry *with* him. That would be pointless, like much of what Nicholas did, but Seiji didn't find it totally objectionable.

"Sometimes...," said Seiji. "Sometimes when I look at Nicholas, I see Jesse. I don't know why that would be, but it's true. I was—angry with Jesse, and it made me furious with Nicholas."

His father's voice was mild, in the way it was when he pointed out unassailable facts on business calls. "Well then, you're going to stop that, aren't you? Because you want to play fair."

Seiji nodded to himself.

"I will. I have another question. Do you think I should do my hair differently?"

His father sounded surprised by the question. "It might be time for a change. A lot of people tell me that my ponytail is dashing."

"I am not ready for a ponytail," Seiji said flatly.

His father laughed. "Whatever you want. You're a very handsome kid. You take after me, how could you not be?"

The sun was rising on a troubled sea, giving every choppy wave a golden crown. Seiji was somewhat abashed by his father's words, and he was still deeply worried about the day to come, but it was like making up with Nicholas. Seiji was glad he'd called.

"Thanks." Seiji paused. He didn't want to seem like those people who only wanted to fence Seiji for the victory, calling his father purely to get something. He offered, "Next time, I'll call just to . . . chat."

He wasn't sure what he would say, but he would figure it out.

His father sounded as though he was smiling. "Looking forward to it. Say hello to Nicholas from me."

"I will," promised Seiji. "Later he's helping me trespass."

"Um," said his father. "What?"

Right. Nicholas had made it clear that the first rule of petty crime was not alerting authority figures.

Seiji told his first lie of the day. "Oh no," he said. "The connection of this international call has gone wrong. You're breaking up. We can't continue the conversation."

"Seiji—"

"Goodbye, I love you," Seiji announced stiffly, then escaped from terminal embarrassment and criminal revelations by hanging up the phone.

The sky was pearl white over a slate-blue sea. It was time to face Jesse, but Seiji wouldn't do it alone.

31 NICHOLAS

The last day of training camp was going great so far. Nicholas and Seiji had made up, and now he was going to help Seiji do crime. The first order of business was finding Eugene and Bobby to explain the situation—and Nicholas and Seiji's scheme—to them. That took almost all of breakfast time, with Nicholas waving around his breakfast roll from Seiji to illustrate the master plan.

"I dunno. It's a million-to-one chance," said Bobby.

Nicholas grinned. "...But it might just work?"

"I wasn't going to say that," said Bobby. "I mean, I'm with you to the death, Nicholas, but I'm actually very worried it won't work! Can we get banned for life from Camp Menton?"

"The dream," murmured Dante.

Nicholas appreciated everybody's support.

"Where were you at breakfast yesterday, by the way?" Eugene asked Seiji. "We missed you, bro."

Seiji inclined his head without saying a word, but he did the thing where his mouth wasn't frowning or in a perfectly ruled line, which was something like a smile.

Next up, drills. Nicholas found they were actually going more smoothly than before. A few other teams had to run more suicides than Kings Row.

Aiden had gotten into some kind of trouble, though, so he wasn't at drills. Without Aiden and Eugene, their team felt incomplete. Nicholas couldn't wait to go back to normal, but that meant making sure Seiji stayed at Kings Row where he belonged.

Nicholas had to prowl the training grounds until he found Marcel, then wait for him to finish his bout, then demand Marcel lead Nicholas to Jesse. When he did, they found Jesse standing and chatting in German with two other fencers. Jesse was wearing a sunny, charming smile, and his companions seemed dazzled.

As Jesse's eyes fell on Nicholas, the sunlight drained out of his face. He scoffed, "You?"

Nicholas smiled a wicked, delinquent smile. "Me."

"He says Seiji sent him," Marcel reported.

Jesse hesitated, then nodded to the other fencers, who departed with speed, obviously freaked out by the abrupt change in Jesse's demeanor. Nicholas turned, and Jesse and Marcel followed him out of the practice grounds and through the trees, to the rock by the sea where Seiji stood waiting. Seiji was wearing his fencing whites. Nicholas had argued strongly for Seiji not to wear them, as white from head to toe was the opposite of sneaky.

"I can see you for miles. There's a reason ninjas don't dress this way," Nicholas said in greeting.

Seiji rolled his eyes so hard Nicholas thought he might hurt himself. Jesse was right there, but Seiji was paying attention to Nicholas, so Nicholas felt great about everything.

"Why is this person even here?" Jesse demanded.

Seiji's gaze moved to Jesse. Nicholas stepped in between them.

"I'm helping out my buddy," he announced cheerfully, watching Jesse's mouth go pinched. "You challenged him to a fencing match, right?"

Echoing silence was Nicholas's answer.

"Did you just think it would work out for you, because you expect everything to work out for you?" asked Nicholas. "Lucky thing Seiji has me. I know how to break the rules."

"Seiji, is this person a *criminal*?" demanded Jesse.

"No!" exclaimed Seiji. "Unless you mean in the sense of, *Has he committed certain petty crimes?* In that case, yes."

That caused Jesse to make the only expression Nicholas had ever enjoyed seeing on his face. Nicholas felt someone should frame it and put it in an art gallery, and title the masterpiece *Jesse Coste, Rendered Speechless.*

Nicholas proceeded to explain the plan. "I wanted to have this planning session now, because our team captain is having a fencing match with Bastien. Nobody will overhear us. They're all watching the match. Our coach has put money on it. Actually, many people have put money on it. I think most of Camp Menton is expecting it'll be a fun opportunity to see another lousy American fencer get crushed. Which is hilarious, since Harvard's totally going to win!"

Marcel made a dismissive sound. "Please. My friend Bastien is going to win."

"Of course he is," said Jesse. "He's better than all the Kings Row fencers."

The calm certainty in Jesse's voice made Nicholas's fists itch. He'd wanted to go to Kings Row because his father had gone there before him. Whenever Nicholas walked through Kings Row, he told himself he was walking in his father's footsteps. Being at Kings Row was the closest he'd ever been to his father.

Jesse had all the rest of their father. He shouldn't get to look down on the only piece Nicholas possessed.

"What about"—the words stuck in Nicholas's throat, but he forced them out—"your father? Didn't he go to Kings Row?"

"Exactly," Jesse responded. "If my father thought Kings Row were the right place for a promising young fencer, he would have sent me there. That place, that team, almost dragged my father down. That's why I'm doing Seiji a favor by getting him out of Kings Row."

"You haven't done anything yet," Nicholas reminded him. "You haven't won your match against Seiji. And Harvard hasn't lost his. I don't think he will." He turned to Seiji. "You agree with me, right?"

Seiji gave some thought to the matter. "I'm not certain. In terms of skill, Bastien and Harvard seem fairly evenly matched."

"Seiji!" Nicholas shoved him. "Where is your team loyalty? He's our captain! He's the best captain ever."

"My personal feelings about Harvard and Bastien as individuals don't matter, Nicholas," said Seiji. "Fencing is a game of skill."

Jesse raised a golden eyebrow. "What was your captain ranked again? Thirty-third?"

"He should be ranked higher," Seiji responded in his coolest, most analytical tone. "He's good at defense, but he's flawed when it comes to attacking. He has trouble with his low lines, because he's tall, which I've spoken to him about extensively. Yet instead of concentrating on working on his weak points, Harvard spends a great deal of his free time developing plans for his team and guiding us through drills."

"So you're saying he focuses on the wrong things," said Jesse.

"No," Seiji returned, level. "That's not what I'm saying."

If Nicholas hadn't known Seiji, he would have thought Seiji was entirely indifferent to Jesse's needling. Unfortunately, Nicholas was keenly aware that Seiji was holding himself with so much tension that Nicholas worried he might snap, as even a great sword might when too much pressure was exerted on the steel. Nicholas wished he could help. He wished he could hit Jesse. But he'd promised Seiji he would stay beside him at the party, and he hadn't kept his promise. The least he could do was stay by Seiji's side now.

They walked toward the edge of the trees, heading for the winding road and the botanical gardens.

"What's your plan, then?" asked Jesse.

"It's gonna take some good old-fashioned Kings Row team-work," said Nicholas, and nodded toward the trees.

Bobby and Dante were there. Dante regarded Jesse with silent disdain, which was how Dante regarded everyone. Bobby, who'd been fully briefed that Jesse was the enemy, restricted his natural exuberance to a small wave at Marcel. Thawing slightly, Marcel waved back.

"You invited all of Kings Row to our conversation?" asked Jesse.

"So, here's the plan," said Nicholas, ignoring him. "We're going to sneak into the *salle* during the big party."

Jesse scoffed. "Surely it would be a better idea to sneak in at midnight, once everybody is asleep."

"You're an amateur at crime, Jesse," said Nicholas loftily. "The coaches here are all obsessed with curfews. If a noise wakes them at night, we're all sunk. If they find us when they're patrolling, we're all sunk. The party is when they'll be distracted. The party's our chance. Our teammate Eugene says he'll pretend not to feel well so that we can sneak away. And Bobby and Dante will sneak down to the harbor tonight. If we're not back and people start asking about us, they'll create another distraction and a call for help, so everyone will go looking for them and not us."

Jesse's voice went captainly again. "You two will get kicked out of Camp Menton."

Dante asked, "Promise?"

"If necessary, I'm going to fling myself in the water!" Bobby announced with huge excitement. "Dante will be there to make sure nothing bad happens to me."

He squeezed Dante's forearm appreciatively. Dante, who hadn't been in favor of the *Bobby flinging himself in the water* idea, looked less grim.

"Thanks for helping, both of you," said Seiji.

The tips of Bobby's ears went pink. Nicholas also found the measured amount of warmth in Seiji's voice touching.

"Is this what it's like at Kings Row?" demanded Jesse.

Bobby didn't seem to hear Jesse, distracted first by Seiji's praise and then by a horrible realization. "I can't believe we're missing Harvard's match," Bobby said wistfully.

As if uttering Harvard's name was a summoning spell, a tall boy slipped between one shadow and the next, moving in long strides like a predator.

"I, too, can't believe you're missing Harvard's match," drawled Aiden Kane. "I can't believe you're making *me* miss Harvard's match. What are you planning, freshmen?"

32 HARVARD

Before the match with Bastien started, Harvard had to endure several more trainees coming over and being sympathetic to him. It seemed Harvard had made some friends at Camp Menton. It also seemed as though his new friends were all convinced Harvard was going to get his ass handed to him.

He could deal with that.

As they all gathered around the *piste,* before Harvard and Bastien began their match, Harvard saw Aiden coming. For a moment, there was a burst of ease and freedom in Harvard's chest, the same feeling he got watching a flock of birds alighting from a tree into the air. He thought Aiden would come over and speak to him. Aiden always told him that he was the best captain, the best ever, with faith in Harvard that Harvard had never been able to summon in himself. He hadn't needed to. Aiden was always there.

Aiden made eye contact with Harvard for a moment. Then Aiden averted his eyes and walked directly over to Bastien.

Harvard watched the lovely, wicked curve of Aiden's smile as he whispered something in Bastien's ear. That was much harder to deal with than anything else.

Aiden spoke far too low for anyone but Bastien to catch, but his tone was carried on the warm Mediterranean breeze. Aiden's voice sounded warmer than the breeze, dark and sweet at once, like honey being poured in the shadows.

Harvard dragged his eyes away and searched the spectators to find a friendly face. He would've liked to see Nicholas there to encourage Harvard to believe in himself.

He couldn't see Nicholas. He couldn't see anyone.

When the time came for his match, he didn't see many Kings Row students there to cheer him on. Eugene was there, but not Nicholas, nor Seiji. Even Aiden seemed to have disappeared. Harvard could hardly believe it. He felt oddly bereft, as though he were expected to fence without his épée or his plastron. He always had his team to think of.

A flash of red and white caught his eye. "Go, Harvard!" yelled Coach Williams. "I have money on this, and I don't want to lose it. Teachers' salaries are shamefully low!"

His coach was there to support him, but she didn't need him to support her. Coach had said to Harvard once, *Remember there's a* me *in* team. There was nobody for Harvard to worry about except himself. There was nothing he could do for his team but be the best fencer he could be.

There was something almost freeing in that. He took a deep breath of air, finding steadiness in this strange place.

Well, Harvard thought. Time to find out what he could do.

He stepped out onto the *piste*, the steel strips reflecting the evening-sky blue of the domed ceiling.

Other people were defeated by Aiden all the time. Harvard always beat Aiden. He'd always believed it was because Aiden wouldn't hurt Harvard on purpose, wouldn't cut at Harvard with his sharp tongue until Harvard flinched like all the rest, but Aiden said it was because Harvard was always sure with him.

Perhaps that was true, too. Harvard had always been sure of Aiden, and sure of how they worked together... until this last week.

Harvard was tired of feeling uncertain.

Harvard met Bastien attack for attack, lunge for lunge, and saw Bastien's movements check as he startled. Clearly, he hadn't expected this from Harvard. Harvard was supposed to be reliable, nice, a good sport, a middle-of-the-road fencer. Harvard knew he hadn't fenced like this since he'd come to Camp Menton. Maybe Harvard hadn't fenced like this ever.

Bastien ran him up and down the strip, but Harvard had plenty of endurance. Bastien was very good, landing the most fluid of attacks imaginable, but Harvard had been learning as much as he could at Camp Menton and practicing at Kings Row with skill-smooth Seiji and lightning-fast Nicholas. Defense had always been his specialty. When Bastien went low, Harvard remembered Seiji's stern instructions about his low lines. He could defend against any attack Bastien made.

The points were flying between them, Coach Williams and Coach Robillard both roaring approval and advice. Melodie was yelling encouragement to Bastien like a motivational French banshee, while Eugene yelled even louder for Harvard.

The points were pretty even. But Harvard couldn't keep being on defense forever. The trick was not only to defend, but to make a move against Bastien and make it count.

A captain had to lead by example. This was for his team and for himself. This was how Harvard would prove he was a worthy captain to lead them to victory at the state championships.

Bastien tried for an attack by lunge, which Harvard used all his skill to parry. Then immediately, without pause for breath or doubt, he went for the riposte, the offensive attack made directly after a parry.

His riposte was fast, fast enough that Bastien couldn't counter it. That move was for Nicholas.

Even with the way Harvard had been fencing throughout the match, Bastien hadn't expected such instant aggression. Harvard got through his guard and scored the final point.

He won.

A buzzing rose in his head as though the electrical current in his jacket had gotten into his blood. He couldn't quite believe he'd won. The gleam of the state championship trophy seemed closer somehow, like something in Harvard's future rather than in his dreams.

Harvard pulled off his mask and emerged, blinking, into what felt like new light. Arune and the MLC guys were cheering wildly. So were several of the other fencers, who Harvard had imagined pitied him. Turned out they simply liked him instead.

"I wouldn't have thought you had it in you," remarked Coach Robillard, but in an approving way, even though Bastien was his son.

"I *always* knew he had it in him!" Coach Williams shouted. "Pay up!"

"Good match," Harvard told Bastien, and offered his hand to shake.

As he clasped Harvard's hand, Bastien inclined his darkly handsome head. "Your coach is right to be proud of you."

"Nice that someone believes in me, I guess," Harvard said.

Bastien's mouth pulled out of shape, as though he'd been sampling the fruit on the lemon trees. "Do you know what Aiden whispered to me before the match?"

Harvard remembered with painful acuteness how Aiden had pulled Bastien in to murmur a lilting lover's secret in his ear. Suddenly, Harvard's little triumph felt hollow.

In the end, what did it matter if Harvard had won some stupid match, something that wasn't part of any tournament and wouldn't count toward their hoped-for victory at state? He'd lost

Aiden. His best friend would leave Kings Row and would be with a hundred boys like this one, and Harvard had damaged the friendship between them irreparably.

Then Harvard realized Bastien's eyes weren't gloating. They were bleak.

"Aiden whispered in my ear, 'You're going to lose.'"

Just then, the missing Kings Row students appeared. His team. Nicholas was giving some kind of war cry. Harvard couldn't make it out, because he couldn't look away from Aiden, who was smiling directly at him.

Coach Williams gave Harvard a hug, and the rest took this as their cue to pounce. Nicholas and Eugene both hit Harvard on the back with perhaps too much enthusiasm. Seiji seemed disturbed to be caught in the middle of a group-hug situation. Aiden was laughing.

"O captain! our captain!" Aiden said in his beautiful voice, low and sweet and mocking.

Harvard didn't know where his team had been, but they were here now.

He just wished he could keep them. He wished he wasn't losing the most important one.

33 AIDEN

Aiden couldn't believe he was missing out on Harvard's match to deal with errant freshmen. Yet the freshmen had been mysteriously absent, and Harvard had enough to deal with, so it had been up to Aiden to track them down. And now it was up to Aiden to deal with them.

He studied the guilty faces of his freshmen and the Exton freshmen, who had nothing to do with him. Aiden crossed his arms and glared them all down.

"I heard everything. Sneaking off tonight to have a duel, are we? I see my duty clearly. It's obvious I have to"— Aiden braced himself and sighed and took responsibility—"come with you."

Nicholas and Jesse looked oddly similar when they were surprised, their usual swagger collapsing. Aiden supposed Seiji Katayama had a fencing-partner type. It was a toss-up whether Seiji had traded up or traded down, in Aiden's opinion. Nicholas was a better person, but Jesse had better hair. Maybe it didn't matter, since nobody was getting any action other than fencing action. Tragic individuals, all three of them.

Nicholas cleared his throat. "You're not, uh, gonna stop us?"

"Nah, I don't really feel I can stop you from breaking rules without being a huge hypocrite," said Aiden. "You have no idea how many rules I've broken. I couldn't even tell you about half of them. It would blow your tiny freshman minds. I'm banned from ever returning to Camp Menton, and I'm expelled from Kings Row."

"So, you often get *caught* breaking the rules?" Jesse asked skeptically.

Aiden shot him an annoyed glance. "No," he said. "I've been off my game lately."

Jesse scowled, so Aiden transferred his smile to the other Exton boy, who might be more deserving.

"I'm—" Aiden began.

The Exton boy stared back at him. "I'm Marcel Berré. And you're Aiden Kane," he said. "You dated Alexander Kostansis. He goes to Exton."

Aiden blinked. "I dated who?"

"He told me you ruined his life and crushed his soul!"

"I'm sorry," said Aiden, "but you're going to have to be more specific than that. You're just describing a random Wednesday for me."

Marcel gave him a look that was part fascination and part terror. Jesse's scowl intensified, and he dragged Marcel protectively away. Aiden walked alongside his freshmen through the lemon trees, trying to think of a way to take that desolate, set expression off Seiji's face. Harvard made it look so easy, comforting someone, making them believe they were special. Aiden always knew what people were feeling, but Harvard knew how to make them feel better.

Aiden couldn't do it Harvard's way, but perhaps he could use his own talents for good instead of evil for a change. He thought about what he said to people when he was trying to psych them out, so they would flinch during a fencing match and give him the victory, and then tried to reverse the strategy in his mind.

"Seiji, remember when I mocked you at our fencing tryouts about losing to Jesse?"

"Of course I recall," Seiji said distantly. "I fail to see why you're bringing it up now. It's not helpful."

"I wish to add that you're a maddening person," Aiden went on. "It's why you're so extremely unpopular. You're not easy to get along with. You're difficult and unyielding."

"Wow, Aiden," muttered Nicholas, "that is so mean. I think Seiji is—"

"So *be* difficult and unyielding. You're a disgustingly relentless human being. You don't let anything stop you. You didn't let me beat you the second time around. And you won't let Jesse beat you the second time around, either." Aiden studied Seiji with some concern. "There. Was that helpful at all, or was I just bullying you?"

Seiji paused, the fixed expression on his face easing a fraction. "It was slightly helpful bullying. Thank you."

Aiden felt a small burst of warmth in his chest. It was possible he and Seiji Katayama were having a nice moment.

"Are we going to hug?" Aiden asked in dread.

"Oh, no, thank you," said Seiji.

He retreated behind Nicholas, his human shield from society, with obvious horror. Nicholas eyed Aiden in apprehension.

"Are you gonna try and say something nice to me?" he asked.

"We both wish Harvard were here right now, huh?" Aiden asked in reply.

Nicholas nodded. "Yeah."

They were on common ground, and that was somewhere to start.

Aiden shrugged and tried honesty. "If Harvard were here, he'd say something nice, and he'd mean it. He likes you, Nicholas. And that means there has to be something special about you. Even if I can't see it."

Nicholas smiled, sudden and sweet. "Aiden? Back atcha."

Aiden found himself surprised. He often measured the world through Harvard's eyes, but it had never occurred to him to measure himself through Harvard's eyes and discover he was worthwhile.

Against his better judgment, he slung an arm around Nicholas's shoulders. Just then, Nicholas was distracted by his phone buzzing in his pocket. He pulled it out, checked the screen to see a text from Eugene. He let out a yell of triumph.

"Eugene says Harvard won his match!"

"I knew he would," Aiden said, smiling.

Nicholas returned Aiden's smile. "Yeah, I knew, too."

"Let's go congratulate him," said Aiden. "Then later, my little freshmen, let's show those Exton boys how we do it at Kings Row."

34 SEIJI

On the way to his match against Jesse, Seiji led the way. He ducked his head under the broad stone lintel of the low, small door of the converted chapel, then walked down the stone corridor toward Camp Menton's *salle*. The broad flagstones were worn so smooth they looked like the surface of calm water, but their footsteps echoed on the floor. When they entered the *salle d'armes* itself, the *salle* by night was dark as a cave with a monster lurking within it. On the wall was a plaque bearing a silver sculpture of crossed swords, moonlight striking it so that the silver points looked sharply brilliant.

"Oh, my hair," murmured Aiden, breaking the silence.

"Is something in your hair?" Nicholas demanded. "Is it a bat?!"

"No, I mentioned my hair because

it's beautiful and I believe we should all think about it," drawled Aiden. "Actually, I got a spiderweb in it when we were walking through the woods at night. While in formal attire."

They were all dressed for the party in order to maintain their subterfuge. Seiji had tried doing his hair a little differently, but it had been a failure. Nicholas and Jesse had both given him the same strange look. Now, on top of everything else, Seiji had to bear the knowledge that he looked ridiculous.

Nicholas took hold of the back of Seiji's shirt so he could deploy him as a shield against bats at any time. Seiji shot him an annoyed look. Nicholas grinned at him. Privately, Seiji was grateful that Nicholas was distracting him from the icy fear that seemed to be shot all through him, like cold steel next to his bones.

At least Seiji would never be as ridiculous as Nicholas. That was a comfort.

Seiji took a deep breath and stared around the *salle*.

The seats surrounding them were empty, but it felt as though they were full of people watching Seiji, about to be disappointed. The way Seiji's father and Jesse's father had been during the tournament where Seiji messed up because he was scared of letting his father down.

Seiji recalled his father's voice, beloved and worried, saying, *You should decide when the victory is important. Don't let anyone choose your fight for you.* He remembered Nicholas, talking about how he must painfully unlearn what he'd learned wrong, even though he cared about the person who'd taught the wrong things to him. *Don't play Jesse's game*, Aiden had said, and Seiji thought he understood now.

He took a deep breath of stone-cold air and announced, "I'm not going to fence you, Jesse."

Jesse's voice was incredulous. "What?"

"Correction," said Seiji. "I said I would fence you, and I will. I always keep my word. I will fence you when I want to, in a real match, and not before. Why should you get to choose when we fence? You come to France, and you demand that I fence you, and you set the terms of our bargain. You think you should always get whatever you want. Why should I say *How high?* when you say *Jump?* I'm tired of it. I'm not going to do it anymore. And I'm not going to fence you now."

Jesse looked so utterly stunned he almost seemed lost, like a kid who'd had his present ripped out of his arms on Christmas Day.

Marcel went and sagged on the stone seats encircling the theater like a puppet with its strings cut. "After all that!"

"Strongly agreed, Mordred from Exton," said Aiden, strolling over to join Marcel and stretching his long legs out in front of him. "That is, I applaud and support your decision, freshman, but couldn't you have had the epiphany before you put me through all this trouble?"

"So we broke in, and now nobody's going to fence," Marcel murmured, despairing.

He slid a speculative look toward Aiden.

"I'm not fencing anyone!" Aiden declared. "I already fenced James."

"Jesse," said Jesse.

Aiden smirked. "Jesse James?"

"*Jesse Coste.*"

"Settle down, Sundance Kid. I should be at a party right now. You people and your priorities disgust me."

Jesse turned to Seiji. "I beat Aiden. And I hear *Aiden* beat *you.*"

Jesse's eyes reminded Seiji of the match when Jesse had won, avid on Seiji's face, watching for Seiji to flinch.

"Yeah, I beat Aiden, too," Nicholas chimed in, and Jesse's attention slid away in shock. "At tryouts. Wasn't that hard. Aiden needs to practice more. Also, people shouldn't listen to him talk. He does it too much."

"This doesn't involve you," Jesse said. Then a smile woke on his face, sparkling and alluring, and dread coiled in Seiji's stomach. "Unless..."

There was a certain tension in the air suddenly. Or perhaps it was only in Nicholas, and so Seiji could feel it all through his own body.

"Unless?" Nicholas asked quietly.

"If Seiji doesn't want to fence for some ridiculous reason," said Jesse, "that's all right. I will lower myself to fence with you. Same terms. If you win, I'll acknowledge you as a legitimate opponent.

If I win, Seiji comes to Exton. Here it is. Your one chance to be taken seriously as a fencer. What do you say?"

There was a long moment with Jesse's offer hanging like a bright offering in the gloom. Seiji remembered the way he and Jesse had first met. Seiji was used to other kids his age hating him for showing them up, and Jesse had smiled and said he hoped they'd have a good match.

Then and now, Jesse seemed to offer a golden ticket to belonging.

Seiji could see Nicholas was tempted.

Then Nicholas said, "I'll pass. Stop being gross. Seiji's my friend. I'm not gonna trade him in like a Pokémon."

Seiji felt his shoulders ease down a fraction.

Jesse bit out, "I get it. You're scared, because you know I'll win."

Nicholas rolled his eyes. "I'm not scared of losing. Happens to me all the time."

"Prove it," challenged Jesse.

Nicholas shrugged. "Okay. Marcel, wanna fence?"

Marcel glanced at Jesse, then sighed. "Sure. Someone should fence around here."

He picked up the épées lying on the seat beside him and offered one to Nicholas. Nicholas took it with a grin.

Since it appeared he was about to be a spectator to rather than a participant in a match, Seiji went and sat on the seat beside Aiden. Immediately, Aiden slid away from Seiji. He appeared absorbed in a game on his phone that involved cupcakes.

Jesse sat down on the other side of Seiji. Involuntarily, Seiji glanced toward him. He was startled by what he saw. Jesse looked gray as old stone, all his gold hidden under dust.

"I'm sorry," Seiji told him.

Bewilderment descended on Jesse's face, followed by something even stranger. He almost seemed hopeful.

"For what?"

"I know you came to Camp Menton to fence," said Seiji. "I understand if you feel I wasn't playing fair."

"Seiji," said Jesse. "I don't care about this camp at all."

Seiji frowned. "Then why did you come here?"

"You don't know why?" Jesse asked.

Like Seiji, perhaps Jesse was trying to appreciate world travel more.

"To appreciate the French countryside? Menton is sometimes referred to as the Pearl of France," Seiji said. "Did you know that?"

"I didn't know that," Jesse answered slowly. "Listen—"

Seiji's head turned.

"I can't. I have to watch Nicholas's fencing match now, Jesse," Seiji told him. "We always watch each other's matches. It's what friends do."

Jesse went silent. Seiji thought perhaps he hadn't known that rule.

Nicholas and Marcel assumed *en garde* position. Then Nicholas went on attack, like he always did, though Marcel's technique meant that he was able to beat back Nicholas with ease. Nicholas's form was getting better, Seiji thought with some pride.

He and Jesse had always dismissed fencers whom they could beat, but now Seiji had watched and given a great deal of thought to how Nicholas fenced. He hadn't found it wasted time. Dismissing people, Seiji thought now, might have been a mistake.

Both Marcel and Nicholas moved in that circular space, on a *piste* that gleamed silver in the moonlight. Marcel was an excellent fencer, who moved with the grace of training so ingrained it was instinct. He scored several points on Nicholas, but Nicholas slid away from some attacks, left-handed and lightning swift.

"He's fast," Jesse admitted grudgingly.

Seiji leaned forward, elbows on his knees, so he could watch more closely. "Yes," he agreed distantly, mind on analyzing the match. "Nicholas is the fastest fencer I've ever seen."

35 NICHOLAS

All those drills were paying off, Nicholas had to admit as he fought against an amazing fencer in the *salle d'armes* at the most elite training camp in Europe. He was grateful for both Kings Row and Camp Menton.

Images from his expanding world flew through his mind as his and Marcel's épées clashed. Coach pushing him to work on the basics, Harvard believing Nicholas could do it, Eugene's unfaltering support, Melodie showing him moves she'd learned from both Bastien and Marcel himself. Above all else, over and over, he heard the echo of Seiji's stern instructions, remembered Seiji's relentless drive toward perfection, unyielding in the way only Seiji could be.

He made a space in between breaths to think, even though it

might slow him down, and when Marcel made an attack by lunge, Nicholas instructed himself to combine beat and pressure together to deflect the blade. Nicholas slid into attack and scored a point.

He didn't score enough points to win, but he made a decent showing. When the match ended, Marcel's eyebrows were raised.

"What, Exton boy?" Nicholas asked, trying to sound as indifferent as Aiden.

"Nothing," said Marcel, and offered his hand. "Good match. You caught on to some moves really quickly."

Nicholas beamed and shook. "Yeah, soon enough I'll be the best. Next time we fence, I'll beat you."

"We'll see," said Marcel skeptically. "Anyway, you're all right, for a beginner."

"You're all right for a friend of Jesse Coste."

Marcel's eyes darted toward Jesse, whose attention was fixed resentfully on Seiji. Marcel appeared to come to a decision.

"You're wrong about Jesse," said Marcel. "There's a reason he's the best, and there's a reason he draws the best fencers to Exton. When we face you at state, you'd better be ready."

Nicholas thumped Marcel on the back. "Sorry, buddy. My team's the best, and *we're* gonna win the state championship."

Their promising friendship was cut off when Marcel looked disdainfully down his nose at Nicholas.

"*C'est impossible*," he said firmly, then shouldered the bag of equipment and made his way out of the *salle d'armes*.

That was as good a way as any to end this. Nicholas turned and made for the stone passageway that would lead them out of the *salle d'armes* and toward his friends and the party. Then he stopped as Jesse Coste blocked his path.

"I'm going to fence you one day," said Jesse.

"Count on it," said Nicholas.

For the first time, Jesse favored Nicholas with one of his golden-boy smiles. "Take all the time you need to learn. Listen to your coach and your captain, attend every training camp you can. Drill with Seiji every day. Reach every bit of your potential. I want you to. I want you to be at your best when I beat you."

Nicholas wanted to scoff at Jesse, but his mouth was dry, and he couldn't laugh. It sounded so plausible, the future Jesse's words painted. Nicholas could handle Jesse being better than him when he thought of that as a temporary thing.

The idea that Jesse would always be better, that Seiji would always think so, that his father would always think so, was much harder to bear.

He and Jesse stood staring at each other until they were knocked apart by Aiden, striding past them and brushing them both off to opposite sides, as though flicking cobwebs off his shoulders.

"Oh my God, you people had your chance for a big, tense

fence-off, and you didn't take it. Knock it off before I bang your twerp heads together. I'm hosting a glamorous after-party, and I'm going to be dazzling in formal wear, and since I had this bonding experience with all of you, I just want to say"—Aiden took a deep breath—"stay far away from my party. Seriously, I hate your faces."

36 HARVARD

"C aptain," said Eugene, "do I look all right?"

Harvard gave him a fist bump. "You look great."

Eugene looked very nervous. He'd said he wasn't feeling great a while ago, and Harvard had stayed with him since the rest of their team seemed to have vanished somewhere. Now Eugene claimed he'd made a miraculous and total recovery, and was wearing one of Harvard's dress shirts, which was slightly big on him, and his eyes were darting around. Harvard presumed he was worried about impressing Melodie.

Nobody else from their team had arrived at the party yet, so it was Harvard's responsibility to stay by his teammate and provide him with moral support.

When Melodie appeared, she was

wearing something other than fencing whites or jeans for the first time during camp. She was wearing a champagne-colored gown that glimmered in the moonlight as she moved. It was definitely a gown rather than a dress. Eugene appeared to be having trouble breathing.

"Wow," Eugene breathed. "You look amazing. Can...we dance now?"

She hesitated, clearly remembering Eugene's dancing from before, then relented and smiled. "We can."

Eugene started to smile. "Even if I can't actually waltz?"

"But of course, Eugene," said Melodie. "I will simply take the lead."

She reached out a hand, rings glimmering in the moonlight, and Eugene took it and let her lead him out onto the dance floor.

"Are they dating?" asked Nicholas, who had suddenly appeared by Harvard's side.

Everyone stared at Nicholas.

Seiji peered over at Eugene and Melodie. "Now that you mention it, I think they are," he said. "Good observation, Nicholas."

Harvard decided to let it go. No matter what they'd been doing earlier, everyone was at the party to celebrate Harvard's victory with him now. Everyone, it seemed, except for Aiden. Harvard looked around unobtrusively, but Aiden was nowhere in sight.

"No doubt Aiden's having fun at his after-party already," said Arune, drawing near.

Obviously, Harvard's looking around hadn't been unobtrusive enough.

"Having an exciting time without the rest of us plebes," Arune continued. "I wasn't invited, obviously, so I'm bitter. Does Aiden hate me? He seems to hate me. Not sure why. I never did anything to him."

"I'm sure he doesn't hate you," said Harvard.

Arune shrugged. "Just thinks he's better than everyone else, then."

Harvard wanted to argue, but he didn't want to spoil the party. This was their last night at Camp Menton, and his victory celebration. Everybody seemed to be having a good time. Coach Williams was wearing an off-the-shoulder red dress. Possibly to celebrate Harvard's victory. Possibly to celebrate her winnings. Assistant Coach Lewis's glasses had almost fallen off her nose when she'd seen the coach.

Seiji was wearing a suit without a jacket, with the sleeves rolled up. His hair was messier than usual. There was a single lock of black hair falling into his eyes, which was huge for Seiji. Several people at the party were staring in a dazed fashion. Good for Seiji, Harvard thought fondly. Not that the kid was ever going to notice the stunned admirers.

The camp had only lasted a few days, but there was a lot more mingling now than there had been earlier. The music was louder, the buzz of voices louder still. People were exchanging numbers. Bobby had persuaded Nicholas to dance, saying they would have fun because they would be like a dancing team. On the dance floor, Eugene was slow dancing with Melodie beneath the swaying lights and lemon trees.

Harvard, sitting at the picnic bench with the MLC guys, smiled down at the fallen leaves.

Good for Eugene.

Arune nudged him. "Yeah, that could be you, Harvard."

"I—uh," Harvard stammered. "Eugene and Melodie are both great people, but if you think I have any interest in either of them—"

"No, I don't," said Arune. "Pretty clear you're hung up on that jerk Aiden."

Oh good. It really was as obvious as Harvard had feared. That wasn't humiliating at all.

Arune continued, in his helpful, friendly way, totally unaware that it felt as though he were peeling Harvard's heart with a dull knife. "You're a good-looking cat, Harvard. And you're a really decent guy. I'm sure you have all these treasured memories of when Aiden was sweet and little and had that epic crush on you, but those days are gone. You can do better."

"Sorry?" Harvard said. "Epic what?"

The enormity of Arune's mistake made him laugh a little.

"Crush," said Arune.

Arune's voice blurred into white static in Harvard's ears. He could feel his heartbeat hammering in his throat. He felt like someone in a horror movie, his heartbeat speeding up. Something huge and terrible was on the edge of his awareness.

"Aiden never had a crush on me," he told Arune firmly, shutting down that ridiculous idea at once.

Arune just stared. "Pretty sure he did, Harvard."

"Trust me, I would know."

"I thought you *did* know!" Arune exclaimed. "Everybody knew! The whole school had bets on it! Maybe it was just that you were the only person in his messed-up life who he could rely on, but he obviously thought you hung the moon, the sun, and all the little stars. The first time I saw you after eight years, I assumed you guys were together because I didn't realize Aiden was a hot jerk now. Aiden gave you all those valentines—"

"Friend valentines," corrected Harvard blankly. He thought back to all the years Aiden had shyly given him valentines, how he would reply with a *Thanks, buddy,* and Aiden would say it was no problem. The year Aiden stopped giving them to him, Harvard had asked him about it.

"No valentine this year?" he'd said.

Aiden had worn a strange, crooked smile and simply replied, "I guess I grew up."

"Friend valentines are not a thing!" Arune said, snapping Harvard back to the present. "He sent you postcards every day whenever he went away, to say, *Thinking of you.*"

"Yeah, because we're best friends."

"Every day, Harvard?" asked Arune. "Best friends who think of each other every day?"

"Yes!" Harvard exclaimed desperately.

He'd never had a best friend other than Aiden, and he thought of Aiden every day. He assumed it was normal best friend behavior.

But it was like a glass had shattered in his mind. Suddenly, all those moments of best friendship flew through his memories, shining in a new light. Aiden coming to the hospital when they were kids and Harvard's dad had been sick, Aiden agreeing to go to Kings Row, Aiden asking him to go to the fair. Harvard felt his stomach sink as he remembered when he asked Aiden to help him learn to date. He thought about how careful and measured Aiden had been, how he had said about them dating, "It's practice for being real. For Neil." And Harvard had confirmed that it was all for a guy Harvard barely knew and didn't really like. Harvard had just *used* Aiden and been wholly oblivious to his feelings.

"This was like the first date I wanted," Aiden had confessed after Harvard took him to the fair.

When Harvard had asked Aiden if he ever had real feelings for anyone, Aiden had said yes, and confessed, "I never said anything to him. But there were things I wanted to say."

And then Harvard had told him their practice dating meant nothing.

Now Harvard's stomach was churning.

"I . . . ," he said weakly.

"Okay," Arune said, in a voice Harvard himself had used on Nicholas and Seiji, a voice that meant, *This person doesn't understand how the world works, and there is too much for me to explain.* Harvard stared at Arune in outrage. "Not the point. My point was, regardless of what was—extremely obviously—happening in the past, Aiden is now a *love 'em and leave 'em without ever learning their names* type, but I know this totally nice guy I could fix you up with."

"I'm not interested," Harvard said firmly.

Harvard knew what he had to do. His stomach still felt as if it were on the open sea, and he felt as if he had been plunged into an ice bath, but he had never been one to back down from taking responsibility.

"Arune," Harvard said, "I have to talk to Coach."

He got up and left Arune and the MLC guys behind him. He pushed his way across the dance floor, cutting through groups and couples, completely ignoring the annoyed glares he was getting. He was only concerned with the need to get to Coach as soon as possible.

When he reached her, Coach Williams lifted her cup at him in a toast.

"Coach, I need to tell you something," Harvard said.

"Go ahead, my favorite captain," she said.

Harvard blinked. "I'm your only captain."

"So, clearly, my favorite. Hey, I don't want to rain on your

315

victory parade, but *as* my captain, I was thinking—now that Aiden's expelled from Kings Row, does Eugene stay reserve or does Nicholas? What's your advice? I know Eugene has more experience, but I have a good feeling about Nicholas."

"That's what I came here to say." The words stuck in Harvard's throat. "I can't give up on Aiden yet."

Not as part of the team. Not as part of Kings Row. He'd thought they would always have that.

Coach said gently, "I don't want to, either. I have such high hopes for you guys, you don't even know. I thought I was really getting through to Aiden, back when we did our team-building exercise, but he's been a mess ever since the night of the team bonfire."

Harvard flinched away from the memory of that night, the night he'd told Aiden that they couldn't continue with his terrible fake-dating idea. Aiden had agreed. Harvard had been sure Aiden was relieved.

Looking back on it, he wasn't sure at all. When he told Aiden, *I can't think of anything worse than falling in love with you,* Aiden's expression had gone blank as a closed door in a wall. The door hadn't been opened again since that day. Since that moment.

"I have to be able to trust my team," Coach continued.

"You can trust Aiden," Harvard said reflexively. "I do. The same way he trusts me."

You were the only person in his messed-up life who he could rely on, Arune had said. Terrible guilt consumed Harvard, as though

316

he'd had something precious in his hands and let it drop and fall into deep water.

Aiden had trusted him, but Harvard had lied to him. He hadn't wanted anything to change, hadn't wanted his heart any more broken than it already was. He had been a coward. He hadn't trusted Aiden, had been afraid Aiden would treat him like everyone else, when Aiden had never treated Harvard that way in his life. Aiden had always made it clear he thought more of Harvard than he did of anyone else.

Harvard had taken solid ground away from Aiden, and then wondered why Aiden was drowning.

"You trust him?" asked Coach. "Are you sure?"

Harvard said, "*Yes.*"

There would be no giving up on Aiden, and the way Arune and Coach talked about Harvard was making Harvard deeply uncomfortable. Harvard was sick with guilt. He'd done this, too. He knew better than anyone else how good Aiden was at living down to people's expectations.

"There's been something really wrong ever since that night," said Coach. "We can't help Aiden if he won't talk about it."

Harvard didn't need Aiden to talk about it. Harvard already knew what had happened. Aiden had come to Harvard with trust in his eyes, and Harvard had lied.

Harvard swallowed. "We keep asking what's wrong with Aiden. What if we all made a horrible mistake? What if there's nothing wrong with Aiden? What if there's something wrong with *me*?"

Harvard was the one who had lied when Aiden depended on him to tell the truth. He was the one who'd been doubting and defending himself and acting like a coward, while leaving Aiden at sea.

Coach Williams's face was terribly, carefully sympathetic. "Harvard, I know sometimes you feel you're responsible—"

"Yeah, and sometimes I *am* responsible!" said Harvard. "Coach, I have to go. I have to fix this."

Coach protested, but for once Harvard wasn't listening. The party was a blur of gold on black, everyone's faces indistinct. He couldn't think about anything else right now.

He had to go to Aiden and tell him the truth.

37 AIDEN

The yacht had several bathrooms, one with a Jacuzzi. After a long shower to get the freshman stupidity out of his hair, Aiden climbed back into his tux, sat down at the dressing table to admire his astonishingly great hair in the mirror, and didn't look at his reflection at all. Instead, he thought about Harvard winning his match—he'd known Harvard would—and Seiji refusing to have his, and about courage.

He took out his phone and called Brianna back. When she answered, there was a lot of rustling fabric and clicking hangers, so either she was at a boutique or packing for a romantic vacation. Aiden didn't ask which.

"Hey, Almost Stepmother. I figured since delegation's the name of the game, I can do it, too," said

Aiden. "Even if I can't stay at Kings Row, I'll never be like my father. Tell him that."

Her voice sounded strange for a moment until he figured out she was crying.

"I would," Brianna replied, "but actually, he cheated on me and I'm leaving him. I'm packing up my stuff right now."

He couldn't even feign surprise.

"Right," said Aiden. "Awkward. Sorry I said anything."

"No, I was glad to hear it. That's great," Brianna told him. "You stick to that. You seem like a good kid, Aiden."

"No, I'm not," Aiden said. "I am devastatingly good-looking, however."

Brianna laughed, then sniffed. "Sorry I won't get to meet you."

He'd always expected to grow up like his father, Aiden realized. But he hadn't been raised only by his father. There had been a succession of beautiful, brilliant women. Some of them had cared about him. Most of them hadn't. All of them had left, because his father was who he was. Still, in the end, Aiden would rather be like his gorgeous and not-entirely-evil stepmothers.

"You can still meet me," Aiden proposed. "I'm planning to get-together with another almost stepmother of mine, someday soon. You could come, and we could all trash my dad at a Michelin-star restaurant and put the bill on his tab."

"We'll see," Brianna answered, but Aiden thought it sounded like she was in for a meeting of the Almost-Stepmothers Club.

He hung up the phone and looked around the ballroom of

the yacht. Catering had set up a huge buffet, so Aiden wandered over to the desserts and took three cupcakes. He ate only the icing off the top, though that was depraved cupcake hedonism. He was feeling low, and so it was off with the cupcakes' heads.

He was getting kicked out of Kings Row, and it was all his own fault. Everything he'd ever tried to make himself feel better, to feel less alone, hadn't worked.

He texted the relevant group chat that his after-party was off.

There were several boys at Camp Menton, and several more in Menton, who would come running if Aiden called. They always did.

Long ago, Aiden and Harvard had been walking across the Kings Row campus together, and he'd been trying to ask Harvard out on a date. Harvard hadn't understood, maybe because Harvard didn't want to understand, and Aiden was feeling thoroughly dispirited. Then another guy had whistled at him, and Aiden had thought, *Why not?* Why shouldn't he get to feel wanted? Why shouldn't he take a little comfort where he could? Harvard wouldn't care. It was like being under a highly ironic curse, being irresistible to everybody except the one person who mattered.

There had been comfort at Kings Row, as well as everything Aiden truly loved: Harvard and fencing. Kings Row was the first place where Aiden had ever fit in, felt wanted, realized all his dreams of being extraordinary, lived with someone who he loved and who loved him back. He would never get to go back again. There was nothing Aiden could do to make himself feel better, in the face of this loss.

38 NICHOLAS

Several hours into the party, Nicholas was carrying cups of lemonade, which was fizzy in Europe, when he spotted Eugene sitting on a picnic bench all alone and oddly forlorn. He made a detour away from the clearing of fairy lights and music, toward his teammate.

"Hey, bro," he said, wandering over and gently watering Eugene's head with lemonade. "Having a good party? Did you see Seiji's hilarious non-dancing? Where's Melodie?"

"Uh," said Eugene. "She's with her friends, I think. She dumped me an hour ago. Said now was that special time in a girl's life when she must devote herself entirely to the blade."

"Right," said Nicholas. "Tough break."

Actually, he could see Melodie's

point, though he definitely wouldn't have put it that way. Still, he felt bad for Eugene.

"Ah, I see your teammate has come to comfort you," observed Melodie from a sheltering tree. "As it should be. I simply wanted to check on you, but since I am here let me say my goodbyes. Nicholas, you need to bulk up, but . . . to my surprise, it's been a pleasure."

Nicholas glanced uneasily at Eugene, not wanting to be a traitor, but Eugene nodded encouragement. Nicholas leaned forward and bumped his fist against Melodie's.

"For me, too," Nicholas told Melodie.

She had already turned her attention back to Eugene, her keen gaze melting.

"Eugene," said Melodie. "You make the best protein shakes I ever tasted. You're a loyal friend, and you are right about many things. Including hypertrophy specific training. I won't forget you."

"I won't forget you, either," said Eugene.

He stared after Melodie wistfully as she rejoined her friends. Bastien hesitated, then looked Nicholas's way.

"Nicholas, I meant to say, thanks for the match. It was great."

"Ha, no, it wasn't," said Nicholas cheerfully. Bastien reflected Nicholas's grin back to him. "Would you show me a couple of those moves you made, but in slow motion?" Nicholas asked with hope.

"I'd be pleased to," Bastien told him. "But you mustn't feel bad if you can't get the hang of the moves right away. They are rather advanced. I feel a little bad for showing off, but the prize was a date with Aiden, so I felt I must win in style."

"Well, since the prize for winning the fencing match was a date with Aiden"—Nicholas raised his eyebrows—"it was kinda a relief I lost."

Bastien laughed. "Anyway. I'm sorry, Nicholas."

"Forget about it," said Nicholas.

Bastien turned back to Marcel and Melodie. The Bordeaux Blades enjoying their last night together before Marcel had to go back to America. Across the orchard, the Leventis twins were laughing at each others' jokes, and Nicholas couldn't tell which was the one who usually frowned. He supposed it would be nice to have a twin, someone to learn fencing and laugh with.

Well. Nicholas might not have a family, but he had his team.

Nicholas leaned against Eugene comfortingly. "Sorry, Eugene."

"Hey, no, bro. It's been great to come to Menton, even if I couldn't fence. I've met so many amazing people. You know who's super nice?" Eugene answered his own question without pausing. "Jesse Coste."

Nicholas stared at Eugene in shocked betrayal. Sadly, Eugene took this silence as encouragement.

"He's totally my Camp Menton bro. He helped Melodie with me when I had my allergic reaction, and tonight he sat with me when I was sitting alone, feeling sorry for myself, and told me tough break for getting sick and not being able to train at camp. Get this—he asked if my dad would be mad at me for not fencing. Like, why would my dad blame me for being sick?"

As Eugene told Nicholas about Jesse Coste's great personality, Nicholas thought back to Marcel's words about Jesse being the best and drawing the best to him.

"Wait, do we hate Jesse?" Eugene asked, registering Nicholas's silence. He sounded panicked. "Nobody told me we hate Jesse! I thought we could all be bros."

Nicholas thought of Jesse Coste, who made Seiji go tense as a struck blade, but who was inextricably tangled up with Seiji despite that. Jesse, who had chosen Exton over Kings Row because he didn't have to cling to the only link to his father. If Jesse ever considered anyone a rival, it was Seiji and not Nicholas. Jesse knew with unshakable certainty that he was the best.

"No, Eugene," said Nicholas. "Jesse and I are not, and will never be, bros."

39 SEIJI

Nicholas had forced Seiji out onto the dance floor, which was a hideous experience. Then Nicholas went away and came back with Eugene and a mystifying story of doomed romance that they all had to listen to.

Seiji had heard that bad things always came in threes, and that seemed true. Next, Nicholas and Bobby stunned the populace by doing karaoke. Eugene had gone first with a soulful ballad about lost love, and Seiji had found that horrible. Nicholas and Bobby's enthusiastic duet was much worse.

"I hate everything that's happening," Seiji informed Dante. "Don't you?"

"Nope," said Dante, smiling over at Bobby.

It occurred to Seiji that right now, Nicholas's (terrible!) and Bobby's

327

(rather nice) singing was providing him with a cover. This gave Seiji the opportunity to resolve an issue that had been worrying him.

He made his way to the corner where the adults were talking and had a brief private discussion with Coach Robillard.

Once the duet was over, Bobby and Nicholas returned. Instantly, Dante stood and asked Bobby to go on a walk.

Nicholas came over and slumped gracelessly onto the bench beside Seiji. Almost everyone at the party was wearing some type of formal wear, except for Nicholas, who was wearing ripped black jeans and his Kings Row hoodie. He was drumming his fingers on the surface of the picnic table. He was an irritating mess, and no doubt he would soon pester Seiji into engaging in another uncomfortable social activity.

Overall, Seiji found this to be a pleasant party.

40 HARVARD

Menton harbor after the sun went down was like an oil painting of heaven in the evening. The towers and buildings of the town still glowed sunshine gold, holding on to the sunset like light trapped in amber. The sea was black already but painted with electric lights. Bold, brilliant stripes of color went blurred at the edges against the waves, as though the oil in the painting was running.

It was all so beautiful, and Harvard didn't care. He just wanted to see Aiden.

As he ran down the esplanade toward the waterfront, he passed by Bobby and Dante, taking a walk along the harbor by moonlight. Bobby was shivering slightly in his thin silk top.

"Here," said Dante, taking off his

blazer. "There's a postcard from Italy for you in the pocket," he added when Bobby hesitated.

Bobby's face scrunched in a confused smile. "Why did you get me a postcard when you saw me at breakfast that morning, and you knew you were going to see me that evening?"

Dante shrugged. "Guess I was thinking about you."

Bobby hesitated, then gave a sudden decisive nod, and Dante draped the blazer onto Bobby's thin shoulders. It was extremely big on him.

"Thanks, Dante," said Bobby, wrapping the blazer around himself like a huge blanket. "It's really warm."

"Bobby...," said Dante.

"Yeah?" Bobby glanced up. "Talk to me."

Dante visibly searched for words, failed to find them, and muttered, "Tell you later."

He sent you postcards every day whenever he went away, to say, Thinking of you, pointed out Arune's voice in Harvard's mind, and Harvard winced.

The yachts were lined up in the harbor like tethered white clouds floating on the water. Harvard didn't need to ask anyone which boat belonged to Aiden's father. He knew it would be the largest and most ostentatious.

As he ran along the dock and then scrambled onto the yacht, he saw stars shivering in the sea, faint light wavering on the surface of dark, troubled waters. He was terrified of what he had to do, but he wasn't letting Aiden down again.

The yacht was suspiciously still and silent, when Harvard had expected the happy bustle of a party. He crept through the mirrored hallways until he finally heard the low, familiar murmur of Aiden's voice.

"I shouldn't," Aiden was saying. "It's too wicked. How could I live with myself?"

Harvard hesitated, with his hand pressed to the gleaming mahogany of the door. Was some guy fooling around with Aiden already? A sick, scraping feeling began in his chest, as if there were a trapdoor opening there and all of Harvard's insides were falling through.

"I don't care," Aiden decided. "I have no conscience. I'm eating a fifth cupcake."

Harvard drew in a deep, relieved breath and pushed open the door to reveal a ballroom, a gleaming parquet floor and a chandelier like a multifaceted crystal glass filled with ice. The sliding double doors of the ballroom were folded back to reveal the master bedroom, which seemed to be mostly a wide bed made up with white linen and turquoise silk sheets. Aiden was sitting at the foot of the bed in formal wear. His hair was loose, and his bow tie untied. Harvard Paw was propped up to sit by his side, and he had a frosted cupcake in hand. Aiden was also whispering seductively to his teddy bear, but Harvard didn't feel equipped to deal with that issue.

Aiden glanced up at the sound of the door opening. His eyes widened fractionally, but that was all. Harvard looked at those well-known and well-beloved eyes, a darker green than usual, and thought, *Troubled waters*. This was his fault. He had to make it right.

"Hey, Harvard," murmured Aiden.

"Hey, Aiden," said Harvard. "I love you."

Aiden blinked and put his cupcake down. "I love you, too, buddy," he said in a light, careful voice, his words like the footsteps of someone walking a tightrope over blades. "Is something wrong?"

Yes, something was wrong. Something was wrong *with Aiden*, and now Harvard was looking properly, without his own assumptions and doubts in the way, it was so clear. Aiden's mouth pulled tight on the word *buddy* and always had. How had Harvard not seen before?

"Shouldn't I be asking you that?" asked Harvard. Then it occurred to him that he'd come to confess to Aiden, not force Aiden to any painful revelations. He'd caused Aiden enough pain. He continued, after a brief pause, "What happened to the party?"

"Called it off. I'm not really in a party mood," said Aiden.

"Are you feeling sick?" Harvard asked anxiously, then realized the more likely answer. "Oh God. Am I intruding? Do you have plans?"

Terror was a rapid, continuous rush in Harvard's ears, like the sound of the sea. Aiden only shook his head, his face confused.

"I can go if you do," Harvard told him gently. "I will go. I won't stay long, and I don't expect anything from you at all. I just wanted to say this: Aiden, I'm so sorry."

There was a smile beginning to curl up at the corners of Aiden's mouth, indulgent. It might be the last time Aiden ever smiled at him that way.

"I don't have plans. I thought...what's the point? And I didn't have an answer. Why are you sorry? Whatever it is, I forgive you. If you killed somebody, it's fine. We have the Mediterranean to hide the body in. Harvard Paw and I will provide a foolproof alibi. Come tell me, I'm curious. What horrible thing have you done?"

Harvard had always wanted to do the right thing, to fix problems and never cause them. Because he'd tried to think of other people first, he'd never imagined *he* could have power over Aiden. He'd assumed Aiden had the power, that Harvard was the only one who could be hurt, and Harvard was too scared of being hurt to take down his defences and tell Aiden what he wanted. Harvard was still scared. He didn't know if he could do this.

He looked at Aiden's smile, which Aiden was wearing even though he was in pain. For Harvard's sake. Harvard felt something almost like seasickness. The ground he'd stood on all these years was gone.

This was the person he loved best in the world, the person Harvard would have sworn he'd never hurt. But he had hurt him. He had, and until he told the truth, he would still be hurting Aiden.

Harvard gathered all his courage, and confessed, "I lied to you."

Amusement died in Aiden's voice. "What?"

"I'm so sorry, Aiden," said Harvard. "I know you rely on me to tell you the truth, to always be there for you. I always intended to be that, to be a safe place for you, but I didn't manage it. I didn't want to hurt you. I didn't want to get hurt. Do you remember when I told you that I only wanted to be friends because I didn't want to fall in love with you?"

His voice distant now, Aiden answered, "Of course I remember."

Of course he did. Aiden had trusted him, and Harvard had lied, but it was time to tell the truth now. He was so scared of what would happen when he said it, scared of what might change, scared he was too late. But he had to face the truth.

He couldn't watch Aiden's face when he told him. So he fixed his eyes on the ballroom floor instead, and began to speak.

"That was the lie I told you. I'd only realized what I wanted the night before. I was terrified of losing you. I should have realized how I felt about you before, but how do you see the planet you live on? The air you breathe? It was always there. It was too big for me to see. You were always just there. I could look at you every day, the same way I can look at the stars every day. I never had to think about how much I wanted to look."

"I don't—I don't understand." Aiden sounded fraught. "What are you saying?"

"I love you." Desperate to avoid any further terrible and

painful confusion, frantic to get it all out, Harvard clarified: "I'm in love with you."

Quiet followed, broken only by the sound of the boat rocking.

Harvard waited, his heart a hammer counting the silent seconds. There was a pit in his stomach threatening to swallow him whole. The more the silence grew, the wider the pit yawned. He'd said it wrong, he was too late, he'd missed his chance, their friendship was over, he—

"You mean it?"

Aiden's voice was trembling. He must be really upset.

Harvard had hurt him too much. He couldn't make up for his lie or for the years of accidental cruelty before that. All Harvard could do was be truthful and apologize and leave.

"I do," said Harvard. "I really do. I'm so sorry, I wish I was saying it better. I'm not great at making speeches. But I'm good at meaning them. I love you so much. If I meant it less, I could have told you before."

"That's all I need to hear," Aiden said abruptly. "You don't need to say anything else."

"Okay," said Harvard. "I—thanks for listening. I'm sorry. I'll go."

His plan was to get out of there as fast as he could. But something stopped him. There were arms around his neck suddenly, a body against his chest blocking his way, Aiden sliding in close. When Harvard looked up from the gleaming ballroom floor, startled, Aiden leaned in and kissed him.

Harvard had barely been able to think before, with panic running riot through his veins, and now thought became entirely impossible. Everything was drowned out, as if he were submerged, every sense flooded with the taste and scent and feel of Aiden. Harvard didn't want to surface. He resented it when Aiden pulled back, even a little.

"Fool," murmured Aiden against his mouth, so sweet. "I love you back. I loved you first. You're not going anywhere. You're never getting rid of me now."

"What?" Harvard whispered, not daring to believe it was still true, hardly able to believe it was true at all. "Aiden. You can't mean that. Don't—don't pity me. It's fine, I'll be fine, you don't have to lie. Since when?"

He tried to pull away. Aiden wouldn't let go.

"*Hmm*," said Aiden. "Let me think. Since about the time when you gave me a teddy bear, believing I wanted it because I couldn't stop following you around."

He sounded serious, but he couldn't possibly be serious.

"But—but ...," stammered Harvard. "That was—"

"A long time ago. Yeah."

"You could have had anyone. There were all those guys. . . ."

Aiden began to look not only serious but annoyed. "When did I ever care about any of them? I could not have been more transparently indifferent! I get name amnesia!"

"That's not because—that's just how you are. You never remember anybody's name!"

"Don't I?" Aiden drawled, and the amusement was back in his voice. "Harvard. Harvard. Harvard. I love you."

He was walking backward, pulling Harvard in, pulling him close and still closer. Hearing his own name in Aiden's voice, repeated in that way, let Harvard open his eyes. For just a moment, he let himself believe what he saw. Aiden's eyes were on him, clear, green, and profoundly, shockingly tender. Harvard had been so afraid.

Now Harvard dared to look into the depths of dark troubled waters and found them unexpectedly illuminated. Everything was brilliant and clear.

"Why . . ." Harvard swallowed. "Why did you always send me postcards when you went away, that said, *Thinking of you?*"

"Because I'm always thinking about you," Aiden answered.

He looked as though he might kiss Harvard again, so Harvard foiled his plan. Harvard kissed him first. Aiden was only a shade shorter than he was, but Harvard wanted to keep him close, so he tucked his head down to kiss Aiden and keep him close at the same time. Somehow wanting to cherish and keep Aiden turned a little wild, a bright feeling with burning edges, and Aiden was undoing his shirt buttons as they tumbled down onto the bed.

Aiden's hair, starlight bright, obscured the rest of the world, and he spoke as though he were reading the words written on Harvard's own heart.

"My whole life," he said, "this is all I ever wanted."

He kissed Harvard and twined around him, while Harvard tangled his fingers in Aiden's hair and started to believe.

"Really?"

"Really. And now I have it," Aiden murmured. "You can't take it back. You have to promise."

He rolled Aiden over on the bed, safe in the shelter of Harvard's arms, and captured Aiden's face in his hands. Beautiful and his. He wasn't taking starlight for granted, not ever again.

"I promise," whispered Harvard. "I mean it. You can trust me."

Aiden smiled, grasping hold of Harvard's shirt collar, pulling him down. His hands slipped inside Harvard's shirt. When Aiden's fingers brushed skin, Harvard gasped, and Aiden made a soft noise, wordless encouragement, only the first of many loving, lovely sounds to come.

Aiden said, "Always have."

41 SEIJI

Just because they had been up all night and were going on an international flight, that was no reason for Seiji to give up on discipline and fail to rise at four AM to train.

To his extreme surprise, Nicholas resisted jet lag and joined him, still rubbing sleep out of his eyes, and agreed to train with him on the condition that they went out onto the beach rather than to the training ground. They drew strips with a stick in the white sand. Nicholas said he felt like a pirate.

"We'll get up and do all the training exercises you learned here every day in Kings Row," said Seiji.

Nicholas grinned. "Wouldn't do it for anything except fencing. And you."

Since this was their last day in France, Seiji was allowing them to have a match. They hadn't fenced together since they'd come here. Though Seiji had appreciated fencing with different and more skilled fencers, he had oddly missed this. The chance to observe Nicholas, learning as lightning fast as he moved. The way Nicholas was enjoying himself, and so Seiji was learning to enjoy himself, too.

"More drills and fewer matches in future," Seiji cautioned.

"Aw, Seiji," Nicholas protested, voice light as the sound of blades chiming and birds over the sea. "That's no fun, Seiji!"

"*I'm* no fun, Nicholas," said Seiji calmly. "Haven't you heard?"

"Everyone tells me," said Nicholas. "But I don't believe them."

"What do you believe?"

"You're my match," said Nicholas. "You're the match I'm going to win someday. The one I'm looking forward to the most."

Just looking at Nicholas's face, you could see how much he believed it, and it was almost enough to make Seiji believe it as well.

It had been wrong of Seiji not to trust him, but he would trust Nicholas from now on. He wouldn't let his mind betray him, imagining similarities when there were none.

Nicholas was nothing like Jesse at all.

42 AIDEN

For the first time in his life, Aiden woke early, naturally, and sweetly. The electric lights of night were gone. The dawn threw soft, bright ribbons over water, sky, and cabin walls, so they were wrapped in rose and ivory and gold. Light poured over Harvard's glowing dark skin and the silk sheets, and this day was already a gift.

"So this wasn't all a cupcake-induced fever dream," Aiden said romantically. Then he couldn't stop himself from smiling. "I'm glad."

He stretched luxuriously, lying in the warm curve of Harvard's arm. He'd known for years that Harvard's arms were strong. He'd glanced at them many times, thinking to himself, even objectively—which Aiden in no way was—*wow*, but there was a world of difference between admiration and having that strength used to hold you.

341

"I'm glad, too," Harvard murmured in Aiden's ear. "And I have a question."

"Ask me anything."

"Where did the freshmen go during my match and then at the beginning of the party? Something very suspicious is going on."

"Oh, fine!" Aiden said, and confessed about helping the freshmen sneak out for a late-night fencing match.

Harvard listened with growing horror.

"Hey," said Aiden, trying to recall Harvard to the important matters in life. "I love you."

"I love you, too, Aiden Kane, but you're the worst." Harvard gave him a reproachful look. "We're responsible for them."

"Wow—watch that *we*. I want nothing to do with them. I'm not their captain-in-law," Aiden grumbled.

Harvard tricked him by bending his head over the pillow where Aiden's head lay, giving Aiden a slow kiss that spread warmth through him like sunlight. "No?"

Aiden skimmed his palms up the curves of those arms, then cupped Harvard's head in one hand and brought him back down, ending their horrible separation of three seconds, for another kiss.

"No! You may have heard I'm irresponsible and high maintenance, and it's all true. I have no responsibilities and many demands. Listen up, this is the most important demand. If you're thinking that there's a whole wide world of guys out there, too bad. You had your chance to play the field. Don't you dare look at another guy. We're dating now."

"That's funny. I don't remember being asked out," Harvard teased.

"That *is* funny," Aiden agreed. "I asked you to the town fair twice and asked you out for milkshakes or the movies or anything else over and over. I sent you valentines every February. I would have done anything you wanted. I asked you out a hundred times, Harvard Lee. It's not my fault you weren't listening."

Harvard's kind face crumpled a little at the thought of Aiden suffering, his beautiful brown eyes warm with sympathy. Aiden felt this was only fair, considering how much he had gone through. A truly good person would've let it go, but there was only one truly good person in this relationship, and Aiden wasn't him. Aiden was now planning to remind Harvard often of his tragic past of unrequited pining, in order to get his own way.

"I'm listening now," Harvard promised, tucking his nose in against Aiden's cheek.

Aiden couldn't help smiling. "Are you, Captain?"

"Oh wait," Harvard said. "Oh no. That can't be a sexy thing. Nicholas calls me that. You can't call me that when you're using that voice, okay?"

Aiden let his smile turn wicked and mischievous. It stayed happy.

"Whatever you say," Aiden whispered into Harvard's mouth, "Captain."

He nuzzled at Harvard's jaw, then surged up against Harvard's chest, both tumbling over each other, laughing, sighing, the silk sheets by day turned into a wonderful green sea. Aiden had all his attention now, the way he'd always wanted. Not just a teddy bear, not just friendship, but Harvard himself, Harvard to keep for his own.

By the light of the sun or the light of the moon, in any strange land or at home, this was the only truth he knew. *Aiden loves Harvard*, for far longer than a year and a day.

A long sun-drenched time later, Harvard and Aiden emerged from the yacht and walked down the sugar-white sand hand in hand, barefoot in wrecked formal wear. Aiden thought Harvard looked great like this. Harvard should look like this always.

"I think it's my turn to ask you out on a date," said Harvard.

"You could win me another bear, since I tossed out the last one you won me," said Aiden, sharply regretting that rash action now.

"Actually..." said Harvard. "I took the bear out and kept it. You can have it back."

Harvard had kept the souvenir from their date. The revelation made Aiden smile, delight far sharper than regret had ever been, gleeful as a kid thinking *He likes me!* Finally, finally, Harvard Lee liked him back.

"I'm kicked out of Kings Row, so you might have to mail me that bear," Aiden reminded him. "Are you ready to conduct a courtship via letters? Also frequent texts."

"My mom will have to teach me what the emojis mean," said Harvard.

Harvard and Aiden's romantic morning walk was brought to an early close when they came upon Nicholas and Seiji having a fencing match on the seashore. Because of course, what else would they be doing in their last moments in France?

"Morning," called Harvard, waving to them with his free hand.

"Have I mentioned you're tragic individuals today?" Aiden called out.

An awful revelation struck Aiden. He sort of *was* their captain-in-law.

43 NICHOLAS

Nicholas wasn't totally sure, but he suspected Aiden and the captain were dating again. He was tipped off by the way they were holding hands. He was about to share this observation with Seiji when his attention was thoroughly distracted.

Coach Arquette, Coach Robillard, and Coach Williams approached their group, walking across the golden sands until they reached them. Coach Arquette and Coach Robillard's faces were solemn. Nicholas couldn't read Coach Williams' face.

"Monsieur Robillard and I just wanted to say we're sorry about the confusion, and of course Mr. Kane is no longer banned from Camp Menton," said Coach Arquette.

Aiden blinked at them slowly, reaching out to hold the captain's

347

arm as well as his hand, as though Harvard were his anchor in strange seas.

"I'm—not banned?" Aiden asked.

"That's right," said Coach Arquette.

"But—if I'm not banned from the camp, that means—"

"I've spoken to your school principal. You will be fully reinstated at Kings Row as well," Coach Robillard said in a firm voice.

Aiden looked dazed. "But—"

He glanced at Harvard, but the captain seemed just as lost as Aiden. Apparently, nobody had any answers.

"I explained everything to Coach Robillard," Seiji piped up from beside Nicholas.

Everyone turned to stare at Seiji in astonishment. Seiji gazed sternly around.

"I explained that when it appeared Aiden had broken curfew, he'd merely been searching for me," he reported. "Because I got lost in the woods at night."

"And you all . . . believe that," Aiden said slowly.

Coach Robillard gave an expressive shrug. "Of course I wouldn't with anyone else, but I remember training this kid last year. This is *Seiji Katayama*."

"Yes," said Seiji. "I'm Seiji Katayama."

Coach Robillard shook his head, apparently lost in memory. "He doesn't lie about rules. He got an RA out of bed one night because the other fencers were having an illicit midnight hot chocolate. She said she'd let it go this once, and he said she couldn't let it go."

"They had a match the next day!" Seiji protested, clearly scandalized.

Coach Robillard rolled his eyes. Coach Arquette apologized again to Aiden, and she and Coach Robillard left, leaving Coach Williams with her team.

After a moment of silence, Aiden said, "Coach? About... staying at Kings Row. Did you mention to anyone that I told you I was going to break curfew?"

Coach shrugged. "Must have slipped my mind."

"Did...it...," Aiden said.

"Very pleased you've decided to behave, very pleased my team's not going to be decimated at the state championship." Coach said. "And that's that."

She turned on her heel, leaving the boys standing on the beach.

Aiden cleared his throat. Then he asked Seiji, "Why would you lie for me?"

"You've helped me with Jesse twice now," Seiji answered, earnest as only Seiji could be. "Now I'm helping you in return. That's teamwork: I thought you should know how it goes."

"I'm deeply shamed to be receiving lectures about social inter-actions from Seiji Katayama," Aiden mused.

Before Nicholas could bristle at Aiden's ingratitude, Aiden gave Seiji a weird smile. It was Aiden's smile, dazzling and mocking and coaxing everyone to smile back at him, but there was a certain hardness missing. As though there had always been an invisible shield in front of the smile, and now the shield could be lowered.

"Thanks, Seiji," Aiden added with his new smile. "Thanks, everyone. I mean it."

"Well, of course," Nicholas said, thawing. "You're part of the team. You belong at Kings Row."

If Aiden wasn't expelled, then everything would be right with Kings Row and Nicholas's world.

Camp Menton had been great, but his team and Kings Row were the best. Nicholas was ready to go home.

Bastien Robillard, Colm from Ireland, and several other guys looked crushed about Aiden holding Harvard's hand as they climbed onto the bus. Bastien pulled himself together and called out instructions to Nicholas about a few moves he should learn before the Kings Row team had to leave. Bastien was cool, Nicholas thought, but he still believed Aiden had picked the right guy.

On the bus, Aiden slept serenely with his head on Harvard's shoulder, Harvard humming a contented tune all the way to the airport. The rest of them sat at the back and gossiped.

"This is such a wild, exciting, romantic ride!" Bobby enthused.

"I'm glad they are back together," Seiji said, to the surprise of all. "I think Aiden was sad. And that was bound to affect his fencing."

"Wow, Aiden has *feelings*?" asked Nicholas.

Seiji, sudden expert on feelings, elbowed Nicholas in the ribs. Nicholas looked to his other friends for help, but Bobby was wearing an expression that strongly endorsed Seiji's elbowing.

Once on their first plane, Seiji revealed he had prepared several books for Nicholas, as well as a brief fencing quiz. Nicholas appreciated the thought but wanted a trade, so he made Seiji watch a movie he liked about ice hockey and plucky underdogs. Seiji spent much of their second flight darkly observing that the plucky underdogs weren't training properly and didn't deserve to win.

On the bus ride back from New York, Nicholas couldn't settle with any of Seiji's books or even a quiz. He found himself pacing up and down the aisle of the bus, feeling as though he had an itch in his brain, restless until they reached their destination. He wondered if this was how it felt to be homesick. Nicholas had never experienced that before.

However uncomfortable the itch in his brain was, it was nothing compared to the relief when the bus turned the corner and laid out before them all were the deep evergreen woods and not the lemon trees, the deep lake and not the sea. Waiting for them down the long driveway were the redbrick, white-windowed buildings of Kings Row.

With immense satisfaction, Nicholas studied the school logo depicted over the door as they drew closer. A shield wearing a crown, with two swords crossed behind it. An inverted *K* against a background of gold and blue, and an *R* against gold and crimson. Underneath were the words *Unitatis Mirabile Vinculum*, which Nicholas knew meant *The Wondrous Bond of Unity*. It meant being together as one.

Harvard's friends Kally and Tanner were walking by a window, and when they saw the bus roll up, they leaned out and yelled a welcome home. Nicholas observed the way their eyes flew right to Aiden and Harvard's joined hands, noted how they whispered to each other and beamed. Kally and Tanner were clearly happy for them, and Nicholas realized he was happy for them, too. He watched as Harvard lifted Aiden's hand to his mouth and kissed the back, and saw the way Aiden looked at Harvard's bent head.

The best part of a journey was coming home. That was something new for Nicholas to learn.

In that moment, Nicholas was sure he felt the wondrous bond of unity with his school and all the people in it. Especially the people in this bus. Sparkly Bobby and solemn Dante, having one of their unbalanced conversations that seemed to balance. Seiji and his stern face, still cranky about plucky underdogs succeeding without training. Aiden and Harvard, so surprisingly and unmistakably happy. And Nicholas, the scholarship kid who shouldn't belong here, but might anyway. He turned his head and caught a grin Coach Williams tossed his way.

"It's good to be home, kids," Coach announced. "Home's our first step to victory."

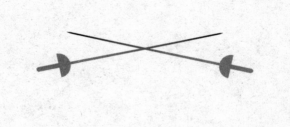

ACKNOWLEDGMENTS

I must begin with many thanks to C.S. Pacat and Johanna The Mad for inviting me into the Fence universe. What a fun universe, and what a journey to go on! Johanna's covers and illustrations for both books have been so amazing and beautiful. I know C.S. Pacat had a particular vision for this novel, and I hope I fulfilled it.

Huge, devout thanks to Suzie Townsend, my knight errant agent; Dani Segelbaum; and the whole amazing team at New Leaf literary agency.

Thank you so much to Susan Connolly for our WhatsApp writing room during the lockdown. Many apologies for the times I put my head down on the kitchen table and cried. Thanks also to C. E. Murphy, Ruth Frances Long, Leigh Bardugo, Robin Wasserman, and Holly Black for writer check-ins during this our year of quarantine.

Thank you to Mary-Kate Gaudet and Regan Winter for their great patience during a wild ride. Also, to fabulous publicist Thandi Jackson, Savannah Kennelly, brocean Lindsay Walter-Greaney, and the whole team at Little, Brown. And many thanks to Kerianne Steinberg for a wonderful copyedit. Thank you to Dafna Pleban, Shannon Watters, Sophie Philips-Roberts, and the team at BOOM! for continuing to make me feel welcome onboard, and especially to Shannon for being nice about my dreadful title suggestions!

The Fence fandom have become dear to my heart by opening *their* hearts to me! Shout-out to faeriereverie (that art!), Seijisrow, babyephant, Harvardpaw, fencedits, laurents-laces, im-your-rival, theninthmember, seijikatayama-stan, dkafterdark, theangry-Inch, elucreh, angst-iguana, michellejackson, nicholas-zero-cox, scathieedraws, metalandmagi, dncngthrghlife, magiclamd, sei-jistan, softerstorms, fenceseiji, aideninparis, nicholaskatayama_, gael_me, fadingintotheforeground, anico_art, allarica, hyosagi, qodious, and many others. Please forgive me for not being able to mention everyone. Thanks so much for embracing *Striking Distance*, and I super hope you enjoyed *Disarmed*. You're all champions.